The sky above the western horizon was drained of color and angry with flashes of intense light, brighter than the midday sun. It was all the world's lightning in concert, a blinding stroboscopic show that could be seen and felt for a radius of one hundred miles.

Scott looked into the face of it, hands shielding his eyes from random bursts of unearthly whiteness. *The assault has begun*, he told himself with a mixture of excitement and terror.

Annie stared at the sky in wonder. "Is it some kind of storm? A tornado, maybe?"

Rand and Rook exchanged grim glances. "I wish it was," Rand told his young friend. Basso sounds were rumbling across the sky, seconds late of the explosions that birthed them.

"It has to be Admiral Hunter," Scott said behind them. Squinting, he could discern dark shapes streaking through that celestial chaos. *Hundreds* of shapes—fighters, mecha, and surely Invid ships launched to engage them. "Let's move in," he said firmly. "We can't just stand here and watch."

The ROBOTECH™ Series
Published by Ballantine Books:

ROBOTECH™ #12:
SYMPHONY OF LIGHT

Jack McKinney

A Del Rey Book

BALLANTINE BOOKS • NEW YORK

FOR THE WEST COAST CONTINGENT:
JULIA, JESSE, AND DANIEL

CHAPTER
ONE

*I am intrigued by these beings and their strange rituals,
which center around this plant their language calls "the Flower
of Life." This world, Optera, is a veritable garden for the plant
in its myriad forms, and the Invid seem to utilize all these for
physical as well as spiritual nutrition—they ingest the flower's
petals and the fruits of the mature crop, in addition to drinking
the plant's psychoactive sap. The Regis, the Queen-Mother of
this race, is the key to unlocking Optera's mysteries; and I have
set myself the goal of possessing the key—if I have to seduce
this queen to make that happen!*

Zor's log: *The Optera Chronicles* (translated by Dr.
Emil Lang)

IT WAS NEVER SCOTT'S INTENTION TO MAKE CAMP AT
the high pass; he had simply given his okay for a quick
food stop—if only to put an end to all the grousing that
was going on. Lunk's stomach needed tending to, Annie
was restless from too many hours in the APC, and even
Lancer was complaining about the wind chill.

Oh, to be back in the tropics, Scott thought wistfully.

He had always been one for wastes and deserts—
weathered landscapes, rugged, ravaged by time and the
stuff of stars—but only because he knew of little else.
Here he had been to the other side of the galaxy and
remained the most parochial member of the team in spite
of it. But since their brief stopover in the tropics, he had
begun to understand why Earth was so revered by the
crew of the Pioneer Mission, those same men and women
who had raised him aboard the SDF-3 and watched him
grow to manhood on Tirol. In the tropics he had had a

1

glimpse of the Earth they must have been remembering: the life-affirming warmth of its yellow sun, the splendor of its verdant forests, the sweetness of its air, and the miracle that was its wondrous ocean.

Even if Rand *had* insisted that they try that *swimming*!

Scott would have almost been willing to trade victory itself for another view of sunset from that Pacific isle . . .

Instead, he was surrounded by water in the forms more familiar to him: ice and snow. The thrill the team had experienced on reaching the Northlands and realizing that Reflex Point was actually within reach had been somewhat dampened by the formidable range of mountains they soon faced. But Scott was determined to make this as rapid a crossing as was humanly possible. Unfortunately, the humanly possible part of it called for unscheduled stops. It was Lunk's APC that was slowing them down, but there was that old one about a chain being only as strong as its weakest link.

The land vehicles were approaching the summit of the mountain highway now. Rook and Lancer, riding Cyclones, were escorting the truck along the mostly ruined switchback road that led to the pass. The ridgeline above was buried under several feet of fresh snow, but the vehicles were making good progress on the long grade nonetheless.

Scott was overhead in the Beta, with Rand just off the fighter's wingtip. Short on fuel canisters, they had been forced to leave Rook's red Alpha behind, concealed in the remains of a school gymnasium building in the valley. Scott planned to retrieve it just as soon as they located a Protoculture supply rife for pilfering. Down below, Annie and Marlene were waving up at the VTs from the back seat of the APC; Scott went on the mecha's tac net to inform Lunk that a rest stop was probably in order.

The two Robotech fighters banked away from the mountain face to search out a suitable spot, and within minutes they were reconfiguring to Guardian mode and using their foot thrusters to warm a reasonably flat area of cirque above the road and just shy of the saddle. By the time they put down, the sun had already dropped below one of the peaks, but the temperature was still almost preternaturally warm. The weather was balmy enough for the two pilots to romp around in their duotherm suits, especially with the added luxury of residual heat from the snow-cleared moraine. There was a strong breeze rippling over the top of the col, but it carried with it the scent of the desert beyond.

The rest of the team joined them in a short time. Lunk, Rook, and Lancer began to unload the firewood they had hauled up from the tree line, while Rand went to work on the deer he had shot and butchered. Moonrise fringed the eastern peaks in a kind of silvery glow and found the seven freedom fighters grouped around a sizzling fire. The northern sky's constellations were on display. Scott had developed a special fondness for the brilliant stars of the southern hemisphere, but Gemini and Orion were reassuring for a different reason: They reinforced the fact that Reflex Point was close at hand. He had to admit, however, that it was foolish to be thinking of the Invid central hive as some sort of end in itself, when really their arrival there would represent more in the way of a beginning. He wondered whether the rest of the team understood this—that the mission, as loose as it was, was focused on destroying the hive, or at the very least accumulating as much recon data as possible to be turned over to Admiral Hunter when the Expeditionary Force returned to Earth for what would surely be the final showdown.

Glancing at his teammates, Scott shook his head in wonder that they had made it as far as they had, a group of strangers all but thrown together on a journey that had so far covered thousands of miles.

Scott regarded Lunk while the big, brutish man was laughing heartily, a shank of meat gripped in his big hand. He had done so much for the team, yet he still seemed to carry the weight of past defeats on his huge shoulders. Then there was Annie, their daughter, mascot, mother, in the green jumpsuit that had seen so much abuse and the ever-present E.T. cap that crowned her long red hair. She had almost left them a while back, convinced she had found the man of her dreams in the person of a young primitive named Magruder. It wasn't the first time she had wandered away, but she always managed to return to the fold, and her bond with Lunk was perhaps stronger than either of them knew.

Rand and Rook, who could almost have passed for siblings, had had their moments of doubt about the mission as well. They had formed a fiery partnership, one that seemed to rely on strikes and counterstrikes; but it was just that unspoken pact that kept them loyal to the team, if only to prove something to each other.

More than anyone, Lancer had remained true to the cause. Scott had grown so accustomed to the man's lean good looks, his lavender-tinted shoulder-length hair and trademark headband, that he had almost forgotten about Yellow Dancer, Lancer's alter ego. That feminine part of the Robotech rebel was all but submerged now, especially so since the tropics, when something had occurred that had left Lancer changed and Scott wondering.

But the most enigmatic among them was the woman they had named Marlene. She was not really a member of the team at all but the still shell-shocked victim of an Invid assault, the nature of which Scott could only guess. It had robbed her of her past but left her with an uncanny ability to *sense* the enemy's presence. Her fragile beauty reminded Scott of the Marlene in his own past, killed when the Mars Division strike force had first entered Earth's atmosphere almost a year ago. . . .

"You know, just once I'd like to sit down and eat steak until I pass out," Lunk was saying, tearing into the venison like some ravenous beast.

"Just keep eating like you're eating and you might get your wish," Rand told him, to everyone's amusement.

"I've never met anyone who had such a thing for food," Rook added, theatrically amazed, strawberry-blond locks caught in the firelight.

Scott poured himself a cup of coffee and waited for the

laughter to subside. "You know, Lunk, we've still got a full day left in these mountains, so I'd save some of that for tomorrow if I were you." *Always the team leader*, he told himself. But it never seemed to matter all that much.

"Well, you're not me, Scott," Lunk said, licking his fingertips clean. "Sorry to report that I've eaten it all."

"You can always catch a rabbit, right, Lunk?" Lancer told him playfully.

Annie frowned, thinking about just how many rabbits they had dined on these past months. "I'm starting to feel sorry for rabbits."

Rand made a face. "They like it when one of them gets caught, Annie. It gives them a chance to go back to the hutch and—"

Rook elbowed him before he could get the word out, but the team had already discerned his meaning and was laughing again.

Even Marlene laughed, eyes all wrinkled up, luxuriant hair tossed back. Scott was watching her and complimenting Rand at the same time, when he saw the woman's joyous look begin to collapse. Marlene went wide-eyed for a moment, then folded her arms across her chest as though chilled, hands clutching her trembling shoulders.

"Marlene," Annie said, full of concern.

"Are you feeling sick or something?" Lunk asked.

But Lancer and Scott had a different interpretation. They exchanged wary looks and were already reaching for their holstered hip howitzers when Scott asked: "Are the Invid coming back, Marlene? Do you feel them returning?"

"Form up!" Rand said all at once, pulling back from the circle.

"Weapons ready!"

Annie went to Marlene's side, while the others drew their weapons and got to their feet, eyes sweeping the snow and darkness at the borders of the firelight.

"Anyone hear anything?" Rand whispered.

No one did; there was just the crackling of the fire and

the howl of the wind. Rand had the H90 stiff-armed in
front of him and only then, a few feet away from the fire,
began to sense how cold it was getting. There was mois-
ture in the wind now and light snow in the air. Behind
him, he heard Rook breathe a sigh of relief and reholster
her wide-bore. When he turned back to the fire, she was
down on one knee alongside Marlene, stroking the frightened woman's long hair soothingly.

"It's all right, Marlene. Believe me, you don't have a
thing to worry about. We're safe now, really."

Marlene whimpered, shaking uncontrollably. "What's
wrong with me, Rook? Why do I feel like this?"

"There's nothing wrong with you. You just have to understand that you had a terrible shock, and it's going to
take a while to get over it."

Lancer put away his weapon and joined Rook.
"Maybe I can help," he told her. Then, gently: "Marlene,
it's Lancer. Listen, I know what you're going through. It's
painful and it frightens you, but you have to be strong.
You have to survive, despite the pain and fear."

"I know," she answered him weakly, her head resting
on her arms.

"Just have faith that it'll get better. Soon it'll get better
for all of us."

Still vigilant, Rand and Scott watched the scene from
across the fire. The young Forager made a cynical sound.
"That sounds a little too rich for my blood."

"Optimistic or not, Rand, he's right," Scott returned.

Rand's eyes flashed as he turned. "I only wish I felt
that confident."

Not far from the warmth and light of the fire, something monstrous was pushing itself up from beneath the
snow-covered surface. It was an unearthly ship of gleaming metals and alloys, constructed to resemble a life-form
long abandoned by the race that had fashioned it. To
Human eyes it suggested a kind of bipedal crab with massive triple-clawed pincer arms and armored legs ending in
cloven feet. There was no specific head, but there were

aspects of the ship's design that suggested one, central to which was a single scanner that glowed red like some devilish mouth when the craft was inhabited. And flanking that head were two organic-looking cannons, each capable of delivering packets of plasma fire in the form of annihilation discs.

Originally a race of shapeless, protoplasmic creatures, the creators of the ship, the Invid, had since evolved to forms more compatible with the beings they were battling for possession of Earth. This creative transformation of the race had its beginnings on a world as distant from Earth as this new form was distant from the peaceful existence the Invid had once known. But all this went back to the time before Zor arrived on Optera; before the Invid Queen-Mother, the Regis, had been seduced by him; and before Protoculture had been conjured from the Flower of Life. . . .

The Regis had failed in countless attempts at fashioning herself in Zor's image but had at last succeeded in doing so with one of her children—the Simulagent Ariel, whom the Humans called Marlene. Then, upon losing her through a trick of fate, the Queen-Mother had created Corg and Sera, the warrior prince and princess who were destined to rule while the Regis carried on with the experiment that would one day free her race from all material constraints.

It was Sera's ship that surfaced next, the heat of its sleek hull turning the glacial ice around its feet to slush. Purple and trimmed in pink, the craft was more heavily armed than its companion ship, with a smaller head area sunk between massive shoulders and immensely strong arms. Momentarily, four additional ships of the more conventional design surfaced around the Humans and their windblown fire.

Sera heard the Queen-Mother's command emanate through the bio-construct ship that had led the squad to the high pass.

"All Scouts and Shock Troopers: you may move into your attack positions at this time! Sera, you will now take command. You are personally responsible for the elimination of these troublesome insurgents."

Sera signaled her understanding with a nod of her head toward the cockpit's commo screen. She had dim memories of a time not long ago when she had fought against these Humans in a different climate, and accompanying this was a dim recollection of failure: of Shock Trooper ships in her charge blown to pieces, of an inability on her part to perform as she had been instructed by the Regis ... But all this was unclear and mixed with a hundred new thoughts and reactions that were vying for attention in her virgin mind.

"As you command, Regis," she responded as confidently as she was able, her scanners focused on the seven Humans huddled around the fire. "We now have them completely surrounded. And with our superior abilities, we will succeed in carrying out your...your orders." Somewhat more mechanically, she added, "Nothing will stop us."

Had the Regis heard her falter? Sera asked herself. She waited for some suggestion of displeasure, but none was forthcoming. It was only then that she allowed herself to increase the magnification of her scanner and zero in on the Human whose face had caused her lapse of purpose.

It's him! she thought, once again taking in the fine features of the one whose strange, seductive, and achingly beautiful sounds had drawn her to that jungle pool; the one who had surprised her there, stood naked before her, holding her in the grip of his strong hands and assaulting her with questions she could not answer. And it was this same Human she had glimpsed later during the heat of battle when her own hand had betrayed her....

"Sera! You're waiting too long!" the Regis shouted through the bio-construct's comlink.

Sera felt the strength of the Queen-Mother begin to creep into her own will and force her hand toward the weapon's trigger stud, but one part of her struggled against it, and at the last moment, even as the weapon was firing, she managed to swing the ship's cannon aside, so that the shot went astray. . . .

Lancer was just commenting on the beauty of the snowfall when the first enemy blast struck, flaring overhead and erupting like a midnight sun in the snowfields near the grounded VTs—a single short burst of annihilation discs that had somehow missed their mark. Scott was the first to react, propelling himself out of the circle into a tuck-and-roll, which landed him on his knees in the perimeter snow, his MARS-Gallant handgun raised. But before he could squeeze off a quantum of return fire, a second Invid volley skimmed into the team's midst, sending him head over heels and flat on his face. He inhaled a faceful of snow and rolled over in time to see a series of explosions rip through the camp, brilliant white geysers leaping from plasma pools of hellfire. On the ridgeline he caught a brief glimpse of an Invid Trooper before it was eclipsed by clouds of swirling snow.

The rest of the team had already scattered for cover. Scott spied Lancer hunkering down behind an arc of moraine slide and yelled for him to stay put as Invid fusillades swooshed down into a gully below the ridge, throwing up a storm of ice and shale. Rand, meanwhile, was closing on the Alpha Fighter, discs nipping at his boot heels from two Invid Troopers who had positioned themselves just short of the saddle. Running a broken course through the snow, he clambered up onto the nose of the Veritech and managed to fling open its canopy. But the next instant he was flat on his back beneath the radome of the fighter, a Shock Trooper towering above him. Frantically, Rand brought his hands to his face, certain the Trooper's backhand pincer swipe had opened him up. But the thing had missed.

Now, he thought, *all I've gotta do is keep from being roasted alive!*

Radiant priming globes had formed at the tip of the cannon muzzles; as these winked out, platters of blinding orange light flew toward him like some demon's idea of

Frisbee. Rand cursed and rolled, thinking vaguely back to that deer he had killed down below. . . .

Two hundred yards away Scott was on his feet, blasting away at the Invid command ship positioned on the ridge. Unless his eyes betrayed him, it was the same ship that had been sent against them during their ocean crossing to the Northlands. And that was a bad sign indeed, because it meant that the Regis had finally gotten around to singling the team out as a quarry worthy of pursuit. He squinted into the storm and fired, uncertain if the ship was still there. The wind had picked up now, and icy flakes of biting snow were adding to the chaos. From somewhere nearby he heard Lancer shout: "Behind you, Scott!" and swung around to face off with a Trooper that was using the Veritechs for cover. Scott traded half a dozen shots with it before a deafening explosion threw him violently out of the fray; he felt an intense flashburn against his back and was eating snow a moment later. Coming to, he had a clear view of the ridge, of the pastel-hued command ship standing side by side with a somewhat smaller Trooper. The Trooper had lifted off by the time Scott scrambled to his feet; it put down in front of him, sinking up to its articulated knee joints in the snow. Scott stumbled backward, searching for cover, while the Invid calmly raised its clawed pincer for a downward strike.

A short distance away, Rook sucked in her breath as she witnessed Scott narrowly escape decapitation. Fortunately, the snow beneath his feet had given way and he had fallen backward into a shallow ravine at the same moment the Trooper's claw had descended. But now the thing was poised on the edge of the hollow, preparing to bring its cannons into play. Rook turned her profile to the ship, the H90 long gun gripped in her extended right hand, and fired two blasts. Given the near-blizzard conditions, it was too much to ask that her shots find any vulnerable spots—although her second burst almost made a hole through the ship's eyelike scanner. The Trooper swung toward her, almost the impatient turn one would direct toward a mischievous child, and loosed two discs in response, one of which tore into the earth twenty yards in front of her with enough charge to blow her off her feet.

By now, five Invid Troopers had put down in the cirque; their colorful commander was still on the ridge monitoring the scene. The team, meanwhile, had been herded toward the steep glacial slope at the basin's edge. Scott leapt up out of his hollow after Rook took the heat off him and waved everyone toward his position. "Everyone over the side!" he yelled into the wind. "Slide down the slope back to the tree line!"

"But the mecha!" Rand returned, gesturing back to the basin.

"Forget it! We've gotta make for the woods!"

Scott saw Annie go over the side and ride down the chute on her butt, trailing a scream that was half fear, half thrill. Lancer and Marlene took to the slope next, then Lunk and Rand. Scott waved them on, yelling all the while and triggering the handgun for all it was worth against the Invid who had nearly taken his head off a few moments before. He managed a lucky shot that blew the thing's leg off, and it settled down into the basin snow and exploded.

Only Scott and Rook remained in the cirque now, along with the four undamaged Troopers that were moving toward them with evil intent.

"Rook! Are you all right?!" Scott yelled.

She gave him the okay sign and started to make her way toward his position, pivoting once or twice to get a shot off at her pursuers. The Invid were pouring a storm of discs at them, so they had to flatten themselves every so often as they attempted to close on the chute. Scott continued to send out what his blaster could deliver and wasn't surprised to see the enemy split ranks and head off for a flanking maneuver. Rook was a few yards in front of him when the two of them went over the side. Scott tried to dig his heels in, then realized why the rest of the team had disappeared so quickly. Under a thin layer of snow the chute was a solid sheet of glacial ice.

*   *   *

Sera saw the apparent leader of the group whipping down the slope and lifted off to pursue him. She paused briefly on the edge of the slide to issue instructions to her troops, then engaged the thrusters that would send her down toward the tree line along the Humans' course.

Although Lancer might have given Sera pause, she had no bonds with the rest of the team. She came alongside Scott, realizing that he could see her through the command ship's transparent bubble, and trained her cannons on him. But at the last minute, Scott's heels found a bit of purchase and he suddenly ended up somersaulting out of harm's way, each of Sera's shots missing him as he rolled down the slope.

The Invid princess came to a halt at the bottom of the chute where the others had taken up positions behind groupings of terminal moraine boulders. Lunk was loosing bursts against the cockpit canopy that made it impossible for Sera to tell in which direction the leader had headed.

Sera allowed the brutish Human to have his way for an instant, then turned on him, aware of the blood lust she felt in her heart. But all at once one of the Human's teammates ran from cover and pushed the big one off his feet and out of the path of her shots. Angered, Sera traversed the command ship's cannons to find him, realizing only then that it was the lavender-haired Human.

Her hand remained poised above the weapon's oval-shaped trigger, paralyzed.

Elsewhere, the rebels and Shock Troopers continued to trade fire.

Marlene cowered behind a boulder as lethal packets of energy crisscrossed overhead, her hands pressed to her head, as if she were fearful of some internal explosion.

"Fight or die!" she screamed, her words lost to the storm. "There must be another way . . . another life!"

Then, a moment later, the fighting itself surrendered.

Scott heard an intense rumbling above him and looked up in time to see enormous chunks of ice fall from the buttresses surrounding the cirque, avalanching down into the basin, scattering the Invid Troopers and burying the Cyclones and Veritechs under tons of crystalline snow.

CHAPTER
TWO

Scott had assumed that the "waning" [sic] of Yellow Dancer had something to do with Lancer's infatuation with Marlene; but while Scott was certainly on the right track, he had the wrong cause—a fact that contributed to the rivalries that arose later on. Had the two men sat down and talked things out, perhaps they would have realized that Marlene was not the amnesiac Scott wanted to believe she was, nor Sera the Human pilot Lancer assumed her to be. Time and time again this failure to communicate would undermine the team's movement toward unity, right to the end.

Zeus Bellow, *The Road to Reflex Point*

IT WAS SCOTT'S IDEA THAT THEY SEPARATE INTO three groups. The avalanche had indeed buried the VTs and Cyclones, but at the same time it had forced the Invid out of the basin area and bought some breathing space for the team. Reunited, they had picked their way farther down the mountainside, splitting up when they reached the tree line. There they left obvious evidence of their separate paths in the snow, hoping the Invid commander would similarly redeploy her Troopers. This way, Scott hoped, his irregulars would stand a better chance of circling back to the chute and retrieving the mecha.

Somehow.

The squall had moved through, but the temperature had actually risen a couple of degrees. Nevertheless, the freedom fighters were soaked to the skin and feeling the chill. Annie felt it more than the others—her jumpsuit had little of the thermal protection afforded Rook by the

Cyclone bodysuit, and she simply wasn't as inured to the cold as Rand. As a result, she had ridden piggyback into the woods, her shaking arms draped around Rand's neck.

"It'll get better when we get into the trees," Rand had assured her. "I can't promise you a fire right away, but at least you'll be out of this wind."

At this point Rand had no real plan beyond finding temporary shelter where they could regain some of their strength. All of them had taken a beating, and Rook had some severe facial burns. Rand didn't imagine that Scott and Lunk were in much better shape, and even though Lancer had been spared real harm, he had Marlene to look out for, which was in some ways worse than being out there alone. Rand had berated himself for having left his survival pack in the Alpha. For the past few weeks he had been complaining to Scott that everyone was becoming too reliant on the mecha systems for survival, and now here he was out in the woods with nothing more than a handgun and his fenceman's tool. But a few steps down the forest's wide trail his attitude began to improve considerably, especially after he spied the snare.

Evidently at one time the place had been occupied by others who were less than sympathetic to the Invid. There were three small, almost igloolike shelters containing foodstuffs, tools, and lengths of cord and cable, but more important, the trees along the trail had been rigged to repel intruders.

Rand left Annie in Rook's care in one of the shelters and went off into the moonlight to investigate. That the designers of the traps had been after big game was immediately obvious, but each of the tree and cable mechanisms was in need of attention, and Rand realized that he was going to have to work fast if the snares were to serve their purpose. So while Rook and Annie warmed themselves, he went to work replacing worn cables, resecuring counterbalances, and sharpening stakes. He had to fell several medium-size trees, but he had been careful to select only those that would topple with the least amount of noise. And thus far there had been no sign of the Invid.

He was busy on a final piece of handiwork now, down on his knees in the snow using cutters on the cable that guyed the central snare.

"Aren't you finished yet?" he heard Rook ask behind him.

He turned from his task to give her a wry look. She was ten feet away, arms folded and a smirk on her face. "Hope you and Mint have been comfortable," he answered with elaborate concern.

Rook made an affected gesture. "Oh, we'll manage until the servants arrive. Have you been having fun with your cat's cradle?"

Rand twisted a final piece of cable around itself and stood up, regarding the contraption in a self-satisfied way.

"Sometimes I amaze myself."

Rook walked over and gave the wire a perplexed tug. "*This* is the better mousetrap you promised us?"

"You two just stay put in the shelter and leave the metal nightmares to me, okay?"

She scowled. "Your confidence is underwhelming."

"*Pretend* to believe in me," he quipped.

Just then Annie ran into the clearing, breathless and pointing back toward the foot of the chute.

"They're coming!"

Rand told Rook to see if she could do something about the tracks they had left in the snow, so she and Annie went to work with conifer switches while he smoothed the snow around the snare. He briefed his teammates on its workings and ran rapidly through the contingency plan he hoped they wouldn't have to resort to. Fifteen minutes later, he was climbing up into one of the trees and Annie and Rook were back in the shelter.

Rand squirreled around a bit until he found a good place for himself in the upper branches, then cupped his hands to his mouth and shouted, "Help! Help me, I'm hurt!" directing his false alarm along the trail that led to the base of the snowslide. Rook and Annie heard his call and hunkered down in the shelter, peering out at the clearing through a narrow slot in the wall. Soon they heard the sound of heavy footfalls, and a Trooper lumbered into the clearing, its blood-red scanner searching the trees.

Rand drew his H90 and reminded himself to remain calm. He could see that the Trooper was following the footprints they had purposely left intact on the trail.

"A little farther..." Rand encouraged, whispering to himself through gritted teeth.

The Invid took two more perfectly placed steps, which brought each of its cloven feet down into the trap's ring mechanisms. Cables cinched and tightened, while others grew taut, straining at turnbuckles and activating pulleys that had been concealed high in the surrounding branches. Elsewhere, poles and trees began to spring loose, groaning as they straightened up, released at last from their bowed bondage. The Trooper's feet were pulled out from under it, and suddenly it was being hauled into the air, captive and inverted.

Grinning in delight, Rand moved out onto the branch to view the hapless thing's ascent. But a moment later his smile was collapsing: the snare had been well engineered but underbuilt. Either that or the lashed trees had seen too many seasons. One after another they were beginning to splinter under the Trooper's weight; cables stretched and snapped, and pulleys were ripped from their moorings. As the ship plummeted headfirst toward the snow, Rand armed his weapon and squeezed off four quick shots, only one of which connected. But all that served to do was alert the Invid to his presence. Before he could react, the Trooper's cannons came to life and discharged a blast that connected squarely with the trunk a few feet below his shaky perch. The tree came apart, and Rand and the upper section were blown backward by the explosion.

He and the Trooper hit the ground at almost the same instant, both of them knocked senseless by their falls. But the Invid was the first to stir. As the Trooper rose slowly to its feet, Rook and Annie saw the ship's scanner wink into awareness. Rand was still unconscious, facedown in the snow, one outstretched arm hooked around the base of the tree he had slammed into on his way down. Annie began to scream.

Horrified, Rook watched the Invid take three forward steps and position itself over her fallen teammate. She barreled out of the shelter, yelling for Rand to wake up, raising her blaster even as the Trooper was raising its claw. She had to put five shots into the alien's back before it swung around, and when it did, it was clever enough to use its pincer as a shield. Undaunted, Rook continued to fire until she saw those telltale globes of priming light form at the ship's cannons; then she spun around and hastily tried to retreat. The Invid dropped her with a disc that threw her into a headlong crash. She rolled over, struggling to regain her breath as the Trooper approached, uncertain if she should be thankful that the thing had let her live. Suddenly she heard Annie's taunting voice close by and watched amazed as her diminutive friend began to pelt the towering ship with snowballs.

Rook raised herself and resumed fire, hoping to draw the Invid's attention before Annie succeeded in enraging it. Rand had meanwhile come around and was contributing his own bursts, and together they somehow managed to send the Trooper to its knees.

"Go, go!" Rand yelled, motioning Rook and Annie past him.

They both knew what he was up to and broke for the trail where Rand had rigged the second trap. Rook turned around to see if he was following.

"I'm right behind you!" she heard him yell.

And so was the Trooper, looming up over them and the trees, monstrous-looking in the moonlight, like the nightmare it was.

But it performed just as Rand had expected, stepping boldly along the path, unaware that one area held a special surprise. And in a moment the Trooper was sinking to its waist through the snow, down into a pit that had been dug underneath the trail.

"Cut your lines!" Rand shouted to the women.

Rook ran to the area he had indicated and drew her knife. She severed the cables as he called out the numbers. Instantly, sharpened logs swung down toward the trapped Trooper from the surrounding treetops. Thrusters blazing against the pit's hold, the Invid dodged the first two and parried the third with its pincer targone, but the fourth punched through the ship's scanner and immobilized it. The Trooper was lifted up out of the pit and sent flat on its back in the trail. The sharpened log protruded out of its blood-red eye like a stake thrust into a vampire's heart.

"God . . . we did it," Annie said in disbelief.

Rook wiped sweat from her brow. "Too close this time, just too close."

"Not bad." Rand smiled, striding over to the bleeding ship. "A bit primitive perhaps, but I had confidence in it."

Rook scoffed at him. "Sure thing, Rand. And I suppose almost getting yourself killed was part of the plan?"

"That's always part of my plan," he told her. "Just to impress you a bit."

"You're never scared?" Annie said, taken in.

Rook looked over at Rand, then down at Annie. "Only when no one's looking at him," she told her.

Somewhat closer to the chute, Scott and Lunk were attempting to bring their own primitive plan into play. They had skirted the edge of the woods, keeping themselves just above the tree line, then worked back toward the western buttress of the cirque. As hoped, the Invid commander had split its forces—*her* forces, Scott was now telling himself—but two of the four Troopers had picked up their trail and were narrowing the gap.

The avalanche had touched off secondary slides in several of the tributary crevasses below the basin, and in one of these, an exposed grouping of moraine boulders perched precariously above the gully's narrow floor. Scott thought that if they could lure the Troopers into the ravine, then somehow manage to loosen those boulders . . .

Lunk was skeptical, but he didn't see that there were any alternatives. The VTs and Cyclones hadn't been completely buried by the snow, but they couldn't even think about reaching them until they had cut the enemy down to size. So he volunteered to go up top and see if he could pry some of the rocks free, while Scott set out to bait the two enemy ships.

Lunk had found what he considered to be a persuasive boulder that would force the entire group into a slide, and he had his shoulder to it when Scott entered the ravine at a run, the Troopers right behind him. The lieutenant reached the end of the ravine and turned to fire a few shots at his pursuers, meant more to antagonize than to inflict any damage. But more than that, Scott's short burst was aimed at keeping the Troopers at bay for just the few seconds Lunk needed to send the boulder crashing down toward them.

"Hurry!" Lunk heard between H90 reports. "They're in position!"

Lunk shoved his bare shoulder to the stone, boots trying to find purchase in the snow. Down below, one of the Troopers opened fire on Scott. The anni discs threw up a fountain of snow that momentarily buried him, but Lunk saw Scott shake himself out of it. And perhaps it was the sight of his friend's peril that gave him the extra push he needed, because all at once the boulder was toppling over and commencing its slide and tumble toward the pack.

Scott heard the rock impact the mass and decided to help things along by training his weapon on the ledge itself. The charges from his MARS-Gallant did what sheer momentum alone couldn't, and in a moment the whole mass was avalanching toward the bottom of the ravine with a ground-shaking, deafening roar. Scott threw himself up the opposing slope, figuring the Invid would blast free of the ravine, giving him and Lunk a chance to reach the VTs. He never hoped they would actually catch the Troopers unaware, but that was exactly what happened. They had both tried to lift off, but the bounding rocks had shattered the ships' sensors, and in the confusion the things got caught up in the slide and were overturned and buried.

When the snow settled, Lunk appeared at the top of the ravine, a triumphant look on his face.

"Not bad, eh, Commander?!" he yelled down.

Scott surveyed the damage they had wrought and could only regard it in wonder. "Yeah, great, pal," he called back. "Just like we planned."

Lancer and Marlene had run clear through a finger of woods. They were not far from Rand and the others, but their trail had led them to the edge of a deep gully, with a river of snow several hundred feet below them. They had no way of knowing that the one Trooper on their tail was the last of the four.

Marlene seemed unaware of where she was or what it was they were running from. Lancer had simply pulled her along like a helpless child, often shielding her with his body from debris flung up by the Trooper's discs. But now all he could do was gaze hopelessly across the ten feet of empty space that separated them from the gully's opposite face.

"Maybe if we hurry we can double back around," Lancer told her, trying to make it sound feasible.

But as he took hold of her thin wrist again and prepared to set off, he saw the Trooper emerging from the woods, closing in on them fast. Marlene understood that they would have to jump across the abyss. She nodded to Lancer, her forehead wrinkled up in apprehension.

They gave themselves several yards of runway and made a mad dash toward the ledge, hand in hand as they soared across the chasm. And they almost made it. But they fell short by a foot, catching hold of the edge—which was really little more than snow—and falling backward to what they thought would be the chasm bottom.

Instead, however, they landed on a narrow ledge approximately ten feet below the lip.

Lancer was thinking that things couldn't get much worse, but of course they could. Above them, the Invid command ship came into view. But to his surprise, he watched as the control nacelle sprang open and a Human pilot jumped down from the padded cockpit. It was the same brainwashed captive he had seen on the island: a slim female of medium height with punked out green-blond hair and eyes as red as a Trooper's scanner. She wore a bodysuit of colored panels that emphasized the body's major muscle groups in swaths of black, purple, and pink—like the colors of the command ship itself.

"I know you," Lancer called to her as she peered down at them. "Why are you fighting for the Invid?"

The woman's only response was to mock him with a short laugh.

Lancer pointed at her accusingly. "You're a traitor! Answer me: Why are you fighting for them?"

Sera continued to stare at the Human, angered and confused at the same time. *I should destroy this thing called man*, she thought. *But for some reason I cannot.*

The Trooper who had pursued Lancer and Marlene through the woods appeared on the opposite ledge now, but it, too, held its fire.

Lancer regarded the ship warily, then swung back around to confront the woman, who was obviously in command of the situation. "Can't you understand me?!" he demanded. When he failed to get a response, he altered his tone to one of cynical surrender. "Then get it over with. But spare this woman. She's done no wrong."

Marlene and Sera met each other's gaze. And during the exchange, which Lancer thought brief, a wealth of racial memories was transmitted.

That face . . . thought Marlene. *It's as though time has stopped and I can look into my past and my future simultaneously* . . .

Sera's face had dissolved, but Marlene seemed to follow those flashphoto eyes on a journey through space and

time. Cosmic vistas opened up before her, stains and
weblike filigrees of brilliantly hued clouds, swirls and
spirals of galactic stuff strewn like diamonds on velvet.
She beheld a vision of Optera through Sera's eyes, of the
Invid as they were before the coming of Zor, of the
Flowers before the Fall. Then Sera's unconscious un-
locked for her the horrors of days since. Marlene saw the
quest for their stolen grail; the transmutation of the race
to an army of relentless warriors, burdened with a need
for mecha and Protoculture that rivaled the Masters'
own; the trip across the galaxy to this planet they now
called their own; and the dispossession of its indigenous
beings, just as they themselves had once been dispos-
sessed. . . .

And there was a voice in Marlene's mind—one that
she could not identify but that at the same time seemed to
be her own:

*"Reach into the cosmic consciousness of your race,
Ariel,"* the voice told her. *"And although you feel you are
dreaming, watch and observe the beauty of your home.
For we are a race of powerful beings destined to control
the universe with our intellect and power, and you, Ariel,
are a part of that power. Come back to us, my child; come
back, Ariel, and rejoin the hive. . ."*

Marlene stared at Sera as her face took form once
again, the journey through space-time concluded, and
thought: *I know her: we're like sisters somehow. . .*

Then without warning, explosions were rocking the
ledge and erupting around the base of Sera's command
ship. Scott and the rest of the team had positioned themselves on the ridgeline above the gully and were firing
bursts against the command ship and its sole minion.

Momentarily confused by the renewed fighting, Sera
broke off her contact with Marlene and returned to the
cockpit of her ship, lifting off at once and joining her
charge on the opposite side of the chasm. But no sooner
did she touch down than the ledge gave way and the two
dropped together, impacting rocks and outcroppings as
they fell.

Lunk and Rand pulled Lancer and Marlene to safety. It seemed unbelievable that they had all survived and that all their crazed plans had worked. But even more unsettling was the Human pilot who had once again demonstrated a bewildering ambivalence. Scott refused to believe that the woman had purposely stayed her hand; he pointed out how she had fired on him earlier without compunction. Lancer, however, knew better than to accept Scott's explanation that the woman had been *distracted* by their sudden fire. And he also saw that something inexplicable had transpired between the woman and Marlene. Both Rand and Annie had been touched by the Invid consciousness in the past, but their psychic encounters had been brief and transient. Marlene, on the other hand, had been profoundly affected.

"I don't belong with you," Marlene told Lancer later, when the others had moved off in the direction of the buried mecha. "Please, Lancer, I'll just bring trouble for all of you. . . ."

He tried to comfort her as best he could by offering himself as her protector. And that did seem to calm her a bit. But it brought him little succor.

Who would be next to feel the enemy's mind probe? he wondered, shivering as he led Marlene away from the abyss.

■ ■ ■ ■ ■ ■ ■ ■ ■ ■ ■ ■ ■ ■ ■ ■ ■

CHAPTER
THREE

*In quieter moments I find myself wondering about the men
and women I have served with during these long campaigns. I
think about the ones left behind, like Max and Miriya, and the
ones sent away, like John Carpenter, Frank Tandler, Owen,
and the rest. The list goes on and on. Would I have joined that
crew had it not been for the Sentinels; abandoned these dark
domains for even a chance at seeing Earth's blue skies once
again? I think: Absolutely. But what can my homeworld offer
me now? Certainly not peace, that endangered species. Retire-
ment, perhaps. How Lisa would laugh!*

> Admiral Hunter, as quoted in Selig Kahler, *The Tiro-
> lian Campaign*

F REEING THE VERITECHS AND CYCLONES FROM THE
snowslide proved to be a greater challenge than anyone
had expected. The team brought the collective heat of
their MARS-Gallant H90 hand blasters to bear against
the massive chunks of ice that had been loosed during the
avalanche, by sunrise they had succeeded in defrosting
the Alpha Fighter. Tango-9 explosive and the VT's thrusters did the rest of the work in a tenth the time, but Annie
and Marlene sustained mild cases of frostbite nonetheless. And despite Scott's optimistic projection, it took the
team several false starts and another two days to cross the
Sierra range. But waiting for them was the desert with
those warm highland winds, and with it came a renewed
sense of purpose and determination.

This was the same arid expanse crossed by pioneers
and adventurers during North America's push toward its
western horizon, but few would have recognized it as

such. Over the course of the last two decades the region had seen periods of devastation to rival those of its geoformative years. Dolza's fleet of four million had not overlooked the cities that had grown up here, and neither had Khyron after New Macross had risen to the fore. Vast stretches of the territory were cratered from the thousands of annihilation bolts rained upon it, host still to equal numbers of rusting Zentraedi dreadnoughts, thrust like war lances into the ravaged land. Just north of the team's present route were the remains of Monument City, which had played such a pivotal role in the Second Robotech War.

Population centers had grown up in some of the craters, but most of these were abandoned now, their onetime residents returned to life-styles more befitting the territory's original nomadic tribespeople than the Robotechnologists who had once tried to breathe new life into the wastes.

Scott had listened intently to Lancer and Lunk's information; he of course had read and heard accounts of Macross and Monument, and the team's propinquity to those legendary cities filled him with an awe usually reserved for sacred places and archeological power spots. It made him think about the long road that had taken him back to this land of his parents' birth and the treacherous one that lay ahead. The team was close to Reflex Point now—the presence of an Invid tower assured him of this much—but he had to wonder how many more twists and turns they would have to negotiate before they stood at the portal of the Regis's central hive, how many Invid stood in their way, and how many more deaths their journey would entail.

There were many such communication towers placed around the hive complex, and Scott knew from past experience that the team's further progress toward Reflex Point would depend on how many of these they could circumvent, or better still, destroy. Options were discussed while the team made temporary camp near a meandering river where cottonwoods and conifers provided a narrow green ribbon of safety and shade. In the end it was decided that Scott and Rand would recon the outlying area; nearby were the ruins of a deserted city and what appeared to be an inhabited town. Annie insisted on tagging along, hoping they would run across a cowboy or two.

The three freedom fighters set out on Cyclones, Annie in her customary place on the pillion seat behind Rand. Only Scott was suited up in battle armor. Rand had tried to talk him out of it but soon recognized that Scott fancied himself the only law and order between here and Reflex Point.

A short ride brought them into the town they had glimpsed from the Veritechs, a curious combination of high-tech modular buildings and wooden structures fashioned after centuries-old designs, complete with elaborate facades, shaded boardwalks, and hitching posts for horses and pack animals. The dirt streets were empty, but this no longer came as any surprise. Scott was certain the townsfolk were well aware of their arrival and were merely concealing themselves until the proper moment. As they powered the Cyclones down the town's main street, he could almost feel the weapons being trained on them from upper-story windows.

The one thing he hadn't figured on was getting arrested.

But that's just what the residents of Bushwhack had in mind when they finally did show themselves, twenty or so strong, dressed in Twentieth-century garb and armed with antique rifles, shotguns, and revolvers. They formed a broad circle around the rebels and ordered Scott and Rand away from their mecha. Scott was willing to comply—even to go as far as removing his battle armor —until he saw the ropes come out. But by then it was too late to do much about it. He and Rand were stripped of their weapons, tied up, and led by the jeering mob to the sheriff's office.

He was a short, stocky man with curly black hair and a handlebar mustache. He was wearing a beat-up felt fedora and a sheepskin coat. Scott didn't see any badge displayed, but when the sheriff pointed a six-gun at him, he stopped looking.

"Anybody who goes around dressed like that is just *lookin'* for trouble," the sheriff told him, gesturing to the heap of Cyclone armor Scott had piled in the street. "I reckon you're under arrest, strangers."

"But we haven't done anything!" Rand protested, struggling against the rope coiled around his arms. Silently he cursed himself for having listened to Scott's harebrained logic about uniforms and earning respect.

"Well, you look like you *might* do something," the sheriff answered him, putting the muzzle of the revolver close to Scott's head.

"It's illegal!" Scott argued, trying to step away.

"Yeah, you can't arrest us without charges," Annie added.

The sheriff's dark eyes narrowed. "Z'at so? Well, I reckon I'll be the one to decide that, young 'un. You renegade soldiers and your catch try to take over everything. But we're not lettin' you take over this town."

"Who'd want to, anyway?" said Annie.

"But we're not renegades," Scott argued. "I'm from Mars—"

"From Mars?!" The sheriff laughed and turned to the crowd. "Here that, folks? He's from Mars!" The crowd started whooping it up. "Reckon you better tell it to the judge, robby."

"Fine," Scott said through gritted teeth. "Lead us to him."

The sheriff flashed a smile and pushed his hat back on his head. "You're lookin' at 'im."

Again the crowd got into the spirit, laughing and jeering. One dangled a noose in front of Rand's face, while a second began to inspect Rand's boots with an evil glint in his eye. There was what amounted to a festive atmosphere brewing, so much so that no one took notice of the two strange figures who were watching the scene from nearby. One was perhaps two feet shorter than his com-

panion, but both were clothed alike, in bottletop ₂
helmets, cowls, and full-length cloaks.

"Looks as though these strangers are going to be occupied for a spell," said the taller of the two.

"Then I guess they won't be needin' their Cyclones,
huh, Roy?"

"I feel it only right that we see to it that no harm
comes to them."

"The Cyclones, you mean."

"Now what else would I mean?"

"Well, you coulda meant the strangers."

Roy made a face. "Now, have you ever heard me express any concern for strangers before?"

"No . . . but—"

"And is it *likely* that I would be concerned about the
strangers?"

"Well, no. But—"

"Then I think it would be prudent for you to adhere to
our original plan."

"Adhere, Roy?"

"As in 'stick to.'"

"I should get the truck?"

Roy let out an exasperated sound. "Yes, Shorty, you
should get the truck."

Back at the camp on the outskirts of town, Lancer,
Lunk, Rook, and Marlene were doing what they could to
camouflage the VTs with strategically placed branches
and bunches of sagebrush and tumbleweed. They had
moved the fighters to a kind of natural shelter Lancer
discovered, a rock outcropping with plenty of surrounding scrub. It seemed a senseless task, but at least it was
keeping everyone busy.

Lancer hadn't been in favor of Scott's heading off into
town; whenever Scott disappeared, it usually spelled trouble for the rest of them. It was some comfort to know that
Rand and Annie were with him, but not enough to keep
Lancer from worrying. The major source of his concern,
however, was Marlene. She had said little these past two

days, and it was obvious to Lancer that her confrontation with the Human pilot of the Invid command ship had had a devastating effect. Was it possible, he asked himself, that Marlene herself had once been used in a similar fashion? Perhaps she had escaped after her own command ship had been destroyed. There was a certain logic to it, since, like the blond pilot, Marlene seemed to have no recall of her past life.

I don't belong with you, Lancer could hear her say. *I'll just bring trouble.*

Marlene was aware of Lancer's concerns and smiled weakly at him as she continued to tug handfuls of tall grass from the sandy earth. Then suddenly she was down on her knees, moaning and clutching her pale hands at her temples. Lancer jumped down from the radome of the Alpha, but Rook beat him to Marlene's side and was already stroking the tortured woman's long hair and speaking soothing words into her ear by the time Lancer got to her.

"She must be sensing the Invid again," Rook told Lancer and Lunk. "I *told* Scott this would happen if we camped too close to that communications tower."

Lunk shook his head. "We're not that close to the thing. But maybe there's a Protoculture farm around here."

Lancer knelt down to take Marlene's hand. "Marlene, can you tell us what you're feeling? Can you tell from the pain whether it's a patrol or a hive?"

Marlene pressed the heel of her hand to her forehead and made an agonized sound.

"You're asking a lot of her, Lancer," said Lunk.

"Look," Lancer said, turning around. "I know what I'm asking. But it could be that Scott and Rand are in danger, and Marlene might be able to lead us to the source of it."

Rook looked at him as though he had just sentenced Marlene to the rack. "The closer she gets, the more unbearable the pain becomes. I don't have to tell you that."

"No, you don't. But *all* of us are at risk here—not

just Marlene." He touched Marlene's cheek with his fingertips, and she opened her eyes. "The decision's yours. Do you think you can lead us to the source of your pain?"

"I can . . . try," she responded weakly.

Lancer tightened his mouth and nodded. "Then we're going out together," he said, getting up.

Rook and Lunk were dead set against it, but Lancer convinced them that there was really no other choice. Marlene was part of the team, with strengths and weaknesses just like the rest of them. And it only made sense to exploit her strengths, especially when that early warning system of hers was kicking in. So an hour later Lancer and Marlene were cruising out over the wastes, side by side in the APC that Lunk had reluctantly given up.

"Are you all right?" Lancer asked her after they had been driving for some time.

She nodded without saying anything.

"Is the pain still there?"

"Not now. It's like someone just switched it off inside me."

"It would help if you could remember something about your past."

"I feel like I was born on the day you people found me, Lancer. There's nothing beyond that—I'm empty."

He looked over at her. "Still, you *had* a life. We just need to find out who you were."

Marlene shrugged. "How much do you remember about the day you were born?"

"Not very much," he started to say. Then all at once there were two men on horseback positioned in front of the vehicle. Lancer brought the APC up short, instinctively extending his right arm across Marlene; the horses reared, their riders leveling rifles.

"One false move and I'll make a lead mine outta yer innards!" warned one of the men. "How's that fer threats?" he asked his partner.

The second rider repeated the warning to himself and shook his head. "I don't like it. Too . . . *cryptic*." He brought his rifle to bear on Lancer. "Supposin' you tell us what yer doin' in these here parts, Lavender Locks."

Lancer suppressed a grin. The man had on a bandanna and a tiny pair of tinted goggles. His voice sounded like sandpaper on cement. "We were just out driving around, and we got lost," he told them sheepishly.

"Yeah?" said the first rider. " 'Pears to me you had sumthin' on yer mind 'sides yer drivin'." He began to laugh knowingly, leering at Marlene.

Lancer smiled and put his arm around Marlene, pulling her close. "Well, shucks," he mimicked the rider. "Iffen you have to know, we're newlywed honeymooners."

"Well, no wonder yer all distracted," the rider exclaimed, lowering his weapon. "I would be, too!"

"Stop cackling and tend to business, Jesse," his cohort told him. "You folks might not know it, but there's an outlaw gang operatin' out here, an' yer lucky ya didn't go and git yer car 'n' everythin' stole out from under ya." He disarmed his weapon.

"Worse'n that, yer headed right smack dab straight into Invid territory."

"Garldarn," said Lancer, playing it up. "Me and my little bride 'preciate yer bein' so neighborly as to warn us like that."

The gruff-voiced man seemed to offer a grin beneath the bandanna. "Seems we speak the same language, stranger, so I tell ya what we're gonna do: We're gonna show ya where you can buy some mighty fine weapons to defend yerselves." He tugged at the reins to bring his mount about. "Ya jus' follow us."

The two riders began to gallop off. Lancer kept the APC close behind. Their trail angled east along the remains of a once-broad highway.

"Why are you trusting them?" Marlene asked.

"I'm not. But I'm curious about these weapons. Maybe there's a resistance group operating around here."

The highwaymen led them down into one of the devastated crater cities Scott and Rand had flown over earlier that day. Its once-tall towers were nothing but empty shells now, burned and collapsed like fallen layer cakes. Some time ago a river had altered course and turned most of the crater into a polluted lake. But adjacent to the resultant waterfall, practically beneath its thunderous flow, was a massive tunnel that led to an arena of some sort, and it was into this that the riders disappeared. "Hole in the wall," they called it. Inside, however, was an even greater surprise: the rusting remains of a Robotech battle fortress. It had put down on its belly and somehow seemed to be fused to its ruined surroundings.

Lancer couldn't help but register his astonishment. The ship was nothing like the cruisers developed during the Second Robotech War; it had more in common with the organically fashioned Zentraedi battlewagons of the First. And yet it was not quite Zentraedi, either. The sleek sharklike bow and massive triple-thrustered stern were closer to the hybrids he had heard about—ships constructed on Tirol and sent home under the command of a certain Major John Carpenter. Lancer said as much to the two riders. They had dismounted and doffed their helmets and cowls; in place of the techno-outlaws who had stopped the APC stood two silver-haired old-timers with thick mustaches and faces aged from a myriad of suns.

"Yep, and she's old and rusty, just like her crew," said the one called Jesse, who affected a headband and had a crazed way of laughing.

"Then you were part of Admiral Hunter's command," said Lancer.

"That's something we don't talk about around here, sonny," returned Frank, who may have had a few years on his saddlemate. His hair was shorter than Jesse's, and his mustache lacked the same outlaw droop.

Just then a third member of the gang stepped through an open hatchway in the grounded ship. He had a cooking pot in one hand and a ladle in the other. With his clean-shaven face and trimmed black hair he appeared to

be much younger than either of his companions; more-
over, he wore a sky-blue uniform that bore some resem-
blance to Scott's. Lancer saw, however, that there was no
sign of life in the soldier's dark eyes. He tried to question
the man as he passed by the driver's seat of the APC but
got no response.

"Don't pay no attention to him," Jesse told Lancer.
"Gabby hasn't spoken a work to anybody since he came
here."

Frank motioned them toward the ramp that led to the
hold of the battlecruiser. "Come on in here, stranger, so's
we can show you what we got."

Lancer and Marlene followed them in. Piled high inside were high-tech crates Lancer knew to contain laser-
array ordnance of all description.

Jesse made a broad sweep with his arm. "Welcome to
the best-stocked tradin' post in the whole West!"

Back in town, the sheriff was trying to follow the
rapid, angry flow of Scott's words. He and his men had
tossed the three renegade soldiers into a cell, but it hadn't
put an end to the leader's ranting and raving.

"Just in case you're interested, *Sheriff*," Scott was saying now, his hands gripped on the bars of the cell, "I
happen to be an officer with Mars Division. We were sent
here from Tirol by Admiral Hunter to liberate Earth from
the Invid's hold. As far as I know I'm the only survivor of
the assault group, but regardless, my orders are to locate
and destroy the Invid Regis and the central hive at Reflex
Point. Short of that I—"

"Enough!" the sheriff shouted, holding up his hands.
The man had been going on like this for more than an
hour, and he couldn't take much more of it—all this talk
about assault groups and an attack fleet on its way to
Earth from the other side of the galaxy.... Every so often
one would hear this sort of thing from people who had
come wandering in off the wastes looking like they had
just received communiqués from the Lord Almighty, but
that didn't mean that he had to sit still and listen to every

last one of them. "You're just wastin' your breath if you expect me to believe such a cock-and-bull story. Besides, I heard tell of a better one than that by the last group of waste wackos who showed up here."

Scott was about to take up the argument from a different front when he heard a shot ring out from outside the sheriff's office. A moment later one of the sheriff's men burst through the front door.

"Rustlers, Sheriff! They got the motorsickles!"

Scott shook the bars and cursed.

Rand shouted: "Don't let them get away, Sheriff!"

The sheriff made it to the door in time to see two of his men emptying their revolvers at a truck that was tearing down the main street. He could just discern a figure in the open back, a cloaked and helmeted figure yelling above the noise of gunfire: "Much obliged, Sheriff! We never woulda gotten away with 'em iffen you hadn't locked away the strangers!"

The sheriff glanced in at the jail cell through the open office door, then once more at the truck.

"You're responsible for this, Sheriff!" Scott called out, furious.

"You've endangered our entire mission," said Rand.

"You dumb hick!" Annie added.

The sheriff contemplated his position: the rustlers were well known to him, and he certainly didn't fancy tangling with them. At the same time, he was responsible for the strangers' property. So it only made sense to let the strangers go after their own machines. He turned to one of his deputies and said: "Saddle up a coupla fast horses."

"This model must date clear back to the war against the Robotech Masters," said Lancer, hefting one of the samples from the opened crate. It was really not much different from the laser rifles the team was used to, except that the muzzle was somewhat thicker and the trigger mechanism more complex.

"Gen-yoo-wine army issue," Jesse said proudly.

Lancer brought the rifle up to high port position. "Guess it wouldn't be considered good taste to ask where you got them, huh?"

"Why should you care?" Jesse wanted to know.

"Good customers don't ask too many questions," cautioned Frank, swigging from a bottle of whiskey.

Jesse laughed. "Frank's right, Lavender. But I reckon there's no harm in tellin' ya."

He came across the hold to explain himself, close enough for Lancer to see the space madness in his eyes.

"Way back when, we was soldiers. The army issued these weapons to us."

"So you're part of this ship's rusty old crew." Lancer grinned. "Then why aren't you out fighting the Invid with all this firepower instead of playing rustler?"

Jesse scowled and looked away for a moment. "We had our fill of fightin'. We were with Admiral Gloval on the SDF-1; after, we signed up fer duty with the Expeditionary mission. Traveled clear across the galaxy, sonny, a godfersakin' place called Tirol. Then we made one heck of a mistake and tied in with Major Carpenter. 'Course, we finally made it back all right, but by then General Leonard and his boys had their hands full with the Robotech Masters. So we jus' kinda *retired*, if you know what I mean. Now we sell supplies to resistance fighters, so I reckon we're doin' our part."

Marlene saw Lancer's face begin to flush and did what she could to calm him down by sliding under his arm and laying her head against his shoulder. But Lancer's anger was not so easily assuaged.

"Making a nice profit for yourselves, aren't you?"

Jesse laughed. "Reckon we are at that."

"You're nothing but a pack of deserters," he started to say. But suddenly there were new sounds wafting in from outside the hold. A truck had pulled up in the arena. Lancer heard someone shout: "Look what we got!" followed by a wild "*yaahoo!*"

Jesse and Frank were standing by the hatch. "Wonder

where they stole those?" Jesse said before the two men stepped outside.

Lancer heard the Cyclone engines.

"Why don't you see if you can make a little more noise?" yelled Frank. "I don't think them thangs can be heard more'n twenty miles away!"

"Aw, the sheriff didn't even bother to send a posse after us," the new arrival yelled back, laughing as wildly as Jesse had a moment before.

"Keep that talk down, Shorty," Frank ordered. "We got company."

As Lancer and Marlene were stepping down the hold ramp, Jesse swung around to ask them if they were interested in buying a couple of Cyclones. Lancer saw two men in cloaks and helmets astride mecha they had ridden out of the back of the truck. It took him a moment to recognize the Cycs, and he had to quiet Marlene before she said anything.

"Young folks, meet Roy and Shorty," said Frank, gesturing to the men. Roy was tall, with a blockish, bald head. Shorty had crossed eyes and a pinched-up face. He bristled at Frank's introduction.

"I told you not to call me Shorty, Frank!"

"Well, we gotta call you *something*," Frank answered him.

Jesse leaned across the Cyclone's handlebars to thrust his chin at Shorty. "We'd call ya by your real name if ya could remember what it was, *Shorty*!"

Shorty raised himself on the footrests. "That ain't funny!"

It looked as though he might have taken a swing at Jesse just then, but Gabby appeared out of nowhere with his pot and put a quick end to it by ladling some hot stew onto Shorty's bare hand.

Shorty screamed and clutched himself, while the rest of the band had a good laugh.

"Gabby ain't too fonda Shorty," Jesse told Lancer and Marlene. "Ain't that right, Gabby?"

Gabby stood still, almost catatonic, oblivious to it all.

"Fact is, Gabby ain't too fond of nobody," Frank chimed in. "He's a little funny in the head."

Lancer looked over at the uniformed man and experienced a rush of compassion. Gabby seemed to pick up on it and walked toward the hatchway, proffering the pot of stew to Marlene.

"Look out, folks!" Shorty warned them. "He might throw it at ya!"

But instead, he simply held the pot out until Marlene took it from his hand.

Frank felt his chin. "Well, I'll be hornswaggled. He's offerin' it to you."

Marlene thanked him.

"Well, isn't *this* a day for surprises?" said Roy.

Shorty nursed his burned hand. "First time I ever seen him do anything nice for anyone."

"He tried to rejoin Hunter's outfit when those kids from the 15th ATACs got hold of Jonathan Wolff's ship," Frank explained. "But his Veritech got shot down before he could make it."

Jesse snorted. "Durn fool wuz tryin' to git back into the war agin. He's gotta be crazier'n a bedbug."

The four old veterans collapsed in laughter.

CHAPTER
FOUR

Dr. Lang considered him an army brat and tried on more than one occasion to instill him with some sense of objectivity, but Scott was a lost cause. If he couldn't persuade, his inclination was to force. And this kind of behavior was simply not tolerated in the lab. Lang would tell him: "You can't force experiments or people to conform to your world view! The universe just doesn't work that way!" Scott heard him but was not so easily convinced. He had little patience in those days and was often accused of being arrogant and judgmental. Type A, all the way.

Xandu Reem, *A Stranger at Home: A Biography of Scott Bernard*

LANCER ASKED HIMSELF HOW SHORTY AND ROY could have come across Scott and Rand's Cyclones. There was some talk about a local sheriff and how he had been foolish enough to leave the Cycs unattended. It was beginning to sound like Scott had gotten himself into another fix, but Lancer had yet to find out why or where his teammates were being held. He had barely enough scrip to purchase one of the laser rifles, let alone buy back the Cyclones, but he wondered if he couldn't persuade the Robotech veterans to rescue Scott for old time's sake. After all, they had all been on the SDF-3 together, and chances were that Frank or one of them had at least *heard* of Scott Bernard, the Pioneer Mission's youngest member.

They had all moved back into the hold of the cruiser, which functioned as the group's living quarters as well as their high-tech trading post. Marlene and Lancer had gorged themselves on Gabby's delicious stew. The shell-shocked soldier had taken to them and, in his eerily silent fashion, was treating them more like honored guests than potential customers. Frank, Jesse, Roy, and Shorty were engaged in a wild game of cards that required two full decks and seemed to be a hybrid of gin rummy and draw poker.

"Come on, Lady Luck," Shorty was saying now, "give me the card I want." He took one from the facedown stack just as Jesse was throwing one faceup beside it.

"You can have this one, Shorty."

But Shorty was too busy kissing the card he had picked to respond to Jesse's offer. "Jus' the one I wanted," he crowed. "How 'bout that!"

Frank looked at his hand and made a disappointed sound. The cards were an inverted fan in his left hand; his right gripped a whiskey flask.

"Don't need this 'un either," said Jesse, discarding another.

"Gentlemen, I fold," Roy announced stiffly, although he kept the cards in his hand.

Shorty started bouncing up and down in his seat. "Frank, y' ole coot, ya gonna play or not?"

"Hang on, I'm jus' tryin' to decide how much to raise you."

"Yer bluffin'!"

Gabby served a cup of steaming tea to Marlene, who smiled and thanked him. Lancer watched the man shuffle off into an adjoining compartment separated from the hold by cinched curtains. Gabby sat down at a communications console and began to throw switches.

"Is that transceiver in working condition?" Lancer asked loudly enough to cut through the card-table conversations.

Frank answered him. "Like everything else around here, it's wore out." Dismissively, he threw his cards to the table. "We still receive transmissions from the Expeditionary Force, but we can't respond to 'em."

Jesse grunted and laughed. "Gabby keeps turnin' it on like maybe he's expectin' a message from somebody."

Gabby seemed to hear the men ridiculing him; forlornly, he got up from the console and left the hold.

"What do the transmissions say?" Lancer asked after Gabby had gone.

"Who knows?" Shorty cackled. "We don't pay no attention to 'em."

Lancer leaned back in his chair. *What a sad bunch*, he thought. *Soldiers who have lost the will to fight . . .* He was about to launch into the speech he hoped would rekindle their spirits, when Marlene suddenly shot to her feet and let out a low groan of pain. Lancer stood up and took hold of her quaking shoulders; she had her eyes closed, her fingertips pressed to her temples.

"What is it, Marlene? Are you hearing the Invid broadcasting towers again?"

The four veterans voiced a shocked "*Whaaatt*?!"

"The tower must be broadcasting again," Lancer explained without thinking.

Alarmed all at once, Frank stood up. "You mean she can hear 'em?" He gestured to the others. "Git 'em, boys! I reckon these two to be Invid spies!"

"You're wrong," Lancer told them, shielding Marlene.

"Well, I think Frank's right," Jesse said menacingly.

"I knew there was sumthin' funny 'bout 'em," snarled Shorty.

Frank leveled a hand blaster that resembled an antique short-barreled staple gun. "Don't make a move," he warned Lancer. "If she *ain't* an Invid, how come she hears their signals?"

Lancer took Marlene into his arms while she sobbed. "She's been traumatized by them. It affected her hearing somehow—it's more sensitive than ours."

Jesse scoffed. "That's 'cause we're Human and she's an Invid!"

"That's not true," Lancer shouted, leading Marlene slowly away from the couch and closer to the external hatch. "She's suffered more from the Invid attacks than any of you! You can see for yourselves the agonizing pain their broadcast signals put her through."

Shorty took a step forward. "You're whistlin' in the wind, pretty boy. We ain't buyin' it!"

Roy uttered a kind of growl and began to move in bearlike, his huge mitts raised. Lancer backed Marlene against the bulkhead and turned her in his arms. "Think she's an Invid, huh?" He pulled her to him and kissed her full on the mouth. Startled at first, Marlene began to relax and return his tenderness. The veterans went wide-eyed.

"Whoa!" said Jesse. "Don't reckon he'd kiss an Invid like that, do you, Frank?"

"They might be aliens, but they sure ain't *strangers*," laughed Shorty.

"Hol' up, kids, 'fore ya short out our pacemakers."

Lancer broke off his embrace. "That was the most pleasant way to prove a point I could ever imagine," he whispered, looking into Marlene's eyes.

Frank tucked away his blaster and sat down on the edge of the table. "No hard feelings, kids. Consider yourselves among friends."

Lancer saw his chance to enlist their aid. "Does that mean you'd be willing to help us?"

Frank looked at him questioningly. "What possible help could we be? We're just a bunch of old—*huh?!*"

An explosion rocked the ship.

"The telltale sound of trouble," said Roy, reaching for a weapon.

From the hatchway they saw two Troopers complete a pass over the arena. Gabby, some sort of tote bag clutched in his right hand, was running a jagged course toward the ship. A single charge from one of the Invid ships tore into the already ruined street, throwing him off his feet. Roy had a rocket launcher on his shoulder; he fired and caught the Invid with a glancing shot to its underbelly.

"Lay down some more cover fire!" Frank yelled. "I'll go try to fetch 'im!"

"No, wait," Lancer said, pulling the launcher from Roy's grip. "I can move faster. I'll get him."

Lancer raised the weapon and darted out into the arena. The second Trooper was swinging around and preparing for another pass. "Make a run for it!" he told Gabby, helping him to his feet. "I'll keep you covered."

Wordlessly, Gabby struggled to his knees, but instead of heading for the escort, he doubled back to retrieve the tote bag he had dropped. The Trooper, meanwhile, was coming in low overhead. Lancer seated the launcher on his right shoulder, centered the ship in the weapon's laser sight, and triggered the missile. His shot was sure, straight to the Invid's optic core; a brief fireball and the enemy disintegrated.

Gabby was still on his hands and knees but now had the bag tight in his arms.

"Leave it!" Lancer barked, hearing the sound of the first Trooper's thrusters. "Whatever it is, it isn't worth risking your life!" But he had begun to wonder. Gabby looked up at him, words of explanation in his eyes, and fumbled with the bag's latch. Puzzled, Lancer went down on one knee to gaze at the contents: it was Gabby's battle armor.

All at once the ground rumbled. Lancer reshouldered the launcher and twisted. The first Trooper had put down behind them, its right pincer raised for a crushing blow. Lancer squeezed off a second projectile, which tore into the Invid's scanner, dropping it instantly. He was on his feet watching the thing bleed green when he heard Rand's voice in the distance.

"We've been looking all over for you!"

Rand was waving at him from atop a heap of slacked steel that had once been part of the arena's superstructure. Scott and Annie were with him, along with the horses they had ridden in on.

Not exactly the cavalry arriving in the nick of time, Lancer said to himself while returning the wave, but it was good to see them just the same.

* * *

Lancer led his teammates to the Robotech ship; Scott filled him in on their brief incarceration and the theft of the Cyclones, and Lancer primed Scott for the surprises in store. Everyone remembered the incident with Jonathan Wolff, and Rand especially was concerned about Scott's reaction to all this. It was certainly good news that the Cycs were safe, but Rand knew that Scott wouldn't let it go at that—not when the rustlers were soldiers who had once served with the illustrious Expeditionary Force.

The veterans claimed never to have heard of Scott Bernard. This didn't surprise Rand, given the fact that some of them apparently couldn't even recall their own names. Besides, from what Scott had told him, the Pioneer Mission had had an enormous crew, and Major Carpenter's contingent had separated from the main body of the force early on in the mission. They had been lost in space for approximately ten years, but Scott wasn't about to cut them any slack.

Frank was the first to catch Scott's wrath—square on the side of his jaw.

"You cowardly scum!" Scott raved, sending the old man backward into the arms of his companions. "I hate to even dirty my fists on you."

Rand kept his mouth shut, but he wished for once that Scott could control his temper.

"We ain't soldiers any longer," Jesse was telling Scott, wagging a bony finger in the lieutenant's face. "And we don't take orders from the likes of you or anyone else! So if ya wanna attack the Invids, you'll jus' have to do it on yer own!"

"You're all traitors!" Scott bellowed back, grabbing Jesse by the shirtfront and glaring at him.

Lancer put his hand on Scott's shoulder. "Back off, Scott, you're wasting your time. They fought bravely against the Zentraedi, but the fight's gone out of them. Obviously they're no match for the Invid now."

Scott growled and propelled Jesse backward into Roy's arms. It looked for a moment like he was ashamed of himself, but just then he caught the telltale sounds of the transceiver. He rushed into the adjoining cabin, where Gabby was seated at the console.

"A working transceiver?" Rand heard Scott say before roughly snatching the headphones from Gabby's grip and shoving him aside. "Calling Admiral Hunter," Scott began. "Come in, Admiral Hunter..."

Frank, Jesse, and the others burst out laughing until Scott turned on them.

"What's so damned funny?"

"The transmitter doesn't work," Lancer explained while the old men tried to stifle their chuckling. "Just the receiver."

Scott looked at the console in disbelief. "It what—"

Suddenly the monitor screen flashed, and the external speakers crackled to life. "This is the Expeditionary Force calling all Earth stations. Do you read us? Come in Earth stations...."

"We receive you, com base," Scott spoke into the headset, desperation evident in his voice. "This is Earth station receiving Expeditionary Force command...."

The face of a young man began to resolve on the screen. It was a clean-shaven face with blue eyes, fine-featured and framed by shaggy brown hair.

"If anyone is reading this message, your orders are to rendezvous with the Expeditionary Force at Reflex Point. Ships of the main fleet will be entering Earthspace within two weeks Earthtime this transmission...."

"Admiral Hunter jus' won't give up," Jesse commented.

"He's sure a spunky one, ya gotta give 'im that," said Shorty.

The image had de-rezzed by now. Through it all Gabby had been staring at the screen as though he had seen a ghost. While Scott continued to fiddle with the console controls, Gabby shuffled mindlessly toward the hatch.

"We've got to take out the broadcast towers," Scott was saying to no one in particular. "If we can cripple even some of them... Hey! Where's he going?"

Rand stepped back to permit Gabby access to the hatch; he noticed that the man was clutching something in the palm of his hand, but he couldn't make it out. "Let him go," he told Scott. "He can't help, anyway."

Lancer volunteered to take the APC out to the camp and bring in Rook and Lunk. It was dark by the time he returned, and in addition to Rook and Lunk, the APC carried what remained of Gabby's body. Lancer explained that they had seen flashes of annihilation disc fire in the vicinity of the broadcast tower; they had gone in when the fighting stopped and discovered the flaming wreck that was Gabby's jeep. Close by, they had found Gabby, clad in the battle armor he had retrieved only a short while before.

They had the man laid out in the escort hold now; Gabby's fractured helmet sat on the floor next to him, and the holo-locket taken from his burned hand lay atop the sheet Lunk had thrown over the body.

"He was a brave and loyal soldier, all the way and then some," Frank said soberly.

Shorty tugged in a sob. "We're gonna miss ya, Gabby."

Marlene stooped to place a flower on the sheet; she gathered up the holo-locket, accidentally activating it as she stood up. A handsome, uniformed youth appeared in an egg-shaped aura of purple and gold light. "Hi, Dad," the holo-image saluted. "Like father, like son; so here I am in the army now, and I just hope you'll be as proud of me as I am of you." Marlene thought she recognized the youth but said nothing.

"Poor Gabby," Jesse said, kneeling down to lift a corner of the sheet.

All at once Frank grabbed Jesse by his lapels and pulled him to his feet.

"Are we gonna jus' sit around and let the Invid kill us off one by one, or are we gonna do somethin' about it?!" He shoved his friend aside and drew his blaster. "I'm gonna finish the job Gabby started!"

Lancer came up behind Frank and caught him up in a

full nelson, trying to reason with him. "You can't do it alone, Frank."

The old man told Lancer to butt out but ceased his struggling as a second transmission began to flash from the communications console. On the screen was the face they had seen earlier, and the young man's message was much the same: The Expeditionary Force was preparing for an offensive, and all resistance groups were urged to move against the central Invid hive, designated Reflex Point.

Marlene reactivated the holo-locket and compared the two images.

"It's him!" exclaimed Jesse. "That's Gabby's boy on that screen!"

Lancer let go of Frank. "No wonder he spent so much time trying to make that transceiver work," he said, turning to the body. "With it he could stay in touch with the one person he loved the most."

Frank hung his head. "It's a goldurn pity. Gabby could see his son, but the boy couldn't see him. An' he never told us nuthin' 'bout it."

"Listen to me, everybody," Scott said in his best take-charge voice. "I'm going to get that broadcast tower if it's the last thing I do. How about it—are you with me or not?"

The team, of course, rallied, but the veterans remained unmoved.

"What's your plan?" Rand thought to ask Scott as the freedom fighters raced toward the hatch.

"We'll decide on the way!"

Terrific, Rand said to himself.

"But what about the old cowboys?" Annie wanted to know, gesturing to Frank and his men.

"You heard them, Annie," Scott told her. "Their fighting days are over!"

Frank knew what he had to do; he just couldn't seem to bring his body to understand. It was as if the young lieutenant's words were true after all: The fight had gone out of him. He had, however, gotten as far as suiting himself up in his rusting armor and struggling his way to the bridge of the ship. He was sitting in one of the command chairs now, trying to bolster his courage with long pulls from his flask, but even the whiskey was failing him.

"This ain't no help," he muttered, giving the flask a toss toward the rear of the bridge.

"Thank ya, Frank, but we don't need it either."

Frank swiveled in the chair to find Jesse grinning at him, the flask gripped in his right hand. Roy and Shorty were with him, all three of them squeezed into armor that barely fit them anymore.

Jesse laughed, shutting his eyes. "You ain't goin' nowhere without us, Cap'n."

"Reportin' fer duty," saluted cross-eyed Shorty, hand to the helmet he was rarely without.

"He's correct," said Roy, a smile playing across that sagging face of his, his bald pate gleaming in the console lights.

Frank rose out of the chair, suppressing the smile he wanted to return. "Well, what're ya waitin' for, then? Git to yer battle stations."

Jesse tossed the flask back to him and straightened his headband. "Aye, aye, sir!" he said smartly.

A moment later the aged cruiser's lift-off thrusters came to flaming life. Like some predatory fish, the ship began to rise, disentangling itself from the techno-debris that had ensnared it for so long. And in response the devastated city rumbled its applause, buildings and ruined roadways vibrating in sympathy. At an altitude of five hundred feet, the ship's Reflex engines kicked in, triple-thrusters blazing like newborn suns, to direct it along its final course, straight into the heart of the Invid domain.

The blunt top of the broadcast tower resembled the glowing hemispherical hives Scott and the others had already gone up against, except for the fact that it was set atop an organic-looking stalk some eight hundred feet high. As the three Veritechs closed on it—Scott's Alpha and the uncoupled Betas—scores of rust-brown Pincer Ships poured out to engage them. And the odds had never been worse.

"God, there are too many of them!" Scott yelled into his helmet mike, suddenly questioning the impulsive nature of their attack. Two of his three heat-seekers found their targets, but the skies were literally dotted with alien ships. "We'll never get through them!" As a storm of annihilation discs was directed against him, he loosed a cluster of four more missiles. Three more Invid ships exploded, sending teeth-jarring shock waves and flashes of blinding light clear into the VT's cockpit. Scott zigzagged through a second salvo of enemy fire and was triggering off another missile flock when he heard Rand's voice cut through the tac net.

"Scott, look! Those crazy old men have actually gotten that junk heap off the ground!"

Scott edged himself up in the seat; he saw the cruiser off to the right below him, barely above treetop level.

"Watch your mouth, sonny," Frank was telling Rand. "This ain't no junk heap, and we're gonna prove it by showin' you whippersnappers what a real combat crew looks like!"

Scott wanted to take back all the things he had said to them. He had heard those words of newfound courage before, and the ending was always the same.

"Get that ship out of here!" he roared.

"Jus' like the good ole days!" Jesse yelled over his shoulder to Roy. He had the base of the broadcast tower centered in the console's targeting screen, but it was not the tower he was after—not yet. First there were all those ships to take out. So he flipped the weapon selector switch to maximum burst and depressed the trigger button.

A fan of laser-array energy spewed into the field, annihilating countless ships. But the combat troops were quick to even up the score. Ignoring the Veritechs for the moment, they massed against the cruiser and refocused the might of their collective firepower. Without shields, the Robotech ship had little immunity to the discs. Fiery explosions erupted across the cruiser's bow as blast after blast flayed armor and superstructure and blew away gun turrets.

On the bridge Shorty was thrown screaming from his station as an angry white flash holed the ship.

"Dadburn it!" Jesse cursed, seeing his friend go down. "I'll show 'em!"

He slammed his hands against the trigger button again and again, but for every Invid ship that flamed out there were two more returning fire. They were buzzing around the cruiser now, slashing at its damaged areas with their pincers and opening irreparable wounds in its hull. Discs found their way into these, and soon the warship was a flaming, smoking wreck locked in a new struggle with gravity itself.

Scott watched helplessly as the cruiser began to fall. "Use your escape pods!" he pleaded with them. "Abandon ship while you've got time!" But Frank spoke the words Scott knew he would hear:

"No way, sonny. This crew don't give up."

"Don't be foolish, old man! There's nothing more you can do!"

"There's still a job to be done," Frank told him weakly.

Scott was alongside the ship now, trying to get a look in through the bridge viewports. "You're not going to prove anything by this!"

"We can prove we ain't cowards, Lieutenant."

Scott realized that they were trying to pilot the cruiser into the very base of the broadcast tower. He would have given anything to have been able to prevent them, and yet the tower had to be taken out, and it was doubtful that the Veritechs could do it alone. So Scott pulled up and away from the ship's suicidal plunge, ordering Rand and Rook back at the same time.

The cruiser pierced the stalk like a lance, some two hundred feet below the hemispherical cap.

On the bridge, Roy turned a knowing look to Frank at the adjacent station. "I've removed the safety locks from all the missiles, Commander."

Frank nodded. "Are we all in agreement about what must be done?" he asked his crew. "Shorty, what d' ya say?"

Mortally wounded, Shorty had managed to struggle back into his seat. His head was resting on the console. "Commander, how many times do I have to tell you? Don't call me Shorty."

Scott's voice boomed through the speakers. "There's still time. Set the charges and get yourselves to the pods. We'll come in and pick you up."

"Sorry, sir," said Frank. "Our radio's been damaged, an' we can't hear a word you're saying." Rand tried to make them understand, but Frank just shook his head. "No, it's better this way. . . . Shorty, you ready?"

Shorty coughed once. "It's a funny thing, Commander, but I just remembered what it really is—my name, that is. It's—"

Frank brought the heel of his fist down on the self-destruct button.

The tower exploded, a stalk in a firestorm.

The three Veritechs swooped in for a flyby.

"We mustn't let the world forget them . . . loyal, courageous . . . *soldiers*."

"They'll be awarded medals of honor," Scott said softly.

Down below, Lunk, Annie, Lancer, and Marlene watched the fireball climb and mushroom overhead.

"Who were they, anyway?" Annie asked.

Perplexed by the conflicting emotions she felt, Marlene thought back to Gabby's kindness, Jesse's laugh, Frank's gruffness, the brief holo-locket image of Gabby's son. . . .

"They were heroes," she sobbed.

CHAPTER
FIVE

> *They thought they had stumbled into Denver, but in fact they had lucked into Delta-Six, a top-secret subterranean installation attached to the Cheyenne Mountain complex, constructed to ensure that America's heads of state would survive any form of attack leveled against the continent. But they weren't thinking of the Zentraedi then, and certainly not of Dolza's four million.*
>
> "Northlands" *History of The Third Robotech War*, Vol. LXXXVI

THE TEAM SWUNG NORTH, THEN EAST, LEAVING THE desert behind and entering the foothills of the Northlands central range. The Rockies, they were told. They chose to avoid southern routes across the continental divide in favor of the less traveled northern passes, even though this made for more difficult ascents. But there were numerous satellite hives in the warmer valleys to the south, and since the team's reserves of Protoculture were low, they couldn't afford to risk all-out engagement. They had managed to procure a few canisters of fuel, but Scott had insisted they be used for the red Alpha, which Rand and Rook had retrieved.

The weather was against the team, however, and although a week went by without an enemy encounter, their progress was slow. When at last they crossed the spine, they began to sense the nearness of the prairielands beyond. But tectonic upheavals brought about by the

Zentraedi Rain of Death had so altered the terrain here that they often felt off the map; and given their precataclysm charts, indeed they were.

It was snowing now in this final pass that had no right being there. Fearful of calling attention to themselves and careful to conserve what little fuel remained, they had decided to keep the Veritechs grounded. Lunk had secured chains for the APC and fashioned skids and tow bars for the fighters using plate and barstock he had scavenged from what had been a recreational ski area. They had the APC rigged as a kind of tow vehicle, but most of the real propulsion was derived from battery-driven thrusters in the VTs' raptorlike legs. Annie and Marlene were riding up front with Lunk; the rest of the team was currently on foot.

"It's so cold," Annie whimpered to Marlene, shivering and clutching the hooded poncho to her neck. "It feels like my nose is going to fall off or something."

Marlene pressed herself closer to Annie and brought some of her own poncho around Annie's shoulders.

Scott, Lancer, and Rook, similarly attired in cold-weather ponchos, were alongside the red Alpha at the middle of the caravan. "Soup," said Rook, daydreaming. "Nice, hot soup. A cup of thick soup, a *bathtubful* of piping hot, steaming soup . . ." She felt Lancer's hand on her shoulder.

"Don't. It only makes it worse."

Then she heard Rand: "Hold up a minute, guys!"

He was behind them at the Beta's wingtip, preoccupied with his latest acquisition—the thermograph Jesse had given him shortly before the assault on the broadcast tower. It was about the size of a small chain saw, with a muzzlelike sensor and top-mounted carrying handle. Rook saw that he was kneeling down, sweeping the instrument across the snow.

"Lunk! Stop the sleds!" Scott called out over the wind.

"It's amazing. . . . There's something underneath us!" Rand was saying as Scott, Lancer, and Rook approached.

"Yeah, we know. It's called ice," Rook told him.

Scott motioned her to lighten up. "What are you picking up?"

Rand double-checked the indicator readings. "A large heat source. Massive, way off the meter."

"Volcanic?"

Rand shook his head, loosing wet snow from the poncho. "Definitely not."

"Then the thermograph is on the fritz," Rook said through chattering teeth. "Either that or it's your brain."

Rand ignored the comment and began pushing snow aside, as if to get a glimpse of something beneath the ice. "It's gotta be a generator of some kind . . . just below this layer of snow . . ."

Rook made an impatient sound. "Come on, man, you're wasting our time."

He looked up knowingly and got to his feet. "Wasting our time, huh?" All at once he was beside her, pushing her toward the window he had excavated.

"Quit your shoving!" she protested.

"Well, Miss Know-it-all, why don't you take a look for yourself?"

She glared at him for a moment, then went down on her knees, wiping away flakes of new snow and peering in. The ice was virtually transparent, as clear as Caribbean water. But her mind refused to accept what her eyes were telling her: she seemed to be looking down on a turn-of-the-century building bathed in artificial light— one of those twenty-story milk cartons she had seen pictures of. There was steam or something issuing from exhaust elbows on the roof, and below that she could discern other buildings and lit streets.

Overwhelmed by a sudden sense of vertigo, she had to turn away.

"It's a city!"

"Told you," said Rand.

Scott looked at both of them and frowned. "Sorry, guys, but it's no time to play archaeologist."

"We just need a pickax and some ropes!" Rand said excitedly. He was already up and running toward the

APC. "Think of the food and supplies that are down there!" He threw off his poncho and made a mad leap for the vehicle's shotgun seat, mindless of Lunk's bewildered cries. He was rummaging around in the storage compartment beneath the seat when the ground started to give way.

It was too late for the warnings Scott and the others were shouting out; the APC fell through, almost dragging the VT caravan with it. Instinctively, Scott grabbed hold of the Beta's skids, but momentarily the fighter train came to a halt of its own accord, with the blue Alpha perched precariously at the edge of the hole, its radome dropped, like the beak of a bird searching for worms in a hole.

Down below, Annie felt herself for broken bones. She looked around and saw that Rand, Marlene, and Lunk were performing similar self-examinations. She had no idea what they had fallen into or onto, but it seemed to be some sort of roof. The APC was upright nearby, the chains that had connected it to the lead Veritech snapped. Overhead, Scott and the others were leaning in to inquire if everyone was all right. Annie got to her feet and felt a strong uprush of heated air.

"Hey, I think we can get down to street level!" Rand was shouting. He had thrown open the door to a boxlike structure that housed the building's stairway. Atop it were the jetting exhausts Rook had seen from above.

Rand disappeared through the door, and Annie followed him without a thought.

The rest of the team had lowered themselves to the roof by now and had discarded their ponchos. Above the jagged rend in the ice the snowstorm was still howling. Scott moved to the edge of the roof and looked around in amazement: It was indeed an underground city, intact and apparently deserted. He turned to gaze up at the hole and realized that the city was not only subterranean but fully enclosed by a protective dome of what appeared to be fabriplex. Somehow the place had been spared destruction by both the Zentraedi fleet and subsequent geological shifts. Over the years it had become buried by earth and snow. He wanted to run this by Lunk and Lancer, but Lunk had other concerns on his mind.

"The landing gear's been damaged," he told Scott, indicating the undercarriage of the still suspended blue Alpha.

"I guess that means we're stuck here for a while," said Rook, not exactly unhappy about it.

Scott scowled. "Another delay," he muttered under his breath.

Rand and Annie, meanwhile, had hit the streets. They had taken the forty flights warily, and Rand had his blaster out even now, but there was no sign of activity. The ground-floor levels of many of the buildings were illuminated, as were numerous signs and street lights. Still, there were indications that the place had been abandoned in haste, and it was an eerie feeling to walk through it all. There were no vehicles, and the only sound was that of the city's self-contained atmosphere being sucked toward the breach they had opened in its protective umbrella.

Annie wasn't quite as put off by the emptiness as Rand. "It's magical," she enthused. "I've never seen a city this big in my whole life."

Rand holstered his weapon.

"I wonder what keeps it running. It looks like it dates back to the prewars period." He caught a glimpse of Annie's look of enchantment and laughed. "And to think, it's been buried here just waiting for you and me to come along."

"Like out of a fairy tale!"

Rand took hold of her hand, and they ran off to explore.

Scott sent Marlene and Rook off to locate Rand while he, Lunk, and Lancer carefully disengaged the caravan and piloted each of the Veritechs to the roof of the building. A search for tools brought them down into the lowermost of the building's subbasements, where Lunk discovered the source of the city's power: a generator that tapped thermal power deep within the Earth itself. Lancer also came up with something that explained where they were: it was a teletype evacuation notice addressed to the residents of "Denver," issued on the eve of Dolza's devastating barrage of death.

"They were in such a big hurry, they forgot to turn out the lights," Lunk smirked. "They're gonna get stuck with *some* utility bill."

Rook had managed to find Rand. It wasn't difficult: she simply started with the toy stores, then worked her way through the supermarkets and delis.

She was off gathering supplies now, while Rand, Annie, and Marlene were sampling foodstuffs from the plastic wrapped, bottled, and canned goods smorgasbord they had spread out on the floor around them. They had found bags of marshmallows and jars of peanut butter, cookies, dried fruits and frozen pies, cans of soda and bars of chocolate, cereals, beans, soups, and assorted sweets.

"Mmmm, mint chocolate," Annie said with her mouth full. She tore open a second package and broke off a piece for Marlene. "Try it, you'll love it. I could live off this stuff."

Marlene nibbled at it and raised her eyebrows. "It is good."

"Peppermint!" Annie exclaimed, picking another item from the floor. "This is my most favorite thing in the whole world!" She pillowed her head against the bag and closed her eyes lovingly.

Nearby, Rand popped open a Coke. "You got mints on the brain, kid." He gulped some down and took a bite from the hero he had defrosted.

"I don't care what the Invid do as long as they don't take away our peppermint."

"Nice attitude, Annie. But I gotta agree with you: this is the life. Somebody pinch me so I know I haven't died and gone to heaven."

Rook, pushing a cartful of supplies, came by just then to remind him. "How about a kick in the teeth instead?" She gave the three of them her best disapproving look. "What a mess. We're supposed to be foraging supplies, not packing them away in our stomachs. Ever think that Scott and Lancer might be hungry, too?" She shook her head at Rand. "Sometimes you make me wonder."

He showed a roguish grin in response and tossed a can over to her. "Ever seen these before?"

Rook read the label. "Vienna sausages? What's a 'vienna'?"

Rand saw Annie and Marlene's puzzled looks. "You mean none of you have tried these?"

"Are they peppermints?" Annie said, getting to her feet.

Rook made a face and tossed the can over her shoulder to Rand. "What a disgusting thought."

Rand shared a wink with Annie and said, "Let's find out."

She kneeled down and pulled on the can's ring-seal. "Oh, they're cute!" she laughed, fishing out sausages for Rand and Marlene. She popped one into her mouth. "Ter-ri-fic . . . Not peppermints, but pretty good anyway."

Rook was watching them all munching away, her forefinger to her lower lip. "Lemme try one," she said, kneeling down, hands between her knees.

Rand dangled a sausage between his fingers. "I don't know. . . . You think you should?"

"Just gimme it," she barked, snatching it from his grip. She chewed the thing up and swallowed: salty and too soft, but it tasted better than anything she had had in weeks.

Annie saw the look of delight on her face, laughed, and pointed her finger accusingly. "Now our food supply's *really* gonna be in trouble!"

Scott had left the VT repairs to Lancer and Lunk and had gone off to look for Rand and Rook. He couldn't blame them for wanting to explore the city; it was like some museum of prewar life, the life some of the oldest members of the Pioneer Mission had spoken of.

He was standing in front of a bridal shop now, staring at a lovely white dress in the display window. The dress reminded him of a picture he had once seen that was taken on his mother's wedding day. There was even something about the mannequin that reminded him of her, the short upswept brown hair adorned with a red flower. . . . He was so caught up in the memory that he wasn't aware of his teammates' presence until Annie spoke.

"Jeepers, look at that dress! What I'd give to be married in that!"

Embarrassed, Scott swung around, certain they had read his thoughts somehow. Marlene and Rook were nodding in agreement. They had three shopping carts loaded with supplies.

"Hey, Scott, who's the lucky girl gonna be?" Rand joked.

But Scott saw his friend's smile quickly collapse after Rook nudged him on the arm. Now it was Rand who was embarrassed for having forgotten about Marlene—*Scott's* Marlene, who had died during the Mars Division assault.

The foursome began to move off. Scott returned to his musings for a moment more, then called out for them to stop.

"Where do you think you're going? I want to get these supplies to the ships. Maybe you've forgotten, but we have an appointment to keep at Reflex Point."

Rand made a dismissive gesture. "Ah, give it a rest, Scott. What's an hour or two gonna matter?" Then he softened his tone somewhat. "Look, I know this place might not be very important to you. . . ."

"But we were born right here on Earth," Annie filled in. "And leaving this place now would be like turning our backs on our heritage."

Even Rook chimed in. "We deserve a little R&R, don't we?"

The three of them didn't wait for his answer and

started off down the street. But he didn't try to stop them; there was no denying the truth of their arguments.

"You're such an old stick-in-the-mud sometimes," Annie said over her shoulder.

Scott regarded the mannequin once again, only now it was Marlene, his fiancée's face, that he saw there. *Oh, come on, Scott*, he fantasized her saying. *Loosen up a little. It's a beautiful dress. And who knows, maybe they'll give us a break on the price. . . . It is our wedding, after all. . . .*

"Marlene," he said softly.

"I'm right here, Scott," the other Marlene said behind him. "What are you thinking about?"

He turned to her and stammered: "Uh . . . about another dress a long time ago that was similar to this one." She had a sympathetic look on her face. "Do you think they're right about me being a stick-in-the-mud?"

She was about to reply that she had no idea what that meant, when Scott's face brightened suddenly and he put his hand on her shoulder.

"Marlene, how about an unguided tour of the city— just you and me?"

She smiled and let him take her hand but an instant later was down in the street on her butt.

"Whoa, are you all right?" Scott was asking her. He was kneeling beside her on the pavement, regarding her ankle boots and frowning. "We're going to have to find you some better shoes and some warmer clothes."

She took Scott's hand between hers and pressed it to her cheek. "Mmmm . . . You're not cold?"

Scott nuzzled her hair. "No. All of a sudden, I feel very warm."

They walked the deserted streets arm in arm, content to say little and enjoying their closeness. Marlene spied a display of lingerie in a shop window and ran to it, fingertips to the plate glass. Here was a pair of yellow bikini briefs with a matching spaghetti-strapped bra, a lavender camisole, a rose-colored teddy.

"Aren't they beautiful, Scott?"

"Uh, that's not quite what I had in mind," he said from a safe distance, blushing all the while. He put his arm around her shoulders to move her away. "Believe me, you'd freeze in those things," he told her.

In a shoe store, he feigned a foreign accent and tried to interest her in a pair of low-impact approach boots, but she playfully demanded to be shown something more feminine.

"But these things will keep you from churning in the snow."

"Feminine, I said."

He round a pair of white pumps in her size and squatted down to place them on her feet. "They're not very practical," he started to say, but she was already up and twirling around on one foot, laughing.

"There," she told him. "Much better for dancing."

Scott smiled up at her. *Dancing*, he thought. But the more he watched her, the more her face began to blend with memories of his lost love, and ultimately he had to look away. She saw the sadness in his eyes and asked him to talk about it.

"I was just dreaming of a better time, Marlene. Of dancing . . ."

Then all at once he was on his feet, the excitement back in his eyes, putting his hands atop her shoulders.

"And now to complete the picture . . ."

He led her off at a run to a dress shop and rummaged through the racks until he had found what he was after: a strapless gown cut like a mermaid's tail, pale lavender above a kind of pleated base of white skirt.

"It was made for you."

She held it up to herself, flattered by his choice.

"Go ahead, try it on," he urged her.

And she was about to, but there was something vague in her memory that prevented her. Scott picked up on it immediately, even though she hadn't a clue as to why she had stopped.

"Stupid of me," he said, smacking the heel of his hand

against his head. He scanned the shop for a dressing room and when he had located it, rushed over to station himself like a guard by its curtained entrance.

"If you'll just step this way, mademoiselle . . ." he suggested with a theatrical bow.

She disappeared inside and cautioned him about peeking, recalling the way Rand had looked at her when she had innocently stripped off her clothes to swim. . . .

Scott jumped back as though scalded. *She's reading my thoughts*, he told himself. He swallowed hard as he watched her discarded clothes pile up on the floor below the curtains. And when the curtains parted, she was the most beautiful thing he had ever seen.

She stood still, her hands crossed at her neck, allowing him to take her in; then she gathered her hair in one hand and turned her back to him.

"Would you zip me up, Scott?"

He regarded the open zipper and took halting steps toward the dressing room, his eyes fixed on the graceful curve of her back, the pale perfection of her skin.

CHAPTER
SIX

Why the sudden shift from Lancer to Scott? many have asked. But the answer is immediately evident once we are reminded of Ariel/Marlene's original programming as Simulagent. Then it seems entirely natural for her to seek out the leader, and, as it were, the team's weakest line of defense.

Bloom Nesterfig, *Social Organization of the Invid*

RAND SANG TO HIMSELF WHILE HIS INDEX FINGERS worked the machine's flippers: *Sure plays a mean pinball* ... The left paddle caught the ball just right and sent it careening around the cushioned arena, up the forward ramp, and smack into the belly dancer's navel for a bonus score of one thousand points. But propelled free, the steel sphere fell like one of Galileo's own and shot directly through the Flipper Straits, lost to the game's mechanical bowels.

"You Khyron!" Rand cursed, whacking the machine with his hands.

Beside him, Rook made a bored sound at her own machine and moved off to one of the arcade's plastiform seats.

"Don't tell me you're giving up already?" he asked over his shoulder.

"Too boring." She yawned.

"Well, how do you ever expect to improve at anything if you just keep giving up?"

He was still angry with her for the elbow she had given him earlier while they were washing their clothes in the Laundromat. Annie had wandered off, and Rand had spotted Scott and Marlene strolling by arm in arm. He was leaping up to give Fearless Leader a round of applause when the gut shot had been delivered without forewarning.

Of course, it wasn't really the case—that Rook had a habit of giving up—but that was beside the point. In any event, she ignored his comment, so he turned back to the machine, angering it just short of tilt after another ball plunged home.

"No good piece of—"

"This place just makes me feel . . . lonely," Rook interrupted him.

Nice, Rand said to himself. *We finally get to spend a few peaceful moments together and she feels* lonely. "So what does that make me—part of the furniture?" he said without turning around.

He heard her laugh. "C'mon, you don't want me to answer that, do you?"

Rand compressed his lips to a thin line. He was going to place the next shot right between her eyes. . . .

Up on the roof, Lancer and Lunk were making final repairs to the damaged Alpha. Lancer was down on one knee operating the torque wrench. It was a rare occasion when the two men worked side by side; Lunk was continually worried that Yellow Dancer would make some unannounced appearance, and the last thing he wanted to do was to be caught alone with her, er, *him*! But today had been different; they had talked shop, and they had talked about the Invid.

"We've really got our work cut out for us now," Lunk was saying. "These new ships they keep throwing at us are a lot more maneuverable than the Troopers."

"You're right about that," Lancer said absently.

"I mean, we were just plain lucky the last time they surprised us in the mountains. If that ledge hadn't given way . . ."

Lancer recalled the fall of the pink and purple ship. And its female pilot. He found himself wondering if he would see her again—wondering with a mixture of fear and anticipation. But Annie's voice brought him from his musings before he had to grapple with the emotions behind them. She came running onto the roof from the stairway cubicle dressed like a June bride.

"Look what I found!"

The dress was a soft pink, with a white ruffled collar and matching bonnet. But it was at least four sizes too large for her, so she had most of the train gathered up in her arms.

"Just what are you supposed to be?" Lunk asked her.

Lancer laughed and stood up, wiping his hands on his trousers. "She's a bride—and a pretty one at that." He formed his hands into an imaginary camera and brought them to his eye. "What I'd give to have my old Pentax."

Annie put up her hands to stop him. "Wait! I want my bridegroom in this photo!" And with that she jumped up, threw her arms around Lunk's neck, and hung there, the hem of the gown touching the floor now.

Lunk went rigid for a moment, then scooped her up and cradled her in his arms, his dismayed expression unchanged.

Lancer threw his head back and laughed.

"Perfect!" he enthused.

Scott couldn't get that zipper out of his mind, except now he was wondering what it would be like to *undo* it. Since Marlene's death he had been convincing himself that celibacy had been written into his destiny, but suddenly this nameless goddess, this new Marlene, was bringing all the old allegiances into question. Was it wrong for him to be having these thoughts? he asked himself. Would his Marlene have wanted him to remain faithful to her no matter what? He sensed that the phrasing was wrong, perhaps even the questions themselves, because he knew that his love for Marlene could never be extinguished. But these new feelings had more to do with happiness and companionship.

The two of them were exploring a department store. Scott had located the sound system and an original Lynn-Minmei disc—probably the first one she had ever recorded. He knew her well from Tirol, but how different that Minmei seemed from the innocent girl whose bright eyes shone from the CD jacket. It seemed ages ago, Scott realized, before all the troubles with Edwards, before Minmei's devastating encounter with Wolff. . . .

"Stagefright," one of the singer's most popular numbers, was blasting through the PA speakers. Marlene, still in that strapless gown that fit her like a glove, was trying on jewelry. Scott watched her in wonderment. They picked out a silver and brass collar and a bracelet of gold. He found her a leather shoulder bag and a floppy blue hat.

They exchanged meaningful looks. And Scott asked her about love.

"Was there anyone, Marlene? Were you ever in love?"

"Love?" she asked him.

He could see that she had no understanding of the emotion. How traumatized she must have been to have had even that erased from her past!

He began to envy her.

In the next store they separated, as two people might drift apart in a museum, lost in private thoughts and personal moments. It was the toys that fascinated Marlene: wind-up clowns and talking bears, music boxes and transformable gadgets, drummer boys and lively ballerinas. She switched all of them on, filling her world with a symphony of transistorized sounds and songs. She was handling a fragile glass giraffe when the gorilla showed up.

Marlene uttered a frightened scream and fell back, dropping the small figurine to the floor. Of course it was only Scott in a mask, but how was she to know that?

She ran to him after he had taken it off, seeking shelter in his arms. "Hold me, Scott," she whispered. But he held back and gently pushed her to arm's length, his hands on her shoulders.

"Marlene, I . . . I want to know all about you."

She gave him a helpless look. "I wish I could tell you," she apologized. "I wish I knew the words. . . ."

But what he saw in her eyes was enough. "We don't need words," he told her, drawing her in. They kissed lightly, tentatively, exploring each other.

Then suddenly *she* pulled back, overcome first by dread, then pain. "They're coming!" she managed. "It's hopeless, hopeless!" Her mane of red hair was shaking back and forth. "There's no escape from them!"

Scott did what he could to comfort her and began to look left and right in desperation. "We're trapped down here!" he berated himself. "Trapped!"

There was no escape!

Far above them in those displaced mountains that towered over the buried city, Corg, the crown prince of the Invid horde, had zeroed in on the rend the freedom fighters had inadvertently opened in the dome. He was a sharp-featured young man with lean good looks and mysterious oblique blue eyes. His hair, which was also blue, lay flat and fine against his skull, lending itself to his somewhat cruel and ascetic look. Corg had been created from the lifestuff of his race by the Regis herself, to rule at Sera's side in the new order.

His command ship was like hers: somewhat acephalic, top-heavy, and buxom-looking with its heavily weaponed torso pods and power nacelles.

Accompanying him were two Enforcer ships that represented the most recent examples of technological innovation from the Regis's weapons factories. They were not unlike their crablike prototypes but somehow appeared almost naked beside them. They were bipedal and seemingly four-armed, their optic scanners were more Cyclopean in placement, and there was a phallic, muscular flexibility to the top-mounted cannons that was absent in the more cumbersome-looking Shock Troopers and Pincer Ships.

Corg chose to make his own opening in the city's dome and did so with a massive charge from his ship's shoulder cannon. Then he began his hellish descent, his two underlings following him down into the breach.

The freedom fighters were waiting for them, though. Scott had alerted the rest of the team to Marlene's premonition, and they had elected to draw the Invid down into the city and utilize the more maneuverable Cyclones to battle them in the streets.

In Battle Armor mode, Scott, Lancer, Rand, and Rook were assembled at street level when the first two Invid blasts shook the city, impacting against the upper storys of one of the tall towers and showering them with chunks of concrete and shards of plate glass.

"We won't stand a chance head to head against these guys," Scott said over the tac net. "We've got to take advantage of their clumsiness!"

"Gotcha!" Rook returned as everyone took to the air.

Rand lingered behind and was almost slagged because of it. "We'll make mincemeat out of them," he was saying when an energy bolt exploded in the street. He caught up with Rook a moment later in an alleyway, but the newfangled Enforcer had pursued him and loosed a shot that nearly fried both of them where they stood. They launched and took up ground-level positions on either side of the alley's exit and poured return fire into the Invid ship as it rounded the corner.

The Enforcer found Rand first and swung toward him, the triple nodes of its cannon primed for fire. Rand leapt away just in time, amazed to see two steady streams of crimson fire where he had expected annihilation discs.

Elsewhere, Scott and Lancer were facing off with the second Enforcer. They had their backs to the wall as the Invid came at them, its rear thrusters keeping it airborne, a flying insect nightmare in the city's twilight.

"I'll draw its fire," Scott told Lancer. "Get above and do some damage!"

The Enforcer's cannon muzzles came to life, spewing two deadly beams, which converged and struck the base of the building, sending shock waves through the streets. Glass was now raining down from everywhere, along with snow that was avalanching through the dome's ruptured skin. Both freedom fighters jumped aside, but Lancer stayed in the air while Scott attempted to lure the enemy onto a wider boulevard. He dug in at the end of the street and waited for the Enforcer's approach; then, with the thing scarcely two hundred yards away, he launched two time-charged Bludgeons from the right forearms tubes of his battle armor. The missiles detonated in the air over the Invid's back, with a collective force great enough to throw the thing face-first to the street. Lancer was in position now, and on Scott's command he activated nearly all his suit's launch tubes; missiles arced from the open compartments and racks and fell like a fiery hail on the immobilized alien ship, destroying it even while its own cannons were blazing away. To add insult to injury, Scott launched another missile into the dome overhead, loosing a fall of massive ice chunks, which sealed the Enforcer's fate.

Rand and Rook were still being pursued by the first ship, whose pilot was obviously the more experienced of the two.

"Boy, this high altitude's beginning to affect me," Rand told his teammate, fighting for breath.

They had stopped to go face-to-face with the ship after realizing that Scott and Lancer were coming in to outflank it. Now all four of them opened up at once, throwing everything they had against the Enforcer and what was left of the devastated dome, burning and burying it much as they had its companion ship.

But suddenly there was another ship in the arena: a drab gray-green command ship with orange-tan highlights. They had seen this one before and had hoped they wouldn't see it again.

"Scott, behind you!" Rook warned.

The team scattered, but the command ship stuck with Scott, pursuing him through several blocks—literally *through* the buildings, although Scott was using the doorways and the alien was simply making his own. Ultimately they squared off, the giant insectlike ship and the diminutive Cyclone, and Scott flicked on his externals to say: "I had a sick feeling you would show up again."

The Invid raised its cannon arm and would have slagged him then and there had it not been for Lancer and the others, who distracted it with rooftop fire. Scott seized the moment to leap away, but the command ship continued to stalk him—probably angered by the earlier comment, Scott had the temerity to say to himself. Even Lunk, Annie, and Marlene had joined the fray by this time; they were packed into the APC, riding circles around the Invid's feet while spraying it ineffectually with machine-gun fire. Down on his butt with the alien looming over him, Scott wondered how they had gotten the vehicle down to street level, but he didn't dwell on it for long, because the Invid was ignoring the trio and raising that handgun again. . . .

Just then Annie somehow succeeded in angering the thing with some silly comment; the Invid switched targets, reangled its handgun, and fired off a rapid burst that nipped at the carrier's tail. The APC was unscathed, but something had been thrown from the rear seat—something pink and soft-looking . . .

Scott realized it was a dress of some sort but couldn't believe his scanners when he saw that Marlene was running back to retrieve it! Lunk had brought the APC to a halt and was yelling at her to forget about it.

The Invid ship swung around and took one giant step, aiming menacingly at its defenseless prey. In the cockpit, Corg stared down at the sister his race had lost to the Humans and could not bring himself to fire.

Scott, meanwhile, had launched himself straight up, crying out Marlene's name and launching half a dozen Scorpions straight into the Invid's back. Leaking fire from its seams, the alien whirled on him and raised its cannon, but Scott was again quicker to the draw with two more missiles that managed to sever the ship's right arm.

The cannon hit the floor with a thunderous crash, but Corg wasn't about to retreat just yet. He turned and stomped after Scott, shouldering the ship through the walls of the building and out into the street.

There, the reunited rebel team ganged up on the command ship, paralyzing it with missile fire and opening up the rest of the dome. It was as though a dam had collapsed: hundreds of tons of snow and ice were pouring into the city. The Invid struggled against the slides but eventually succumbed to the sheer weight of the fall. It went down on one knee, systems sputtering and shorting out, then tipped to its side.

"To the Alphas, everybody!" Scott commanded.

"Well, there goes the world's shortest vacation," Rand said in response.

Lunk, Annie, and Marlene were waiting for them on the roof. Once more, Scott couldn't figure out how the APC had managed it, but he didn't stop to ask. He reconfigured his mecha to its two-wheeled mode and told Lunk to stow the four Cycs in their Veritech compartments. Marlene was frightened but unhurt. Scott wanted nothing more than to hug her, his battle armor notwithstanding, but he contented himself with simply touching her shoulder.

Shortly they had the Veritechs in the air, the APC slung from the undercarriage of the Beta.

"Sorry about the accommodations," Scott apologized to Lunk, Annie, and Marlene, "but the fresh air will do you good."

Lunk swung himself around in the driver's seat of the APC to look back at the massive holes in the ice dome that had kept the city a secret from its surroundings for the past twenty years. In his hand he held an electronic detonator he had rigged to the computer control system of the city's thermal furnaces.

"Now or never," he said out loud, and thumbed the trigger button.

Five minutes later the city exploded with near-volcanic force; a swirling pillar of fire shot up into the winter skies, vaporizing snow and ice and capturing the resultant thaw and clouds of steam. The sound of follow-up explosions echoed in the mountains, catching the Veritechs in their roar. They fought to stabilize themselves in the shock waves and newborn thermals, the jeep rocking to and fro like a pendulum beneath Scott's fighter.

"What the hell happened?!" Rand's panicked voice boomed over the net.

Lunk flipped on the APC mike. "I rigged the main generator to feed back on itself," he explained.

"Bu-but *why*?!"

"Because that city had no place in this world." There was a kind of anger in Lunk's voice.

"Well, it sure doesn't anymore," Rand said.

"Some fireworks, though," Rook commented.

"Well, golly gee, Miss Rook, sure glad we were able to bring some excitement to your day. Least you won't have to be *bored* anymore."

"Who asked *you*?!" Rook returned.

Scott listened to them go at it, then reached out to lower the volume in his cockpit. He craned his neck to see if he could get a glimpse of Marlene, below him in the personnel carrier. *She knew they were coming*, he told himself. But what was the strange link they shared? What channel had the Invid opened in her shocked mind that allowed her to sense their coming? And could the team somehow tap that frightening frequency?

He thought back to the command ship's momentary paralysis when Marlene had appeared to pick up Annie's lost dress. *Why didn't the alien pilot fire?* he wondered, thinking back to the blond pilot's similar reluctance. The Invid had her right in its sights, and yet it was almost as if the thing had *recognized* her.

Almost as if Marlene was . . . *one of them*.

SEVEN

> *Opinions vary: there are those who give Annie LaBelle's age as thirteen and others who give it as seventeen; and there's enough contradictory background data to give strength to either argument. Subsequent research has yet to reveal enough to persuade or dissuade either camp. Rand, in his voluminous Notes on the Run, states that "Annie was thirteen going on seventeen," while elsewhere he opines that "she may be seventeen, but she acts like she's thirteen." It is a minor controversy, to be sure, but one that is still argued over. Ms. LaBelle has not been helpful in laying this matter to rest.*
>
> Footnote in Bellow, *The Road to Reflex Point*

THE PRESENCE OF INVID SCOUTS PATROLLING THE outer perimeters of the central hive forced the team to keep to the mountains and turn south once again. There was still no sign of Hunter's invasion force, and the Protoculture reserves in the VTs were simply too low to permit any worthwhile reconnaissance behind the enemy lines. No one was really put off by the delay; even Scott breathed easier knowing that Reflex Point was temporarily out of the question. Besides, the snow was behind them, even though the land itself was no less rugged. Travel since "Denver" had been almost due south—into what Scott's maps indicated had once been called western Texas.

Scott, Rook, and Lancer had done most of the flying; Lunk's APC was back on the ground where it belonged, with Rand's Cyclone to keep him company. Annie was in the mecha's buddy seat, urging Rand through the old highway's twists and turns. It was a warm, blue-sky day, and she felt gloriously alive and uncommonly optimistic. Indeed, she had good reason to feel this way.

"It's my birthday!" she shouted into Rand's ear when they had exited one of the road's many tunnels.

"If you don't stop screaming in my ear, it'll be the last birthday you celebrate," Rand warned over his shoulder.

They had lost sight of the VTs on the other side of the tunnel, so he took the turn fast, hoping to spot them before entering the figure-eight switchbacks that led down into the valley. All at once, Rook's red Alpha came whipping around the shoulder, scarcely ten feet above the roadbed. Rand told Annie to hold on and locked the Cyclone's brakes, stabilizing the mecha through a long slide as Rook was setting the fighter down. Lunk had a clearer view of things and managed to bring the APC to a more controlled stop behind the Cyc.

"Why don't you look where you're going?!" Rand shouted even before Rook had opened the canopy.

"Are you trying to kill us?!" Annie threw in.

"Just the opposite," Rook said peevishly over the Alpha's externals. "There's an Invid hive on the other side of the ridge, and at the rate you two were going, you'd have been on it in no time."

Rand's eyes went wide, but instead of thanking her or apologizing, he simply said: "Way down here? Choicest spot around."

Rook was correct about the hive; what she didn't realize was that the Invid were already aware of the team's presence and were heading toward them. About the same time she was warning Rand away, the Invid Regis was issuing new instructions to her troops through one of the hive's bio-constructs.

"Shock Trooper squadron, prepare to relieve incoming patrol drones," she announced. "Projected course of Robotech rebels from last point of encounter should bring them into our control zone during the next eight hours. Evidence of Protoculture activity on the outlying limits of

scanning perimeter indicates possible presence of Robotech mecha within control zone even now. All scanning
systems on full alert."

On foot, Rook, Rand, and the others joined Scott and
Lancer at the top of the ridge, where the two had concealed themselves among some rocks. The VTs had been
shut down and left on the roadbed.

"I don't like the looks of all this activity," Lancer was
telling Scott when the rest of the team approached. He
had a pair of high-powered scanning binoculars trained
on the hive dome. Shock Troopers and Scouts were buzzing in and out of the hemisphere, and several Pincer units
were in assembly on the ground, as though receiving
orders from some unseen commander. "I think they're
expecting us."

"But they weren't expecting us to spot them first,"
Scott said gruffly.

"How does it look?" Rand called out behind them.

Lancer lowered the binoculars and stepped away from
the outcropping. "In a word—bad."

"We've got to double back," Scott told them. "There's
a high road that keeps to the ridgeline above this valley.
We might be able to get through before their sensors pick
us up. It's going to be slow going, but I don't see that we
have any choice."

The refrain, Rand said to himself as he trudged back to
his mecha.

Scott, Rook, and Lancer led the slow, silent uphill pro-
cession, relying once more on the battery-operated thrusters that had seen the Guardian-configured Veritechs over
many a northern pass. But once over the ridge, they
risked increasing the pace somewhat and brought the
Protoculture systems back into play. They kept to the
road nevertheless but were now hovering fifteen or so
feet above its rough surface. But this still wasn't fast
enough for Annie.

"Some birthday," she griped to Rand. "No party, no presents, and no fun."

He had been hearing this for the better part of three hours now and was beginning to tire of it. "Count your blessings," he told her. "We're lucky to be alive. Isn't that right, Marlene?" he added, hoping to gain some support.

But Marlene didn't have much to say beyond a soft "Uh-huh" from the front seat of the APC. Her head felt as though it was splitting open, but she was determined not to let the others see how much pain she was in.

The three pilots became more brazen on the downhill stretches and were soon winging the fighters along at a good clip. Encouraged (and seeing an opportunity to raise the noise level of the mecha above that of Annie's nonstop complaining), Rand began to feed the Cyclone more throttle.

"Mint, what d' ya say we goose this thing a little. That sound good to you?"

Annie hammered her fist against his shoulder. "Don't call me Mint—*Whoa!*"

With a turn of his wrist, Rand saw to it that her words were left behind. The three Veritechs had disappeared around the bend, but with a bit of fancy weaving under the foot thrusters, Rand thought he could not only catch up but pull out into the lead. As soon as he made his first move, however, the first Invid ship appeared on the scene. It elevated into view from the trees at the base of the slope and skimmed two streams of annihilation discs straight into Rand's path. Consequently, he had to bring that fancy maneuvering into play sooner than planned, but he did succeed in dodging the energy Frisbees of the enemy's first volley.

Of course, it meant leaving the road entirely to do so.

But at least we're alive! he screamed to himself as the Cyclone was bounding down the steep slope toward the trees, Annie hanging on for dear life, in and out of the pillion seat half a dozen times before they hit the flat ground at the base of the cliff. Rand risked a look over his shoulder and saw that the APC had also left the ledge roadbed.

What he didn't see, however, was that Lunk's landing was far from smooth. A second discharge of disc fire had forced Lunk to swerve at the last moment; the nose of the vehicle connected with some large rocks and overturned, sending Marlene sprawling while Lunk rode out the roll. The same Invid ship swooped down for a close pass over the fleeing Cycloners, loosing a barrage as it fell, but Lancer's Alpha was on the thing now and holed it before it could manage a follow-up burst. Rand, meanwhile, was closing on the trees at top speed, heartened when he heard the Pincer unit explode behind him, but panicked when he saw two more rise unexpectedly out of the forest.

"They're everywhere!" he shouted.

"Rand! Get into your battle armor!" he heard Scott say over the mecha's tac net. "I'll keep you covered."

Rand halted the Cyclone and began to snatch sections of armor from one of the storage compartments. Off to his right he saw Lunk leading a dazed Marlene to shelter among the rocks at the base of the slope and told Annie to join them there. She ran off, holding her cap on her head with one hand.

Rand struggled into the "thinking cap" and launched for reconfiguration. A moment later he was back on the ground in Battle Armor mode, squaring off with one of the ships. The thing tried an overhand pincer swipe that missed, then a quick spray of disc fire after Rand had aggravated it with two Scorpions from the Cyclone's forearm launchers. The discs tore into the earth at Rand's feet and threw him flat on his back, but he countered with three missiles that found their way into seams in the ship's alloy. The Invid had enough life left in it to attempt a second pincer crush, but Rand rolled out from under it and watched as the ship collapsed onto its face and exploded.

Elsewhere, Rook was in pursuit of the second new arrival; Scott was several lengths behind her as she chased the ship across wooded valleys and dry fingers of foot-hills. The lieutenant's face came up on the red VT's cock-pit commo screen.

"That's enough, Rook—let it go."

"But we can't let this one report that it found us," she pointed out. "We've gotta finish it."

"Forget it," Scott told her more strongly. "They're on to us already, or we wouldn't have had that little skirmish back there. Swing around."

Rook glared at Scott's screen image, then began to ease the VT off its pursuit heading. She couldn't help but notice how beautiful the land was below her—green hills and meadows, in startling contrast to the barrenness of the high ground. She saw a town and alerted Scott to her find.

"It doesn't look like anybody's home," she commented as the two fighters completed a quick flyby.

Scott was silent for a moment, then said: "That'll be perfect."

"Perfect for what?" she asked him. But he had nothing further to say.

They all agreed that the village must have been a de-lightful place when it was alive. Now it was just a motley collection of buildings and houses (spanning several hundred years of architectural styles), but nothing could diminish the tranquillity of the valley itself or the beauty of the surrounding mountains.

Scott ordered the Veritechs in and instructed Rand to assist Lunk with whatever repairs the APC required; af-terward the two men were to join the others in town, but Marlene and Annie were to wait until they received an all clear before coming down from the hills.

A building-to-building search of the place revealed lit-tle in the way of supplies, but Lancer stumbled across one item that prompted a scheme to turn the tables on the Invid Troopers in the nearby hive—as well as carry out the more prosaic surprise Scott had in mind for Annie. What he had found—hidden in a barn on the outskirts of town—was a device known as a bio-emulator, a Protoculture-powered instrument that was capable of mimicking the energy emanations of a supply-sized cache of the pure stuff. It had been developed not by the resistance but by the black market racketeers at the close of the Second Robotech War, for luring Southern Cross personnel to their deaths.

Given top billing in Scott's reworked plan was an unusual building that dominated the town, a circular structure with a columned cupola adorning its domed roof that had once served as an armory. Installation of the bio-emulator setup required a certain amount of group effort to conceal wiring and such, but the original plan, the prosaic one, called for little more than setting up several strategically placed rocket launchers and breaking out some of the supplies the team had brought with it from the Rocky Mountains underground complex. The freedom fighters split up into two teams, with Rook and Rand handling the indoor chores while Lunk and Lancer worked together rigging the armory building with charges. Scott did what he did best: he supervised.

Then Rand was sent to fetch the two women.

The sun was setting, huge and golden, and Annie and Marlene were still waiting in the mountains, sitting side by side on the rock with a western view.

"I guess birthdays are very special days," Marlene was saying consolingly. "I wish I could remember if I ever had one."

"Oh, you've had one," said Annie. "I don't think there's any way around that."

"Do they always make you unhappy?"

Annie brought her knees to her chest and put her head in her hands. "Let's just say that it's hard to be happy when every single one of your birthdays is a disaster."

"But Annie, were they all bad?"

The young girl was sniffling now, her eyes closed.

There was a time, she recalled, when things could have been pleasant but weren't. A time before the Invid invasion, when her parents and Mr. Widget were still alive, when the Northlands were embroiled in war with the Robotech Masters, and the Southlands prospered. Before the bombs . . . when she still had a home.

She could see herself in that simple shingled house, dressed in her yellow pants and blouse, reading the card they had given her and gazing at the cake her mom had bought at the market, left alone to puzzle out why they couldn't stay to enjoy it with her, why they always seemed to have more important things to do. She could hear her mother's voice still: *Your father and I won't be back till late, Annie, so when you've finished your little party, be sure to clean up all the dishes and put yourself to bed at a decent hour, all right? Well, good-bye, honey, and, oh yes, happy birthday. . . .*

"I don't know how many times I prayed that just once I could have a real birthday party with friends and family like everybody else in the world."

"I don't think there's anything worse than being alone on your birthday. Well, I guess I wasn't completely alone . . . at least my friend Mr. Widget was there to help me eat my birthday cake."

"Who?"

"He was my cat. . . . He's gone now. . . ."

"Oh," Marlene said softly, trying to understand.

Annie looked up into a pale yellow sky, wisps of lavender clouds. "Jeez, when did it get so dark? I wonder where the others are." The sun was already down now. "Thank goodness it won't be my birthday for much longer," she sighed.

All at once the two women heard growling noises coming from the trees behind them. They wrapped their arms around each other and waited for the worst. The growling grew louder, and Annie began to scream, clutching at her friend; then Rand appeared out of the darkness with a big hi and a smile on his face.

"Rand, you *jerk!*" Annie yelled.

He snorted and walked over to them. "All right, all right, calm down. I should've known you'd be a nervous wreck by now. But let's get going; we have to go meet the others."

"But where's the Cyclone?" Marlene wanted to know, her arm still around Annie's shoulders.

Rand shook his head. "I'm afraid I can't offer you a ride. It's too risky to use any of our mecha. This whole area is crawling with Invid."

Marlene gasped. Strange that she didn't *feel* their presence.

"Scott and the others are holed up in the village," Rand added after a moment. "There's no way we can get through."

"That tears it. . . ." said Annie.

Marlene gave her a reassuring hug. "I'm afraid it's going to be another birthday without a party, Annie. We're sorry."

Rand made a scoffing sound. "I hate to tell you this, but we've got a lot more important things to worry about than Annie's birthday. Now, come on."

He led them off through the woods to the edge of the hill overlooking town, trying to maintain that same hard look that wouldn't give away the surprise. But he knew that the act must be killing her and began to wonder about the more sinister side of surprises.

"That big house down there on the left," he gestured. "We've gotta try and make a run for it."

"It's so spooky-looking," Annie said, burying her face in Marlene's breast. "I'm scared."

"Are you sure Scott's down there?"

"Everybody's down there," Rand told her. "At least, they were when I left. . . . I hope nothing's happened." He started off down the hill. "Follow me."

It was a simple brick affair with a large chimney, curved-top windows and doors, and two small dormers. They hid together behind a tree at the edge of the walk. Rand ran to the door and motioned for them to join him quietly but quickly. Annie was making frightened sounds.

"It's dark in here, so watch out," he cautioned them as

he opened the door. "Scott, I'm back," he whispered into the darkness. "Where are you?"

Annie was the last through the door, and by that time Marlene and Rand were gone. She called out to them, quietly at first but with increasing panic in her voice. "What happened to everybody?" she asked pleadingly as she moved across the floor, unable to see her hand in front of her face.

"Why does everybody always abandon me?"

"Annie, over here," someone called out from somewhere.

"Rook, is that you?" she answered, her voice a tremolo.

Suddenly there were flashes of light in the blackness, then a brightness she had to hide her eyes from. But again someone called out to her: "Open your eyes, Annie."

And when she looked, she saw all her friends, gathered around a round table that had been set for seven, with plates and wine goblets and platters of food and a large birthday cake decorated with seventeen candles. And everyone was wishing her happy birthday.

Lunk was standing over her with the cake in his hands.

"Are you putting me on?" she asked them.

"It's your favorite," he told her. "Mint chocolate."

"And look what I made for you," Rook said, showing her a knitted scarf.

"Happy birthday, Annie," said Marlene. "At last."

Annie stared at everyone for a moment, found that she couldn't take it, and ran outdoors to weep; there she said thank you to the stars.

CHAPTER
EIGHT

Dad didn't plan a career as a voyeur—at least, not consciously. He just kept finding himself looking here when he should have been looking there, stumbling onto this when he should have been busying himself with that... Until the incident at the baths. But I sometimes wonder how much Mom encouraged Dad's behavior. I asked her about it once, and the only thing she would tell me was that Dad got what he had coming. Then she grinned.

Maria Bartley-Rand, *Flower of Life:
Journey Beyond Protoculture*

THE CAKE, THE SWEETS, AND THE GIFTS WERE ONLY
the start of the surprises Scott and the team had in store
for Annie, but after a few sips of wine it turned out that
Annie had some surprises of her own.

She was playing the celebrity host to their toasts and
compliments now, using her wineglass as a prop microphone and modeling the pink chiffon dress Rook had
given her. Her hair was brushed and parted in the center,
for once free of the funky E.T. cap she was seldom seen
without.

"To the cutest little freedom fighter around," Scott
said from the table, lifting his glass.

"Thank you, thank you, ladies and gentlemen," Annie
directed to her audience. "I would also like to thank my
designer, Miss Rook Bartley, for this elegant gown."

Rook took in the cheers with a noticeable blush. She
hadn't done more than tailor the dress down to Annie's

size. And unfortunately, she had gone a little high on the hem; the dress made Annie look about six years old, but no one was pointing this out. The yellow knee socks and brown pumps didn't help any, but they had taken what they could from the sub city, with little thought given to coordinating an outfit.

"Rook, I didn't know you were so . . . so *domestic*," Scott said from across the room.

Rook saw the bemused look on his face but ignored it. "It looks great on you," she told Annie, throwing the lieutenant a look out of the corner of her eye.

"Thanks! I feel like a beauty queen!" Annie tried a pirouette, giggling all the while, and almost lost her balance.

Cross-legged on the floor, Rand stifled a laugh. "One thing's for sure—you're no ballerina!"

Annie looked at him and shook her head as though to clear it. "And now the moment you've all been waiting for," she said like an emcee. "Approaching the judges' runway is our next contestant for the title of Miss Birthday Girl!"

Lunk and the others caught on to the act and applauded.

Annie switched to a squeaky parody of her own voice. "Thank you," she said into the wineglass. "My name's Annie. I'm four-foot-seven with blue eyes, and I'm often complimented on my personality." As she sauntered by Rand, she flashed some thigh and slipped him a wink. "And my legs aren't bad, either, big boy."

"I'll say," Rand enthused, knocking back another goblet of wine.

Annie cozied up to Lunk next. "Oh, I can't tell you how happy I am to be here! It's just too thrilling for words!" She gave him a light peck on the cheek and moved away from the table, snatching up his glass of wine.

"Hey, wait a second, that's not fair!" Rand protested while everyone else laughed. "If a contestant kisses one of the judges, she's gotta kiss all of them."

Annie had backed away tipsily to clink glasses with Lancer.

"Gee, do I have to?"

"Yep. Them's the rules."

"Well, pucker up then," she said on her way over to Rand. But as he stood up and offered his lips, she stuck one of the wineglasses in his mouth. Annie dismissed the laughter and sidled up to Scott, who was leaning against the wall. "Now, don't anybody move, because my very favorite part is coming up next—the *swimsuit competition*!" As Scott's eyebrows went up, she reached up and shut his eyes with her fingertips. "But *you* don't get to watch, you dirty old man!"

"That's telling him, Annie!" Rook encouraged her.

Rand said, "Well, she's got my vote."

"Yeah," from Lunk, getting to his feet.

Rook seconded the vote, and everyone else said, "Agreed!"

"It's unanimous, Annie," Rook announced. "You are the new Miss Birthday Girl!"

Annie skipped over to the curtained window while they toasted her easy victory. "Jeepers, I don't know what to say!" Then suddenly it was her natural voice once again, full of emotion and sincerity:

"Except that this is the happiest night of my life."

But far above the spirited celebration, some uninvited guests were converging on the deserted village: an Invid patrol from the nearby hive, now under the leadership of Corg himself. He had narrowly escaped being blown to bits by the explosions that had destroyed the underground city, and the Regis had granted him a new command ship of the same design as the original.

"Are we approaching the site of the disturbance?" Corg inquired into his cockpit communicator.

The source of active Protoculture readings recently received by the hive monitors had been traced to the village, and the Regis was certain that the Robotech rebels had made their way here. She was just as certain there would be no escape for them now.

"Estimated arrival time: five point two minutes," she told Corg through the command net that linked her with her troops.

Corg glanced out over the landscape from the cockpit of his ship and thought: *The thrill of approaching victory makes me feel almost . . . Human!*

The women were cleaning up—by choice, not design. Normally they wouldn't have even bothered to tidy up, but there was something about the house and the town itself that brought out sentiments most of them thought they had left behind. Marlene was a little puzzled by it all, but she volunteered to help Rook clear the table and clean the glasses and plates. The luxury of running water was more than enough for Rook, and she really had her mind on the hot bath she planned to take once the supplies were repacked.

"I've never seen Annie so excited," she was telling Marlene now. "This is one birthday she'll never forget." Annie was peacefully asleep in a chair nearby. "I never thought I'd live to see her wearing a dress like a regular little girl."

Scott was outside the window, eavesdropping, his handgun raised. Lancer found him there and wondered what it was all about.

"You're concerned about Marlene, aren't you?"

"Well, what about you, Lancer? Don't you get the feeling there's something mysterious about her? And I don't just mean the amnesia. It goes beyond that . . . like she's never had a past to remember. Like . . ."

"Like what, Scott? Go on, say it."

But Scott simply tightened his mouth and shook his head.

Lancer sighed knowingly but wasn't about to open up his own thoughts if Scott couldn't bring himself to do the same. "I don't think that she's going to murder us all in our sleep, Scott. But I agree that she's an unusual woman. Maybe we just have to give her some time to come out of it."

Scott gave him a dubious look and was about to press the point, but just then Rand broke into the conversation.

"Hey, guys, do you really think the Invid might show up tonight?"

There was something about Rand's tone that suggested more than his usual concern, almost as if he had other plans. But Lancer chose to reply to his remark, not to the unsaid things. "There's no sign of them yet," Lancer told him. "And believe me, that's just the way I want it. I think I've had more than enough entertainment for one day."

Rand tittered, delighted. "Well, maybe you've had enough. But as far as I'm concerned the party's just beginning."

Lancer beetled his brows. "Rand, what exactly do you have in mind?"

When Rook and Marlene finished the dishes, they woke Annie up and surprised her with a bag of peppermints they hadn't brought out at the party.

"Peppermints!"

Rook patted her on the shoulder. "I knew those bags you took wouldn't last."

Annie was handling the bag lovingly one moment, and the next she was crying. "When I think that I'm having a real birthday after wanting one so badly...with peppermints and everything..." She buried her face against Marlene.

"We're just glad you enjoyed it," Rook said, smiling. "The only problem is we only get to do it once a year." She yawned and stretched. "And now, something for the three of us to enjoy together...."

The bathroom was in the rear of the house; it was a completely tiled room with a shower stall and a sunken tub large enough for four. Rand had been there when Rook made the discovery, and he knew it was only a mat-

ter of time before she would go back to avail herself of
the pleasures of an honest-to-goodness hot bath. So he
had already stationed himself below the room's only window well before the time Rook, Marlene, and Annie entered. He couldn't believe his luck when he realized that
all three were about to take the plunge.

He had actually convinced himself that he had no idea
just what the room contained. As far as he or anyone else
was concerned, he was merely standing guard out here
while the rest of the guys dillydallied out front, cleaning
their weapons and waiting for the Invid to home in on
that device Lancer had rigged in the armory. Therefore, it
was entirely understandable that he poke his head up to
that window at the first sign of any unusual noises, because who knew what was lurking around in these supposedly deserted villages?

What he hadn't figured on was the damn window being
quite so high; he was forced to stand on the rather shaky
woodpile underneath it in order to peer in. And it was
only then that he realized the window glass itself was
frosted—not opaque but certainly a lot less clear than he
would have liked. And the steam from all that hot water
wasn't helping any, either.

Nevertheless, he was able to discern a good deal of
what was going on. He knew, for example, that that was
Marlene stepping out of her pants, and Annie discarding
her dress, and Rook slipping off her jumpsuit and bra and
panties. . . . It was just the *details* that were left to his
imagination. And the need to know those details soon
had him on tiptoe atop the woodpile, eyes and cupped
hands pressed to the glass.

Annie was already in the sunken tub when the first
logs began to slip under his feet.

"It sure is warm enough," she was saying. "I feel like a
lobster." Naked, Rook and Marlene were laughing playfully but not loud enough to cover up the sounds from
outside the window.

Rand gripped the windowsill, held his breath, and
tried to *will* the logs silent, but they just kept rolling off

the top of the pile and crashing against the side of the house. At first he wasn't sure if the women had heard anything, nor could he be sure they were looking his way. But the bathroom was awfully quiet all of a sudden. . . .

I'm just investigating these strange sounds, Rand said to himself over and over. *I'm just investigating these strange sounds—*

"Hey, is there somebody out there?!" Annie asked.

Rand heard her and started to back off, but the pile gave way again and sent him down on his butt to the ground. By the time he turned around, the window had been thrown open, and in addition to clouds of steam came a bucketful of ice-cold water that caught him squarely on the back and seemed to lift him right off the ground.

"That oughta cool you down, Rand," he heard Rook saying.

"That's what I get for trying to be helpful?!" he shouted in return, running off toward the front of the house.

Overhead, the Invid squadron closed in on the village, a constellation of evil moving across the heavens.

"Estimated three point seven three minutes to objective," Corg told his troops. "Focus scanning systems on Protoculture activity. And remember: These are Robotech rebels. They are not to be neutralized for the farms; they are to be destroyed."

Scott and the others had moved indoors by the time Rand entered, towel-drying his hair and trying to work some warmth into his scalp. Lunk was spreading out the sleeping bags, and Scott seemed to be spit-polishing the muzzle of one of the assault rifles.

"I'm starting to think maybe the Invid aren't as stupid as we thought they were," Lancer was saying from the window.

"Don't worry, they won't let us down," Scott told him. "Just keep your eyes peeled."

Shivering, Rand draped the towel around his neck. "Whew!" he said loudly enough to capture everyone's attention. "I've never been able to figure women out. They go on and on about how men don't appreciate them, and when we *do* go out of our way to appreciate them, they start screaming bloody murder like it was all news to them."

Lancer threw him a disapproving look. "There's a big difference between appreciating them and leering at them, Rand."

"Ah, what do *you* know about it?" Rand countered angrily.

Scott ignored the two of them and asked Lunk about the so-called Roman candles he had set up outside.

"It's just my part of the surprise for Annie's birthday," Lunk explained.

Meanwhile, the birthday girl was back in the tub having her hair washed by Rook. She asked Marlene if she had ever been in love.

"Scott asked me the same question," Marlene said, soaping herself up, "and I have to give you the same answer I gave him: I know it must sound strange, but I honestly don't remember."

"How can you not remember if you were in love?" Annie said in amazement.

Marlene shrugged. "I've forgotten everything. I'm a living, breathing, walking blank—I can't even remember what my *purpose* in life is."

"Your purpose in life is to find a man," Annie told her with certainty. "Everyone knows that. Rook has found herself a man."

Rook stopped massaging Annie's hair and gently twisted her head around. "If you're talking about Rand," she said into Annie's face, "let me enlighten you about a thing or two. First of all, about this business of *needing* a man—*huh*?!"

Marlene was staring at them in stark terror.

"They've come!" she screamed. "The Invid are here!"

Inside the armory the bio-emulator continued its false siren song.

The men were also aware that the Invid had arrived, and the ships were doing just what the plan called for: forming a circle around the building.

"Remind me to congratulate the wise guy who invented that bio-emulator," Lancer said, arming his blaster. "It's working like a charm."

Scott was the first through the open window. "Lunk, stay with the women. And Rand, grab those detonators on your way out. Time for this evening's next surprise."

While Scott, Lancer, and Rand were stealing away from the house, Corg was issuing orders to his troops. They had put down in formation fifty yards from the circular structure and were spreading out to take up positions. The voice of the Regis came across the communications net.

"You have reached the focus of the disturbance."

"Deploy for complete encirclement of the Robotech rebels," Corg ordered. "None of them must be allowed to slip through our grasp."

"Scanners indicate the Protoculture emanations are definitely Robotech in origin. . . ." the Regis updated as the combat units fanned out.

"We will not fail you this time, my queen," Corg started to say, but the Regis had something to add.

"However, the nature of your readings is disturbing. The Protoculture activity is unusually steady in its dispersal pattern. We detect no modulations or fluctuations of any kind—almost as if the matrix waverings were being synthetically produced."

"Nonsense! Humans are incapable of such deception!" He already had the cannon arm of his ship raised.

The cockpit displays in Corg's ship began to flash as new data was received and transmitted. "Our bio-detectors register no sign of Human movement within the structure," the Regis continued. "Probability cortex indicates likelihood of a trap, increasing by a factor of one hundred for every five seconds you remain in present situation. . . ."

Corg reached out and shut down the audio signals. "Open fire!" he commanded.

Streams of annihilation discs began to tear into the circular walls of the armory, and explosions erupted across the face of the dome, filling the cool air with the sound of thunder and throwing pyrotechnic light into the night sky. Corg continued to scream "Fire! Fire!" urging his troops on to greater heights of destructive catharsis, pouring out all the misunderstood feelings and frustrations that were part of the life the Regis had given him.

But outside the circle of pincer-clawed ships, the Humans had some feelings of their own to express. And suddenly there were explosions coming from the trees that surrounded the building, explosions Corg could not understand. He watched as his Troopers were hurled violently against one another and sent smashing into the building's stone walls. Others were lifted off the ground by the force of the blasts. Claws, scanners, and pieces of hardware became fiery-hot projectiles blown from his decimated squadron. The hull of his own ship was holed with shrapnel and pieces of airborne debris, and all at once he felt himself overturned, felled by a storm of enemy fire. Shock Troopers were taken out while they attempted to lift off, erupting like brilliant balls of flame, raining pieces of themselves throughout the field.

"Easy as shooting fish in a barrel," Rand said from the perimeter.

Lunk, too, was yahooing from the window of the house. The women had joined him in the front room, clad only in bath towels. Annie was so excited, she leapt clear out of her towel, breasts bobbing up and down, but Lunk was too preoccupied with the explosions to notice.

"*Ka-boom!* Yeah! I *love* this stuff!"

"Wow! This is the *best* birthday present of all!"

Meanwhile the few remaining Invid ships, including the command ship, were taking to the skies in retreat.

"Okay, we're free to use the Alphas," Scott told Lancer and Rand. "Let's move it!"

The three men ran past the house to the concealed fighters, waving back to Lunk and their towel-clad team-mates. Lancer stopped to say: "Don't anyone go to bed yet, because we fly-boys have one more surprise in store!"

"Another surprise?" Annie asked him, adjusting her towel. "Just what are you guys up to now?"

"Just you wait and see," Lancer said, running off to catch up with Scott.

Lunk had jumped out of the window and was showing Annie an enigmatic grin. "I've got one of my own," he added, rushing away.

The women exchanged puzzled looks and then some as the sky began to fill with starburst explosions.

Rook laughed. "He wasn't kidding: they really are Roman candle launchers."

Annie looked at her. "You mean you knew all along?"

"Only some of it."

Scott was glad to see that the fireworks had only added to the enemy's confusion. The Invid ships were streaking away, trying desperately to evade the fireworks, fooled into thinking they were some sort of lethal missile.

In fact, Corg was reporting as much to the Regis while he led his ragtag troops back toward the hive.

But Scott didn't call for pursuit. Instead, the Alphas formed up on his lead and went through the unrehearsed moves they had discussed earlier that day.

"It's wonderful, isn't it, Annie?" Marlene said from the window of the house.

"I've never had a birthday like this," the teenager was saying.

"I don't think *any* of us have had a birthday like this," said Rook.

And it's really happening . . . it's not a dream!

The women could see the skywriting now, and Rook read the words: "Happy . . . Birthday. . ."

Up above, Rand said: "I'll bet Admiral Hunter never had you guys doing this with your Alpha Fighters, huh, Scott?"

Scott smiled, then realized that Rand was off course somehow. "What are you doing down there?" he asked.

Rand made no response and completed his part of the skywriting moves. From the window, the three women watched as his Alpha spelled out "Mint" under the birthday greeting.

Rook snorted. "So *that's* why Rand wanted to write your name."

"Oh, well," Annie sighed, turning away from the window for a moment. "I guess it's a lot better nickname than 'Peewee.' "

CHAPTER
NINE

*The planet [Earth] secured, the Regis then had to decide
what to do about the surviving Human population. She knew
from past experience that Humans could be a dangerous lot,
even these Terrans, who seemed somehow inferior to the Tirolian species. Eventually it would occur to her to use a percent-
age of the survivors as laborers in the Protoculture farms, but
that was only after what can best be described as a trial-and-
error period, during which an unlucky assortment were sub-
jected to experiments too gruesome to dwell on. Fortunately,
most of the laboratory cases died outright or soon thereafter,
though a scant few remained to wander their ravaged homeworld less than Human.*

Bloom Nesterfig, *Social Organization of the Invid*

AS RAND TOLD IT:

"The soldiers had been dead a week, but the town was
just getting around to burying them when we rode in . . . I
have to admit that I had put no stock in the rumors we
had been hearing on the road, but sure enough, the town
had its own contingent of Robotech soldiers, Mars Division, like Scott, survivors from that same ill-fated assault
on Earth. It was remarkable enough to come across a
populated village so near the Invid control zone, but to
find fellow soldiers as well was almost more than Scott
could bear. I still have an image of him parked in the
middle of that town's dust bowl of a main street, straddling the Cyc with a big grin on his face and broadcasting
our arrival to one and all over the mecha's externals.
When only a handful of folks wandered out to greet us, I
remember thinking: *Here we go again; just another ghost*

town run by a bunch of rubes and rogues. But then we learned that everyone that counted was at the graveyard.

"That's where Scott ran into the robbies. Not straight away, though; there was a funeral service in progress, so we all just hung around on the outskirts of the action until the crowds thinned. There were church bells ringing in the distance. After that, Scott went in to introduce himself to the one soldier who seemed to be in charge—a tall officer, wearing shades and a high-collared gray uniform like Scott's. I never did catch the dude's name; come to think of it, I don't think the two of us exchanged more than a brief handshake the whole time we were in town.

"It turned out that they had been there for some months; they had put down as a unit somewhere south of Reflex Point and worked their way into the Northlands, hoping to come across other Mars Division survivors. They saw a lot of action early on, but now they were just hanging on, waiting for the big one to go down. They had all heard of Scott and were excited to learn that the Expeditionary Force was indeed on its way. They had a good deal of intelligence dope on Reflex Point, but there was something they needed to talk about before getting down to basics.

"There were three fresh graves in the cemetery, marked by simple wooden crosses, one of which was crowned with a 'thinking cap,' its faceguard shattered. I naturally assumed that the Invid had paid the town a visit and left their usual calling cards, but that wasn't the case. It seems that the three had been gunned down by some lone biker who went by the name of Dusty Ayres. These latest murders brought the total to eleven.

"Scott was flipped out to learn that someone other than the Invid were killing soldiers; he asked the officer about Ayres.

"'We don't know much about him,' the man replied. 'Except that he seems to have it in for soldiers.' The officer threw his men a dirty look. 'Some people claim he can't be killed.'

"I didn't like hearing this, but for Scott it explained

how three soldiers could be brought down by one loner. I
didn't bother to point out that a man needn't be *invulnerable* to get the better of a group, because it was obvious
that Scott was already thinking *Invid*. No *Human* could
do such a thing. As if he had to be reminded about the
sympathizers we had met along the way. Wolff, to name
just one . . .

"'Sounds like a real mystery man,' Lancer offered.
'And nobody knows why he's here, huh?'

"Scott said more firmly, 'You must know more about
this guy.'

"I was glad to see that I wasn't the only suspicious one
among us. But the officer wasn't swayed to say any more
about Ayres. 'I wish I had more.' The man shrugged.
'Everything's just rumors right now.'

"'Dusty Ayres, you say,' Scott repeated.

"'That's the only name I've ever heard him called.'

"Lancer brought up the sympathizer idea.

"Lunk punched his open hand. 'I just wish he'd try to
start something with us. I'd break his face.'

"*Terrific*, I thought. I looked at the three graves and
wondered how our helmets would look on those crosses.

"'He's got to be hunted down,' the officer told Scott.
'Will you join us, Lieutenant?'

"Scott was wary. 'I'm not going to involve any of my
people until I know more about this matter.'

"'Sure thing, Lieutenant. You take your time. While
the rest of us die . . .'

"I sucked in my breath; you just didn't go around saying things like this to Scott unless you were already holding an H90 to his head. Fortunately, Lancer stepped in to
intervene. Only thing was, he actually took it upon himself to volunteer our services. Lunk, the big lug, seconded
it, and I guess that was enough for Scott.

"'You won't regret it, Lieutenant,' the officer thanked
us.

"I, of course, *already* regretted it; but everyone else
was talking tough and anxious to get started."

* * *

"We left Annie and Marlene behind—much to our birthday girl's dismay. After all, she had been 'seventeen' for a full week now, and didn't that entitle her to share in the 'fun stuff'? Those were her words: *'It simply isn't fair!'*

"Rook got a big charge out of this but didn't bring it up until later, after we had split up into several groups.

"'Fair? Did she really say "fair"?'

"I repeated Annie's exact words into my helmet mike and laughed. We were both in battle armor now and cruising side by side across the barren stretch where Ayres had last been seen, close to where the bodies of the three soldiers had been found. The area had once been called 'the Panhandle,' for reasons unknown, but it was just plain desert to us, no different from the wastes we had been traveling through since leaving the mountains behind. Scott and Lancer were off somewhere south of us, and Lunk was riding with a few of the other soldiers.

"I confessed to Rook how pissed off I was by the whole deal. 'I mean, what happened to Reflex Point? Suddenly we're a posse for hire, or what?'

"For once, Rook actually agreed with me. Strange, because she had been ignoring me since the stunt I pulled at the bathroom window. I had been taking a kind of apologetic, conciliatory tone with her ever since and now suggested that we split up to cover more ground. But she didn't want to hear it.

"'If it's all the same to you, I'd feel better about this if we stayed together.'

"I certainly didn't need to be told twice, and I'm sure I was smiling inside my helmet when the Invid ships appeared over the hills.

"'Guess we're just not meant to be together!' Rook shouted over the net just before we separated.

"There were five ships bearing down on us: four rust-brown pincer-armed combat units led by one of the new blue and white monsters we had been up against in the underground city. It was bound to happen—our Cycs were probably putting off the only 'Culture vibes for miles around—and I had said as much before we split up, but nobody wanted to hear it.

"The leader dropped some fire at our tails, but we were flat out now and just out of range. The big guy stuck with me after we separated, but Rook had her hands full with the Pincer craft. I saw her slalom through a field of explosions, then launch and reconfigure to Battle Armor mode. She put down almost immediately and took out one of her pursuers with a single Scorpion loosed in the nick of time. I wanted to applaud her, but I was too busy dodging blasts from that leader ship. There was a low mesa directly in my path, and I used it to my advantage by snaking around its base and going over to Battle Armor before the Invid ship completed its own turn. I hovered near the eroded wall of the butte, trading shots with the ship, but I couldn't zero in on any vulnerable spots. The Invid was up on its armored legs, towering over me, loosing anni discs from two small weapons ports tucked under its chin—guns I didn't know existed until just then. But after a minute of this I took off to find Rook. As the two of us landed side by side, she said, 'We've gotta stop meeting like this.'

"I would have laughed if another blast from the leader hadn't forced us into a rapid launch. And when we put down again, there was panic in Rook's voice. 'It's bad, Rand! There's just too many of them!'

"'It's *always* bad!' I shouted back. 'Just range in on the big one and give it your best shot!'

"The four remaining ships had regrouped and were closing in on us. We both raised our forearm launch tubes, and it was then that Rook spied something atop one of the nearby hills. I turned in time to catch a metallic glint.

"'What is that?' Rook asked.

"I told her I had no idea. 'But if it's not friendly, we're in real trouble.'

"The Invid had also caught sight of the thing, and it was apparent an instant later that they found it to be a more appealing target. The ships zoomed past us without a shot, making straight for the hilltop. I thought it might be Scott or maybe Lunk in the APC, but I had to guess again, because instead of attacking, the ships simply moved off, as though recalled unexpectedly.

" 'I guess it's friendly,' Rook was saying, stepping out for a better view of the thing. But that didn't make sense, I told her, following her lead. If it was friendly to us, it would have been fired upon. My guess was that it was an Invid command ship—perhaps that orange and green one we had been seeing lately.

"But as the thing came into view, we saw that it was some kind of sidecarred cycle, piloted by a man wearing a poncho and Western-style hat. We were trading looks with him when he suddenly fell off the bike, obviously *shot*!"

"The rogue was hurt, but well enough to ride. Rook insisted on seeing what she could do for the wound in his arm, and he led us to a patch of forest that bordered the river we had crossed on our way into town. He was tall and good-looking in a derelict sort of way. His hair was parted in the center and fell below his shoulders, and he was in need of a shave and a good scrubbing, but none of that seemed to bother Rook. She was playing nurse to his silent cowboy and enjoying herself. I pretended to interest myself in the guy's mecha, which *was* unusual—it had twin scrambler-type exhaust stacks and a multimissile launch rack (the thing I had taken for a sidecar)—but I didn't miss a word of their conversation. I had already convinced myself that the guy was an Invid plant. He claimed to be as surprised as we were that the Invid had flown off without frying all of us, but I wasn't buying any of it.

"Rook and I had taken off our battle armor. The stranger was sitting down with his back against a tree, the poncho draped over one shoulder, letting Rook probe around inside his wound with a pair of tweezers from one of the Cyc's first-aid kits. What she fished from his arm turned out to be an old-fashioned *bullet*! But even this didn't seem to faze Rook.

"'This should help some,' she said, dropping the small projectile on the ground and treating the wound with antiseptic solution.

"The man thanked her in the same flat, clipped tone I was already beginning to dislike. A breeze rustled through the woods just then, and I gazed up and saw something that reinforced my suspicions about the guy. The wind revealed what the poncho had intended to hide: that his arm and a good portion of his chest were covered with some sort of gleaming alloy. Rook must have seen it, too, because I heard her gasp while asking the rogue's name.

"'Excuse me, mister. I didn't mean to embarrass you,' she hastened to add. 'What happened to you?'

"'Well, I'm glad you didn't run away when you saw it,' the stranger drawled. 'That's how most react. . . . Let's just say it's a little present from our friends the Invid. You could say I'm just lucky that they left me alive at all.'

"Rook made a face. 'I guess it could've been worse. . . .' She asked the man to remove his poncho and dabbed at the wound with gauze before beginning to dress it. 'At least you got away from them.' Rook winked at him flirtatiously. 'Now, I'm no doctor, so you better not let this rest until you see one.'

"The rogue almost smiled—or maybe that tight-lipped grin *was* his idea of a smile. But in any case, he said: 'What'd you say your name was, missy—Rook? Well, Rook, I just can't thank you enough for helping a stranger out.'

"Rook had a blushing response all ready for him. I saw her gesture to the bullet. 'But this isn't from any Invid,' she started to say. 'They don't have anything this primitive in their arsenal.'

"The stranger was about to reply, but I stepped in with my Gallant drawn and aimed at his midsection. 'You're right, Rook. And those Invid ships didn't just forget about us, either. This rogue's a spy.'

"'What are you doing?!' Rook shouted at me. 'Put that thing away!'

"'Not till I find out what it is about his guy that makes the Invid run away, or how he ended up with a bullet in his arm.'

"The rogue just stared, like he was sorry for me or something. 'If you have to know, the bullet came from my own gun. It discharged by accident. Check near the seat of the cycle if you don't believe me, kid. You'll find an antique six-gun under—'

"'You're an Invid agent,' I snarled, ignoring the bit about the gun because it sounded too much like the truth.

"'If that was true, you'd be dead, kid.'

"This also sounded right, but I ignored it and motioned with the blaster for him to get up. Rook was already on her feet, cursing me.

"'He's not our enemy, Rand. Besides—he's *hurt*!'

"I told her to stand out of the way and ordered the guy to his feet. He got up slowly, almost tiredly, and said we had helped him and he was grateful. 'I don't want anybody to get hurt.'

"I had the weapon straight out in front of me, and I guess I really didn't expect him to go for his gun. I even fired a warning shot into the tree behind him as his hand inched toward the holster, but he went for it anyway, confident that I wasn't about to kill him in cold blood, and caught me in the right hand with a stun blast, knocking the Gallant from my two-handed grip.

"That made *twice* when I should have fired first and asked questions later—first with Wolff and now with Mr. Clint McGlint. But so help me, if I'm ever drawing a bead on someone again . . .

"Anyhow, Rook ran over to me to take a look at my hand, dismissing it roughly when she saw that I was only mildly burned.

"'I hope you're satisfied!' she seethed. "You could have been killed!'

"The stranger threw me a look. 'Like I said, kid, if I was one of them, you woulda never left the sands alive.'

"I looked over at Rook, trying to sort through my feelings, and decided that it was all her fault for being so . . . *friendly*.

"Back then I was still struggling with jealousy."

"I let Rook and the stranger have a few moments of privacy by the river while I nursed my hand and wounded pride. But I didn't let it go on for long. The sun was going down, and I was certain that Scott and the others would be worrying about us. I had all but forgotten about Dusty Ayres and the search that had brought us out here to begin with.

"Rook and her new hero were too far off for me to hear, but I could tell by her posturing that things were getting a little too chummy, so I finally banged the Cyc into gear and rode in to break it up.

"'Sorry to *interrupt*, but it's time we headed back to town,' I told her. 'Thank your friend for his *hospitality* and let's get moving.'

"The stranger regarded me, then turned back to Rook. 'I have to leave anyway.'

"'Sorry to hear it,' I said.

"He ignored the comment. I tried to hurry Rook along and roared off, wanting no part of whatever good-byes the two planned to exchange.

"Rook caught up with me a few minutes later, and we rode a long way before either of us spoke. She repeated that I had been wrong about the man from the start—the man with no name. As he told it, he had been used as a guinea pig in some gruesome experiments the Invid had carried out shortly after they had defeated the Earth forces; apparently, the whole right side of his body had been vivisected and replaced with prostheses and alloy plating. Worse than that, his friends had stood by and made no attempt to rescue him. He was an unusually sensitive man, Rook insisted. and I had acted like a complete moron.

"I don't know why I didn't put two and two together then and figure out who the stranger was; I guess I was just too wrapped up in Rook's attachment to him to see the obvious. 'I have some unfinished business to take care of,' he had told her in response to her invitation to join us.

"Well, by the time we got back to town, I was convinced that I had been wrong and full of forgive and forget toward Rook. The open invitation didn't exactly *thrill* me, but I somehow managed to swallow my protests and keep still about it.

"'Rand, level with me,' Rook said when we were getting off the Cycs. 'Was I wrong to befriend that stranger?'

"'No,' I told her. 'You've gotta follow your feelings sometimes, no matter what.' Naturally I thought she was trying to get to the heart of the possessive feelings I had displayed. It was only later that I realized what was really on her mind: she had known all along just who it was she was helping and befriending. The question had nothing to do with *us*; it had to do with loyalties of an entirely different sort. . . .

"We had tracked down Scott and the gang to a saloon-restaurant straight out of an old Western movie. But if the place took me by surprise, the sight of Yellow Dancer nearly floored me. I suppose I had started to think of her as gone—a missing person—someone who had traveled the road with us for a short while and vanished, a casualty of this bizarre war. So to see Lancer now, in his turquoise tunic and helmet/bonnet, his pink belt and skin-tight pants, filled me with contrasting feelings. Scott and Lunk were at the bar knocking back a few while Yellow sang a very subdued 'Lonely Soldier Boy.'

"A couple of the town's soldiers came in just then, announcing that they had finally dug up a photo of this Dusty Ayres character, and they wanted to pass it around to us. Rook and I stood at the bar with the rest of them as the photo circulated. It was of course the face of our mysterious stranger. The cigarette in his mouth made him look even more sinister than he had appeared in the flesh.

"I was waiting for Rook to say something or at least throw me a look, but she didn't do either. I turned to her, my face all twisted up, and said:

"'You *see*?—I was right all along!'"

If the Ayres incident proved one thing, it was that Humans and Protoculture were basically immiscible. Invid and Protoculture? That was something else, as we shall see.

Mingtao, *Protoculture: Journey Beyond Mecha*

ROOK EDGED AWAY FROM THE BAR AND LEFT THE saloon. The sight of Dusty's photo in the hands of all those soldiers who were eager to see him killed, all those soldiers who had allegedly lost friends at his hands, had brought into question her earlier efforts on his behalf. Her flirtations. She sat in the dark on the saloon steps, while inside the soldiers drank and swore vengeance, and wondered why she always seemed to fall for the bad boys, the loners and rogues. It went back to Cavern City, she supposed, to Romy and the Angels and the days when she had been something of an outlaw herself. She couldn't deny, however, that she had seen something noble in Dusty's character. She thought back to that brief glimpse she had had of his chest plates and prosthetic arm. "My friends did nothing to stop them," she recalled him telling her. "They made no attempt to rescue me, or

at least put me out of my misery. . . . " Not that that justi-
fied his going on a murder spree.

Rook heard Rand's voice and glanced over her
shoulder in the direction of the saloon. He was telling the
men that he knew where Dusty could be found. But he
made no mention of the time he and Rook had spent with
him. He was being his usual protective self, and yet Rook
found that she was angry instead of grateful; she didn't
want to thank him as much as throttle him. Because
Rand, underneath all the arrogance and sarcasm, was actually a pretty sensitive man—in a hick sort of way.

Rook shut her eyes and pressed her hands to her forehead, as though in an attitude of prayer. *I knew he was
the one they were searching for, but it just doesn't seem
possible that he could be so cold-blooded. And maybe
Rand is right—maybe he is an Invid agent.* When she
looked up, she found Marlene standing in front of her.

"Are you all right?" Marlene asked her. "I saw how
upset you got in the saloon."

"I'm touched," Rook said nastily as Marlene sat down
beside her.

Marlene made a puzzled expression. "I guess I must
deserve that for some reason. . . . You see, I don't mean to
pry, but you just looked like you could use a friend."

Rook sighed and took Marlene's hand. "I'm sorry,
Marlene. In fact I was just thinking about friendship."

"Do you want to talk about it?"

Rook made Marlene promise that what she was about
to say would remain between them; then she told her
about the brief skirmish with the Invid ships and the
wounded rider she had helped. "It was Dusty Ayres,"
Rook confessed. "I think I knew right from the beginning, but I just didn't want to believe it. And after he told
me what he had been through, I started to feel sorry for
him. I probably wouldn't have said anything if that photo
hadn't turned up. Now I'm going to have to lie about it."

"But Rand won't say anything. He doesn't know what
you were feeling."

Rook showed a thin smile. "Oh, he knows, Marlene, he knows. . . ."

A light rain had begun, but a moment passed before Rook took any notice of it. She could hear the soldiers in the saloon discussing their plans to hunt Dusty down. Suddenly, she shot to her feet, startling Marlene. "I won't be able to rest until I see him again. Maybe I can convince him to surrender before he gets himself killed!"

Rook raced off, leaving Marlene alone in the rain.

An hour later, Scott was leading a Robotech posse across the sands. Rand was overhead in one of the Alphas (the Beta was close to depleted), directing the five Cyclone riders to where he and Rook had last seen the outlaw Ayres. The APC was trying to keep up with the group; Lunk had two of the town's soldiers with him. No one knew where Rook had gone; Rand had an idea, but he wasn't saying.

A heavy rain was falling, and the barren land had all the charm of a landscape in hell. But Scott was inured to the idiosyncrasies of the Earth's weather. Besides, he was obsessed with Ayres's capture, even though he had wanted no part of it initially. Perhaps it was because he was convinced that there was more to the story than anyone was telling him. A supposedly invulnerable outlaw who was systematically killing off Robotech soldiers . . . And yet the man wasn't thought to be an Invid agent, and *no one* had the slightest idea what was motivating him to murder. It just didn't add up. Scott was even beginning to suspect *Rand* of holding something back. It was obvious from the things he had said back in the saloon that he and Rook had had more than a passing encounter with Ayres. But why would Rand lie about it? Scott wondered. With Reflex Point almost close enough to touch (and with the new information the town's soldiers had supplied him), it was imperative that the mystery be solved so everyone could get back on track.

As if to reinforce Scott's concerns, a squadron of some fifteen Invid ships appeared suddenly out of the clouds.

"Invid at twelve o'clock!" Lancer reported over the net. "A bunch of 'em, too!"

Scott made a motion for the Cycloners to fan out. "Here we go, Rand," he sent up to the Alpha. "Standard battle plan!"

In the Veritech cockpit, Rand had to laugh. *Standard battle plan.* That was their little joke, meaning: *Do your best and we'll all try to keep from killing one another in the process.*

Rand wished them luck and threw his fighter into the thick of things. The squadron was composed of Pincer units and one blue leader that he could see; he managed to destroy one of the ships straight away but spent the next few minutes juking and dodging discs and laser fire from the rest. The blue especially was riding his tail with a vengeance.

"Too many of them!" he shouted over the net, upside down now and enmeshed by angry red bolts and streams of annihilation discs. "Where the hell is Rook when we need her?"

Elsewhere on the sands, Rook was confronting the outlaw. Ayres had almost fired on the red Veritech when it appeared but had stayed his hand at the last minute when he recognized Rook inside the cockpit. She was standing by the fighter's kowtowed nose now, mindless of the rain. Dusty was dressed in the same poncho and hat he had worn earlier; his all-terrain war machine was idling softly behind him. "You took a chance coming out here, Rook," he was telling her.

"I know that. But it was a chance I had to take, Dusty."

He grinned at her knowingly. "So you know my name, huh? And you just had to find out more about the mysterious killer. Is that it?"

"I suppose so," she started to say, wondering if she could bring herself to admit more.

"Well, there's nothing more to find out," he answered

before she could go on. "So get back in your fighter and forget about trying to involve yourself in this."

"But I'm *already* involved," Rook shouted. "I knew who you were this afternoon. I didn't need to learn that in town. And all I'm asking you for is an explanation."

Dusty started back to his cycle. "I've got things to do, Rook. I don't have time for this."

Rook pushed wet hair back from her face. "I guess I was naive to think I could keep you from killing again, so you leave me no choice...." She drew her blaster and leveled it at him. "I'm a soldier, Dusty, just like the rest of them. I have friends to protect."

She could see that she had surprised him, but he made no move for his weapon. "I don't want to hurt you, Rook—"

"Don't move or I'll fire," she warned him.

"You're making a mistake," he said after a moment. "Just put the blaster away and listen to me. Don't make me do something I'm going to regret."

Rook's nostrils flared, but she couldn't keep Dusty's words from undermining her will. She recalled how he had shot Rand, and she recalled the stories of his invulnerability... At last she lowered her weapon, and Dusty thanked her.

"You remember what I told you at the river, Rook? About the Invid's experiments with me?" He tossed the poncho over one shoulder and opened his shirt to give her a good look at the alloy plates that covered half his chest. "My *friends* let this happen to me, Rook. They stood by and let those monsters use me like a laboratory animal. They replaced my entire right side piece by piece with Protoculture-generated organs and these metallic prostheses." Ayres glared at her. "Do you really blame me for hunting them down?"

Rook lifted her head to answer him. "It must have been unbearable," she began on a sympathetic note. "But think about it, Dusty: you were a soldier once. Maybe your friends couldn't get to you. Maybe they tried and failed. And look what you're doing now: you're killing the only people who can avenge you. Your enemies are the Invid. How can you be sure they didn't implant something in your brain when they were carrying out those experiments—something that would *compel* you to attack your own friends."

Rook waited for him to respond. The latter possibility made a lot more sense to her than the former, because if Dusty's friends really had made an attempt to rescue him, why were they now acting like the whole deal was one big mystery to them? It was a moot point, though: Dusty was shaking his head, rejecting what she had said.

He raised his prosthesis into the cycle's headlamp and indicated eleven crosshatched marks engraved into the forearm alloy. "Each mark is a name I'd just as soon forget," he told her. "But I won't forget until I've killed every one of them!"

More than the marks, Rook could see the madness in Dusty's eyes. "I understand," she said softly.

He uttered a short maniacal laugh. "I was hoping you would, Rook." He goosed the cycle's throttle and pulled the hat down on his forehead. "I've got no gripe with your friends, but don't try to stop me—any of you."

Rook allowed him to ride off. *We'll meet again*, she told herself. *And I'll do what I have to do. . . .*

Rand took out another Pincer unit with heat-seekers from the undercarriage launch rakes and reconfigured to Battloid mode, bringing the rifle/cannon out in the mecha's metalshod right fist.

"It looks like we've gotten ourselves into a hole this time," Lunk said from the ground, where the soldiers were pouring fire into the sky.

Employing the foot thrusters to stabilize the ship, he raised the weapon to high port position and bracketed yet another Invid in his sights. He triggered off a burst, catching the ship midsection. "Just keep firing," Rand told Lunk, while the enemy fell like a meteor.

Scott screeched his mecha to a halt and stood up,

straddling the seat to bring his assault rifle into play. In the distance at ground level, he saw a bright light moving toward him. "Something's coming!" he alerted the others.

"Let's hope it's on our side," said Lancer.

Lunk lowered his weapon to have a look at it. "It's sure moving fast!"

Suddenly the Invid ships ceased their attack and began forming up on the blue leader, as though to observe the arrival of the newcomer. Then Rand's voice cut through the net: "That's Dusty Ayres's machine!"

With a dozen Invid ships still overhead, Rand expected Scott would have had sense enough to pull back and regroup, but instead, he heard Scott say, "Let's get him!" and launch himself in pursuit of the outlaw. Two of the other Robotech soldiers followed his lead.

Dusty Ayres saw the Cyclones speeding toward him and flashed a satisfied grin. *Well, well, Steve and Kent driving out with their greetings*, he thought. *How considerate of them.* The launcher's panel slid to, and Ayres let his thumb hover over the trigger button. "Now *die!*" he screamed, and fired.

Missiles streaked from the rack and found their targets; the two riders were blown to bits. Scott squinted as flames geysered up out of the sands, instantly superheating the air and filling it up with the stench of death. "Outflank him!" Scott commanded Lancer and the fifth Cycloner. "We'll try a cross fire!"

The three Cyclones and the APC converged on the lone rider, announcing themselves with a horizontal storm of lethal rounds. But Ayres appeared to be weathering it all; his clothes were torn to shreds and aflame, but the man himself was unscathed.

"They were right, Scott! The guy's indestructible!" Lancer exclaimed.

Ayres answered the challenge with shots of deadly accuracy, first taking out the Cycloner, then picking off the soldiers in the APC one by one before loosing missiles against the vehicle itself. Lunk was thrown a good twenty feet from the fiery wreck; when he looked up, he saw

Scott hovering over Ayres in Battle Armor mode, dumping everything the mecha had against him. Lancer pulled up a moment later, and Scott put down beside the two of them.

"Nice shooting," said Lancer as the three of them regarded the ruin that was Dusty's cycle.

But it wasn't over yet: Ayres—at least something that *resembled* Ayres—was stepping from the flames.

"I must be seeing things!" Lunk cried.

Scott's eyes went wide beneath the helmet faceshield. "I wish I could say you needed glasses, but I'm seeing it, too!"

In the meantime, everyone had forgotten about Rand —all except the Invid Enforcer, that is. The rest of the ships were still in formation overhead, but the commander had pursued Rand to the ground. Still in Battloid mode, he was trying to go one on one with the thing, but his reconfigured fighter was an infant to the enemy's giant.

Fortunately, Rook came roaring to his aid not a moment too soon, somehow managing to pilot her red VT right through the Pincer combat units without a fight. Together, the two Veritechs turned on the Enforcer and brought it down with enough explosive heat to turn the rain to clouds of steam. When the Pincer Ship pilots saw this, they broke formation and fell on the Humans; but by now Rand and Rook were back to back, with the VTs' weapons systems synchronized. On Rand's command they launched all their remaining cluster rockets, and in the fireworks display that followed, every Invid ship was destroyed.

At the same time, Lancer was seeing fireworks of his own. The first to attack Ayres, he was the first down, toppled by a blow from the outlaw's bionic arm. Lunk was already out—he had fainted from shock—but Scott stepped forward now, raising his weapon and cautioning Ayres not to move. Confident inside the reconfigured mecha, Scott reasoned that Lancer's battle armor hadn't been enough to withstand the Human monster's strength, but surely Ayres couldn't bring a Cycloner down. . . .

Scott tried to reason through it again a moment later, when he found himself flat on his back with Ayres standing over him aiming a blaster at his heart. He couldn't even recall the punch Ayres had thrown.

"Stay there," said Ayres. "Don't get up."

Who is to say what he might have done had the two Veritechs not put down on either side of him just then? Rook and Rand had the fighters in Guardian mode now; Rand leveled the rifle/cannon on Ayres while Rook leaped from her cockpit to face off with the gleaming half-Human outlaw.

"You told me it was just revenge, Dusty. That you weren't after the rest of us, remember?"

"They tried to kill me," Ayres threw back, training his hand weapon on her. The implication was clear: if Rand fired, Rook was going to die as well. No one was even certain at this point that the VT could really take Ayres out.

"Well, what did you expect them to do?" Rook screamed. "You're a murderer." She took two steps toward the muzzle of the weapon. "So you might as well start with me, because these people mean more to me than life itself. And if I thought that my helping you had contributed to their deaths, I couldn't live with myself." She gestured to her breast. "Go ahead, Dusty: right here, right here . . ."

Scott, Lancer, and Lunk were urging Rook to get back, but she stood her ground.

Ayres glowered at her and extended his weapon, but a moment later, much to Rand's amazement and everyone else's relief, he lowered it.

"I couldn't do that," he said, unable to meet her eyes. "I just couldn't. . . . Maybe if I'd had friends like you, none of this would have happened. I told you: I've got no argument with any of you people."

In the midst of all this, the Invid Enforcer had struggled to its feet and was now taking halting steps toward the Humans. Scott and the rest of the team swung their guns off Dusty to train them on the approaching ship. But Ayres told them not to worry about it. "I can tell by the way it's moving that it's no threat to us anymore."

Scott, who figured he knew the Invid just about as well as anyone, disagreed and told his team as much. So it seemed that only Dusty was surprised when the ship's cannons flared to life. He pushed Rook aside, raised his handgun, and fired, bull's-eyeing the ship's scanner.

Rook hid her face from the ensuing blinding flash and follow-up explosion. She thought she heard a blood-curdling scream pierce through it all, one of agony and release, and when she looked up Ayres was gone, disintegrated along with a great portion of the Invid ship itself.

The team spent the rest of the night picking up the pieces. Rook filled everyone in, grateful for Rand's efforts to support her but in the end overriding his objections. No one blamed her, really; they had all seen so much in the way of revenge, betrayal, and deceit this past year that Ayres's story was nothing new.

"I told him his real enemies were the Invid," Rook explained. "I'm sure they put something in his head; they had more control over him than he realized."

"More than he wanted to admit, that's for sure," said Lancer. "Those ships pulled back to see what we'd do up against their toy. He was probably an early experiment to see if they could use us against one another."

"And it's obvious they can," Scott added. He exchanged a brief look with Lancer. They were both thinking about the blond pilot they had seen in the tropics and then again in the snow-covered Sierra pass.

And they were thinking about Marlene.

"Well, at least he had a friend in his last moments," Lunk said to Rook.

She gave him a wan smile. "He died for us. . . ."

"Stop it, Rook," Scott said harshly before she could continue. "Don't make him out to be some kind of hero."

Rand saw the hurt look surface on his friend's face and

moved quickly to Rook's side to take her hand. "Scott's right," he said softly. "Dusty wasn't a hero, Rook."

"Then what was he, Rand?" she wanted to know.

Rand's lips compressed to a thin line.

"He was a victim."

CHAPTER
ELEVEN

Oh, what a place this was! A city? The city. These nine-foot techno-horse-headed gestapos with their black armor and fancy blasters... They wouldn'a drawn second looks in this town.

Remark reported by Rand in his *Notes on the Run*

ANOTHER WEEK WENT BY AND THERE WAS STILL NO sign of advance units from the Expeditionary Force. Nevertheless, Scott and his team put the time to good use reconning the southern and eastern perimeters of the central hive complex. Thanks to information supplied to him by the Robotech officer (whose remains were now housed in the same graveyard Dusty Ayres helped to fill), Scott was beginning to form an overview of Reflex Point; it was not, as initially believed, a single hive but rather a group of hives, at the hub of which was the Regis's stronghold. The complex covered a vast territory that stretched from the Ohio River Valley to the Great Lakes and from what had once been Pennsylvania west to Illinois. The week's recon had established that the perimeter was most penetrable from the northeast; this constituted something of a lucky break for the team, as it placed Mannatan (formerly New York City) close enough to their route to justify a short detour. Burdette, the late Robotech officer, had furnished Scott with the location of a relatively unpoliced Invid storage facility within the island city, where there was more than enough canister Protoculture to restock the team's dwindling supplies.

Mannatan was the largest surviving city in the Americas, Northlands and Southlands. It had been shaken and scorched by Dolza's annihilation bolts, but many of its enormous structures had survived intact. So much death had been rained around it, however, that the city had had to be evacuated. Few of the millions of evacuees who had fled into the irradiated surroundings had survived, but by the end of the Second Robotech War, people and mutant birds with condorlike wingspans were finding their way back to the cracked and fissured towers, and the abandoned city slowly began to repopulate. Before the Invid arrived, hopes ran high that the city would rise once again to become the great center it had been in the previous century, but those plans were dashed with the aliens' first wave. Still, the Regis saw no reason to destroy the place; she merely constructed one of her hives atop the tallest structure—the 1,675-foot Trump Building, which the hive encased like a wasps' nest just short of its summit—and moved all potential troublemakers to nearby Protoculture farms. With Reflex Point at close proximity, the city's residents (who numbered less than one-tenth of one percent of the city's prewars population) posed no threat to the Regis's domain, and Mannatan was one of the few places where her Controllers and bio-constructs actually patrolled the streets on foot.

Everyone was naturally eager to visit the city, but Scott was wary about all of them entering at once. He wasn't sure just how closely the Regis had been monitoring their recent movements, but given the reappearance of the green-haired Human woman and the orange and green command ship, it seemed reasonable to assume that the team was still a high-priority concern at Reflex Point. And with access to the city limited to a single two-tiered bridge near the northern tip of the island, Scott was against taking any unnecessary risks. Lancer was the obvious choice for advance man because he had already seen the city—years ago, before the Invid invasion, when Mannatan was on the ascendant. Rand would serve as backup, and Annie would accompany them, if only to keep up appearances. The two men would carry hand blasters.

Scott's intuitions proved correct, inasmuch as the Regis had indeed made elimination of the team one of her top priorities, especially since she had lost Ariel to them, and was noticing a certain reluctance on Sera's part. But in some ways this was as intriguing to her as it was baffling—allowing her to recall her own attractions to Zor so long ago. So she elected to place Sera and Corg in temporary command of the city's central hive to observe the results. She did this mostly because she had pressing concerns of her own at this point. The long-awaited trigger point of the Flower of Life was drawing near, but at the same time there was evidence of the imminent arrival of the Human forces who had battled her husband, the Regent, on Tirol and other worlds. And if they arrived before the Flowers came to full fruition, the entire scheme of the Great Work would be jeopardized.

Nine Urban Enforcers marching in a diamond-shaped formation were patrolling a quadrant in the lower part of the island city just now, an area where the towers were especially tall, making the sunless streets feel all the more narrow. Security had been breached earlier that same day; sensors had detected the presence of an unauthorized entry into the city and the energy signatures of Robotech mecha. Shock Troopers and Pincer Ships were hovering overhead, while Scouts covered the miles of waterfront.

"Urban Enforcer squadron," boomed the Regis's voice over the foot soldiers' command net. "Proceed in formation to the East River, divide into units, and search all abandoned buildings for any sign of the rebels. They must not be allowed to slip through our grasp this time."

The nine were huge cloven-foot, bipedal creatures out-fitted in black-and-white battle armor, with rifle/cannons affixed to both forearm sheaths. Their smooth eyeless heads were almost comically small, almost dolphinlike be-neath the helmets, with a single round scanner for a mouth —a red jewel in the elongated jaws of the helmet. Over what could have been the bridge of the leaders' snout was an inverted triangular marking of rank.

Most of the residents had scattered from the streets and returned to their homes. Street stalls had shut down, and mongrel dogs were having a field day. There were two Humans, however, who made no move as the soldiers approached. They were hunkered down on the sidewalk, their backs to the wall of a ruined building, tattered clothing pulled tight around them, hats pulled low on their heads. Their temerity would have been suspicious had the pair not been representative of that class of Humans who had a penchant for street life and were often addicted to any number of intoxicating concoctions. Nevertheless, in light of the present emergency, one of the soldiers saw fit to stop and investigate the duo.

"Investigating Human life-forms . . ." the Invid told his superior, aiming a scanner. "Sensors indicate no active Protoculture, yet their lack of reaction warrants further observation."

The squad stopped to have a look, but after a moment the leader made a dismissive gesture with its right arm. "Do not waste time with these derelicts."

"But they do not fit the standard Human profile," the soldier began to object.

"Do as I command," the leader said more harshly. "These could hardly be the rebels we seek."

As the soldiers moved off, a whispered and muffled voice rose through the clothing of one of the men. "Can we get up now? I can't breathe—the kid's smothering me in here!"

"Not yet," said his companion, taking care to keep still. "Let them get a little farther down the street."

Shortly, Lancer straightened up, removed the brown cap, and flashed a self-satisfied grin at the now deserted street. "Okay," he said.

Beside him, Rand was in a panic. "Come on, Annie, open up the blanket! I've got about thirty seconds worth of air left!"

Lancer stood up in his tatterdemalion threads, while Annie tossed aside the blanket she had wrapped around her shoulders. She had been sitting on Rand's shoulders beneath the makeshift cape for the past ten minutes or so. Adroitly now, she leapt off him and removed her dark shades and gray fedora.

Behind her Rand was massaging circulation back into his score neck. "My head! Jeez, Annie, why couldn't you have—"

"Lancer, I thought you said they called this place Fun City," she complained, ignoring Rand. "Well, it's been a pretty big disappointment so far! All we've done is dress up like bums and hide from the Invid. When do we get to have some real fun, huh?!"

"When are you gonna learn?" Rand said angrily, waving a fist over her head. "What d' ya think, we're in an amusement park or something? Remember what we're here for."

She made a face and stuck her tongue out at Rand.

Lancer had stripped off his costume and was back to his usual black trousers, tank top, and leather knee boots. "Knock it off," he told Annie. "We have about fifty blocks to cover, so let's move it."

Burdette was right about the place being unguarded. There were a few Urban Enforcer troops stationed out front, but the trio had no problems getting around them and were soon in the basement of the building, closing on the duct system the Robotech officer's map indicated would lead them to the main storage room. It was at this point that they were supposed to head back downtown to rendezvous with Scott, but Lancer insisted that they make certain the information was correct and follow through with the break-in without waiting for the diversions Rook and Lunk had planned.

Rand went along with the idea (Annie didn't have to be convinced), and in a short while they were pushing out the grate of the duct that emptied into the Protoculture storage area itself. It was a dimly lit theater with an elaborate stage, but all it housed now were stacks and stacks of crated Protoculture canisters. Rand went over to one of the crates and pried open the lid.

"There's enough here to take a whole army to Reflex Point!" he whispered excitedly, hefting one of the soda-can-sized fuel canisters.

"Provided we can get it out without being spotted," Lancer said absently.

"Ha! Don't worry about a thing, sir," Rand began to joke. "Protoculture Express at your service! We deliver overnight or you get your money back."

"Guaranteed!" Annie joined in. "In fact, if we don't make good, *we* pay *you*!"

"Now all we've got to do is get back downtown and tell Scott about this," Rand said. "Right, Lancer? ... Lancer, are you okay?"

Lancer was glancing around the theater, amazed. "Sorry," he said, turning to his teammates. "I was just thinking what a beautiful place this used to be."

"What do you mean?"

"This is Carnegie Hall," he explained with a sweep of his arm. "I guess it doesn't mean much to you, but before the Robotech Wars this was one of the finest concert halls in the world. I remember reading about it. The people who used to sing here..." He smiled at the thought. "I used to dream of playing here. Now there isn't much chance of that, I suppose."

"Culture of a different sort," Rand mused. "Maybe the Invid will start holding auditions, huh?"

Lancer ignored the ribbing and allowed himself a momentary fantasy that featured Yellow Dancer on stage, singing "Lonely Soldier Boy" to a packed house....

I won't let the Invid destroy my dreams! he promised himself.

It was that promise that enabled Lancer to justify going along with Rand's spur of the moment plan to take what they could get their hands on straightaway rather than risk a second entry into the place. It also made sense from a practical point of view, because they would have enough fresh Protoculture to recharge the Beta and utilize it in a follow-up raid if it came down to that.

They were in the midst of packing away a few six-packs of the stuff when they heard loud footsteps echoing in the hall and headed in their direction. They had already secreted themselves among the maze of stacked crates when one of the Invid foot soldiers entered, seemingly on patrol.

"Keep under cover," Lancer warned as they made themselves small. "We don't want to fight it out if we don't have to." He and Rand had their handguns drawn. Annie was wide-eyed, trying to hold on to the armful of canisters she hadn't had time to set down.

Lancer cautiously peered over the top of one of the crates. He could see the soldier moving systematically through the aisles formed by the stacks. "It may just be on an inspection tour," he said softly. "It'll probably go away if it doesn't find anything wrong, but be ready, just in case." Silently, he stole across the aisle and repositioned himself for cross fire.

Rand looked over at Annie and her precariously balanced load. "Try not to move. Don't even breathe if you can help it!"

She shut her mouth tightly and rearranged the canisters as judiciously as she could, but there was one that insisted on sliding. She made a nervous sound.

The Enforcer stomped past their aisle and stopped, as though alerted to something. Rand drew a bead on the thing's back. *Here we go again*, he told himself. *Sitting ducks...!*

The Invid began to move off, but Annie was suddenly desperate. "Rand, help me! They're slipping—they're gonna *fall!*"

And a moment later they did, hitting the floor with a sound of toppling bowling pins. Rand managed to stifle Annie's scream with his hand, but the Enforcer had heard enough to warrant a second pass along the aisle.

"They slipped," Annie explained in a panic after Rand took his hand away. "I'm sorry, I couldn't help it—"

"Here comes trouble," he interrupted her, arming the Gallant. "Just keep quiet."

The Invid raised its rifle as it began to retrace its steps, but its pace remained unchanged. Lancer threw a quick nod to Rand and leveled his own weapon, wondering just where you had to hit these creatures to have it count. He chose the scanner as a likely target and bracketed it in his sights.

"Just a few steps closer," Rand was whispering to himself when he heard the cat.

At least it sounded like a cat—a rather large cat at that. It growled twice more and then launched itself from wherever it had been perched. Rand went up on tiptoe and just caught a glimpse of the animal's shadow as it leapt from stack to stack. *It was even bigger than its growl had indicated!* He could see that the Invid soldier had swung its snout to the sound and was also tracking the shadow now. The cat took a few more leaps, making one hell of a racket in the process.

Rand breathed a sigh of relief when he saw the Enforcer's rifle begin to lower. Obviously it was satisfied that the animal had been responsible for the noise. *It's going to fall for it!* he thought.

He let himself collapse in sheer nervous exhaustion when the Enforcer exited the room, and Annie came over to him thinking he had been hit or something. Then suddenly the cat was back, snarling a long meow and executing an incredible tumble from the box seats near the hall's stage. Only now Rand was sure the thing wasn't some ordinary cat.

And in fact it wasn't: it was a young, curly-haired Hispanic boy wearing elbow pads, sky-blue dancer's tights, pale yellow leg warmers, and a tank top emblazoned with a large *J*.

"Well that was easy!" the boy laughed, one leg crossed over the other and hands behind his head after his upright landing.

"Have you been here the whole time?" Lancer said once he had gotten over his amazement.

The youth nodded. "That was my Persian. Wanna hear my Siamese now?"

Annie still didn't get it. "You mean that was you? There wasn't any cat?"

"Okay, so you do a good feline impression," Lancer said warily, gesturing with his weapon. "What are you doing in here?"

The boy's eyebrows went up. "What are *you* doing here is more like it, *mano*. As for me, I hang out here sometimes—but I know a lot of easier ins and outs than using the air ducts."

"So you saw us," said Rand. "Hope you're not nursing any ideas about turning us in . . ."

The youth laughed again. "Wha'—for foraging a little 'Culture? Be real, Red. 'Sides, I'm no symp, if that's what you're thinking." He motioned to Lancer's blaster. "Look, I'm not complaining or anything, but how 'bout lowering the hard-tag?"

Lancer glanced down at the weapon and deactivated it.

"That cop's gonna be making another pass pronto," the youth warned. "We better make tracks, unless you're dying to use your juice."

Rand got up, his H90 casually aimed in the boy's direction. "Lead on, Lightfoot," he told him. "We're right behind you."

* * *

There were indeed quicker ways out of the place than the route they had taken in, and in a short time the youth was leading the trio down an east-west street a few blocks from the Carnegie Hall storage facility. The Protoculture canisters had been safely stashed away for the time being.

"I guess we owe you an apology and our thanks," Lancer was saying. "What are you called?"

"Jorge," the youth answered him. "I've got a nest in the balcony back there."

"You can enter that place at will?" Rand asked, impressed.

Jorge turned a gleaming smile up at him. "Shit, man, there's no place in this whole city we can't go if we want to."

"But the Invid—they're crawling all over this place."

"Yeah, but they don't bother us if we don't bother them."

"That was some display you put on," Lancer said, changing the subject. "You're quite an acrobat."

"A *performer*," Jorge emphasized proudly. "Fact is I was on my way to rehearsal before I had to stop and save your necks." He laughed at their chagrin. "Why don'cha come with me and check us out."

Lancer looked over to Rand, who returned a shrug of consent.

"Well, I'm all for it," said Annie, quick to take Jorge's arm. "I'm gonna have some fun in this place if it kills me!"

"It should be a great show," Jorge was telling them a few minutes later.

He and the rebel trio were on a staircase landing overlooking a small stage, where a dozen male and female dancers were executing syncopated martial kicks under colored lights. It was a kind of historical piece, harkening back to the frenzied, *kata* routines of the turn of the century, with some break dancing and pelvic thrusts thrown in for variety.

"They're good," Lancer commented. *I wonder if their dreams will survive this alien nightmare?*

But on stage some of the performers were wondering whether they would survive the director. He was nothing if not the consummate perfectionist. "Hold it! Stop! Stop!" he was shouting now, an effeminate curl to his voice. He was twice the age of the oldest on stage but well built nonetheless. He had a pencil-thin mustache and brown hair, save for a section of bleached forelock. "This is awful, just aw-ful. Harvey," he continued, pointing, "I swear you dance like a moose in heat. And Arabella: You look like you're waltzing, for heaven's sake. Remember, *everyone*, this is supposed to be 1990, not 1770! So could we please *try* not to embarrass ourselves?"

The dancers had all adopted hangdog expressions by now, and Jorge took advantage of the lapse in the music to call out: "Simon! Hey! Up here!" When the director looked up, Jorge gestured to Lancer and the others. "I brought some friends to watch the rehearsal, okay?"

Simon scowled at him. "Absolutely not! You know my rules about people—" He broke off his scolding and was staring at Lancer. "Am I seeing things? Is that the face that launched a thousand slips?! Lancer, is that you?! Or should I say Yellow Dancer?"

Lancer smiled and went downstairs to take Simon's hand. Jorge, Rand, and Annie tagged behind.

"Lancer, I still can't believe it," Simon exclaimed. "I've thought about you a lot. . . . What's it been, something like two years? In Rio, wasn't it? What are you doing here? I want to hear *everything*."

Lancer looked over his shoulder at Rand. "Well, we're just passing through."

"Passing through?" Simon said, surprised. "Since when does anyone enjoy the privilege of 'passing through' anymore? You can't be serious."

"We've got transportation," Lancer said, holding back.

Simon stepped back to regard the trio quizzically. "Perhaps it's not in good taste to ask too many questions," he said after noticing Rand and Lancer's sidearms.

"Probably not." Lancer smiled.

"Well, you've just *got* to come to the show tonight, that's all there is to it," Simon enthused.

"The Invid are permitting performances?" Lancer asked.

"They haven't tried to stop us yet. I guess they figure it keeps the slaves happy and out of their way."

Meanwhile, in the hive atop the Trump Building, Sera was engaged in an argument with her brother/prince, Corg. The Robotech rebels had not been located, and Corg was in favor of taking matters into his own hands by simply exterminating every Human in the city.

"I will not permit it," Sera told him. "Observation of these life-forms has not yet been completed. They require more study, even if that means the rebels live for a time more."

"Your lenience is a sign of weakness," Corg answered her. "I say destroy them now."

She glared down at him from the massive throne—a monolithic two-horned affair set atop what appeared to be a thick-stalked, flat-topped mushroom, adorned along its outer edge with a band of glossy red discs. Beneath the cap stood two Urban Enforcers, as silent and motionless as statues. The domed room itself resembled the inside of a living neural cell.

"You seem to forget our instructions, my brother. We are to study the Humans' behavior patterns and learn from them."

Corg made a disgruntled sound. "The experiment is as good as complete. It is time to exterminate these life-forms. I'll proceed with my program, regardless of instructions."

She knew that he had been defeated on every occasion and wondered whether this was influencing his behavior, but she didn't want to point this out to him. "I'm warning you, Corg, do not challenge my authority in this matter. The Regis has placed me in charge."

"For the moment," he snarled.

"What makes you so sure of that?"

"It's perfectly obvious. You have no stomach for destruction. But you've known all along that our plan calls for the eradication of these creatures. And I intend to begin that process immediately."

Corg disappeared through the floor of the hive even as Sera was ordering him to call off his attack. She reseated herself to digest his words.

Maybe he is right, she began to tell herself. *Perhaps I don't have the determination to carry out this task.* She had to admit to herself that she had no grasp of the emotions that were keeping her from destroying the rebels—especially that one who had touched her with his voice. Surely she should have killed him when they had faced each other at the chasm. But she had let him live, and now Corg was beginning to suspect her. All at once it seemed imperative that she speak with Ariel, because in that brief confrontation with her lost sister she had come close to understanding some of the changes that were going on inside her.

Sera shot to her feet.

I must try to find her . . . !

Corg wasted no time assembling his Shock Troopers and commencing his murderous assault on the city's Human population.

Across the Hudson River, where Scott and the rest of the team were awaiting word from Lancer, Marlene sensed the warlord's destructive swing and screamed as those hellish emotions assailed her consciousness once again.

Scott was by her side in an instant. "Where?" he asked as he tried to comfort her. "Where are they attacking?"

"The city," she managed to bite out, hands pressed to her head, body rocking back and forth in Scott's arms. "They're going to wipe out the entire city!"

"But you've got to be mistaken," Scott started to say

when the sound of the first explosions reached him. He grabbed a binocular scanner and ran to the edge of the roof that was their temporary camp. Training it on the city, he saw countless flashes of intense light, and within minutes it seemed that the entire northern portion of the island was ablaze.

■ ■ ■ ■ ■ ■ ■ ■ ■ ■ ■ ■ ■ ■ ■ ■ ■ ■ ■

CHAPTER
TWELVE

There is some truth to the claim that Corg contributed to the Invid's defeat, such as it was; but only in the sense that his premature blood lust succeeded in alienating Sera that much sooner. On the other hand, the so-called parallels with the Zentraedi Khyron are rather forced and remain unconvincing. To be honest, who can we point to that did not contribute to the defeat? One might as well blame Marlene, Sera, Zor, for that matter. Lay the blame on love, if you will, on Protoculture.

Dr. Emil Lang, *The New Testament*

ORG ASSEMBLED HIS URBAN ENFORCER SQUAD-rons at the northern tip of the island and commanded them to begin a southward march, sanitizing the city top to bottom. Shock Trooper ships would back them up, creating apocalyptical fires to flush the Humans from their dwellings.

The residents thought they were witnessing some sort of drill until the first streams of annihilation discs hit the streets; then there was sheer panic. People fled from burning buildings only to be caught up in volleys of fire from the Invid ground troops. Block after block burned, filling the evening sky with infernal light. The brick and concrete facades of buildings collapsed into the avenues, sending up storms of glowing embers and acrid ash. Hundreds were trapped in the rubble, and hundreds more perished in the alleyways and streets, in shafts and court-yards. No one could comprehend what was occurring.

Had they brought this on themselves somehow? Had they transgressed or violated some Invid regulation no one had been aware of? Or was this simply the way it would always end from now on? No more old age or disease, no more heart attacks or accidents; just random bursts of blinding light, spurts of systematic extermination . . .

Corg smiled down on the ensuing destruction from the cockpit of his command ship. *There, Princess,* he laughed to himself. *Observe your life-forms now!*

Downtown, in Simon's dance theater, Jorge held a note that had just been delivered by one of the underground's black eagle courier birds. The sounds of distant explosions had already reached into the building, and an atmosphere of dread prevailed. "Listen up, everybody!" he announced. "The Invid are on a rampage. They're offing everyone! Sweeping through the whole city, north to south!"

"Oh, my God!" muttered Simon. "They're through with us! I knew it would come to this someday!"

Lancer looked over at Rand, his face all twisted up. "It's because of us, Rand," he seethed, just loud enough for his friend to hear. "We brought this on. Just our being here . . ."

Rand accepted it with a kind of shrug and took another bite from the sandwich Jorge had fixed him before all hell broke loose.

"We've got to get out of here," one of the dancers was telling the rest of the troupe. "They're getting closer!"

The man was right, Lancer realized; the explosions were louder now, near enough to shake the theater itself. The first blast to strike the building threw everyone to the floor. The lights flickered once and went out; a few people screamed.

"We have to help these people get to shelter," Lancer told Rand when intermittent power returned. Dust and particles of debris filled the air. Lancer had his weapon drawn.

Rand, who had almost swallowed the sandwich whole,

pulled it from his mouth and gasped for his breath. "Get *them* to shelters? What about them getting *us* to shelters?"

Jorge was standing beside them, helping a petrified Annie to her feet. "We can reach the subway from the basement," he said rapidly. "We'll be safe there."

"Depends on how *serious* they are," Rand started to say. But Jorge was already herding his fellow performers toward the exits.

Two more crippling explosions erupted in their midst just then, and all of a sudden the interior of the theater was in flames. Most of Simon's troupe had already made it through the exit doors, but the director himself was standing stock still, as though in shock. Lancer ran over to him and spun him around, catching the look of devastation in his eyes.

"Simon, you've got to leave!"

"My theater..."

Lancer put his hands on Simon's shoulders, steering him away from the blaze that had already scorched both their faces. "Listen to me...The theater's gone. And it won't help anybody if you go up with the rest of it."

"It's over," Simon said flatly, overcome.

"Come on, man. There'll be other shows; we'll get through this."

Simon offered a wan smile. "Maybe..."

A column collapsed behind them, bringing down a portion of the balcony and fueling the fire.

"Of course there will!" Lancer yelled. "Unless we don't get you out of here right now!" Rand was by the door, one hand shielding his face from the heat, yelling for them to get a move on. Lancer grabbed hold of Simon's hand and led him off at a run.

"Unbelievable," Scott was saying on the rooftop across the river. "It looks like they're trying to destroy the whole city and everybody in it." He scanned the infrared binoculars north to south, then lowered them.

Rook and Lunk stood silently by the retaining wall,

mesmerized by the fiery spectacle. Marlene was off to one side, hugging her arms to herself. Scott swung around to Lunk.

"How much Protoculture will we have if we cannibalize the Cyclone power systems?"

"Maybe a dozen canisters."

"We have to act quick," Rook told Scott. "Annie and the boys are somewhere in the middle of that firestorm."

Scott tightened his mouth. *Why haven't they contacted me as planned?* he asked himself, already dressing them down. With a dozen canisters of fuel, they would have just enough to power the three Veritechs for a short time. But unless they were able to resupply afterward, that would effectively finish the mecha, fighters and Cyclones both. And even the instrumentality nodes of Reflex Point were a good three hundred miles west of the city.

"Come on, Scott," Rook was saying, her mind made up. "Let's switch the canisters and get out there."

Scott issued a silent nod of consent and went down on one knee by Marlene's side while Rook and Lunk moved off. "You better stay behind," he told her. "I don't want to risk bringing you any closer to that place. I can see what you're already going through."

"I-I'll be all right here," she stammered, as though chilled to the bone. "But promise me you'll be careful, Scott."

They touched briefly, and he was gone.

In the central hive, Sera had been alerted to the wave of death her brother was unleashing against the populace. She sat rigidly at the top of the mushroomlike dais now, hands clasped tight to the arms of the throne, as views of the destruction reached her via a circular projecbeam.

"This is intolerable!" she screamed to her Enforcer guards, who stood unflinching below the dais cap. "Corg is deliberately sabotaging the experiment! The defeats he has suffered at the hands of the Humans have affected his conditioning!"

Everywhere the projecbeam took her, the scene was

the same: buildings ablaze, Human life-forms in postures of agony, and more. But all at once Sera gasped as an image of Lancer filled the holo-field. He was out in the madness, his Gallant stiff-armed in front of him, returning insignificant blasts of vengeance against the overwhelming power of Corg's war machine.

The Earth rebel who has caused so much disturbance within me! she kept saying to herself. But Lancer's presence meant that Ariel must be nearby. Sera leapt from the dais and headed straight for her command ship.

If Sera had continued watching the projecbeam a moment longer, she would have realized that Lancer's shots were not to be so easily dismissed. True, an H90 seemed insignificant when compared to Corg's mobile arsenal, but Lancer and Rand had nevertheless managed to clear the streets of more than a dozen Urban Enforcers.

"That's that," Lancer was saying now as number fifteen fell, its chest plates laid open and oozing green nutrient fluids.

Annie, Jorge, and Simon stepped out from cover to join them in the street. Most of the ground troops had moved further south, but in their wake the city crumbled and burned, turning night to day.

"At least no one in the company got hurt," said Jorge. "Everyone made it into the subway tunnels in time."

"I wish the rest of the city was that lucky," Annie added, stifling a sob.

Lancer checked the blaster's remaining charge and frowned. "We better get underground ourselves."

Suddenly Annie raised her arm and let out a bloodcurdling scream. Two Trooper ships had dropped to the street out of a slice of orange sky, their cloven hooves ripping into the pavement.

Lancer and Rand raised their weapons at the same moment and fired, instinctively finding the same target. The Trooper caught both blasts just above its scanner and ruptured like a lanced cyst, spewing thick smoke and sickly fluids. The second turned to watch its companion go down, then swung back around, its cannon tips aglow with priming charge. But out of the blue something holed the thing with a perfectly placed shot to the midsection, and it too dropped, almost crushing Rand and Annie on the way down.

Simon, Jorge, and the freedom fighters looked up in time to see three Veritechs swoop through the canyon formed by the buildings and fade into the glow.

"It's Scott!" Rand shouted, amazed. "How the hell did they find us?!"

"I don't think they did," Lancer said, watching the VTs bank out of sight. "Just be glad that they chose to zero in on that particular Trooper." He felt a hand on his shoulder and turned.

"Lancer, I've got an idea," said Simon. "I want you to help us go ahead with the show." He paid no attention to Lancer's look of disbelief. "I know it's a lot to ask, but we're going to need help if this city is to survive."

Lancer thought it over; over Simon's shoulder he could see Annie and Rand nodding their heads in encouragement. "Sure," he said at last.

Jorge flicked his fingers together with an audible snap. *Ejole!* "This'll be the show of a lifetime!"

The three Veritechs flew north to the edge of the worst conflagrations and split up to double back. The thruster fires of Invid Trooper ships were just visible in the southern skies. "Let's make sure the streets are clear of any ground units," Scott told the others over the net. "Then we'll go after the ships."

"Nothing on my scanners," Rook reported a moment later.

"Mine either," added Lunk.

Scott looked out over the city and shook his head in despair. The Invid had cut a north-to-south swath of death four blocks wide along the west side of the island. Searching for any signs of Enforcer activity, he dropped down into the canyons again and was almost at street level when his radar displays suddenly came to life.

"Hold on, I've got something!"

By the time he realized what it was a blast had seared the upper sections of his fighter, nearly destabilizing it, but he managed to pull the Beta up and out of its plunge and soon had a visual on the enemy ship even as the displays were flashing its signature.

"Command ship," said Scott, staring down at the orange and green crablike thing that was hovering below him at rooftop level. "It's that damn command ship! Let's take it!"

Corg, as though reading Scott's designs, chose that moment to loose his first stream of annihilation discs. Scott banked sharply and fell; the Invid ship shot up at the same time, and Human and alien ended up exchanging places, discs, and laser-array fire in an aerial duel. Rook streaked in from behind and landed two heat-seekers, but Corg's ship shook them off and stung back, igniting a row of rooftops with its misplaced shots.

Scott and Rook went wingtip to wingtip to launch a salvo of missiles, but again the Invid outmaneuvered them, diving down into the city's hollows, where Lunk almost fell victim to the command ship's wrath.

"That thing is dangerous!" he shouted over the net as explosive light lit up the inside of his cockpit.

"All right, let him go for now," said Scott. He turned to make certain the Invid was willing to give it a rest and exhaled with relief when he saw the ship arrow off. "We've got to find Lancer."

"Yeah, but where do we start looking?" asked Rook, disheartened by the inferno below, to say nothing of the complexity of the city's intact landscape and terrain.

"Just keep your external receivers open," Scott told her.

Hopeless, she thought. *Just what kind of sign does he expect us to see from up here?*

Two hours later, the three Veritechs were still circling. They were all running dangerously low on fuel, and there had been no sign of Lancer, Annie, or Rand. Or the Invid, which was a lucky break. Then Rook picked up

something on the receiver and reported her coordinates
to Scott and Lunk. She supplied them with the frequen-
cies as they came into view on her display screen.

"Tune in and tell me who that sounds like."

Lunk fiddled with his controls, listened for a moment,
and heard the strains of "Look Up" coming across the
cockpit speakers.

"Hey, that sounds suspiciously like an old buddy of
mine."

Rook laughed shortly. "Scott, you wanted a sign, huh?
Well, how's that one down there at three o'clock?" She
tipped the VT's wings once or twice over the source of the
transmissions: a tall, squeezed pentagon of a building
whose rooftop was currently the scene of some kind of
concert or show.

Scott completed a flyby and signaled Rook in a similar
manner. He could discern the words PAN AM at the top of
the building, above a huge lightboard sign that was flashing the word HERE.

"That's Lancer all right," Scott started to say. Then he
noticed that his radar display was active once again: The
command ship had returned with reinforcements. "Follow
my lead to the street," he told his teammates. "And acti-
vate cluster bombs on my mark."

The Invid ships pursued them just as he had hoped
they would, and when the three VTs were properly positioned, he called for a multiple missile launch. Warheads
streaked from the fighters, arcing backward and detonat-
ing in advance of the Invid ships; several of the Troopers
were destroyed, and even the command ship was brought
up short by the force of the explosions.

"I'm going back for Marlene," Scott reported as the
Veritechs climbed. "I'll rendezvous with you at the
source."

Rook and Lunk kept their fighters airborne until the
concert ended; then they hovered down in Guardian mode,
just as Scott was returning from the Jersey side of the river.
Yellow Dancer, who had borrowed makeup and a

flashy pink outfit for his part of the show, was already out of character by the time everyone regrouped.

"I got a bone to pick with you three," Scott yelled as soon as the VT canopy went up.

"Save it, Scott," Rand answered him from the roof. He tossed a canister of Protoculture fuel up to Rook. "Figured you might be a quart low by now."

Scott lost most of his stored anger while he listened to a quick rundown of the events of the day. He couldn't really find fault with their actions, especially in light of what had followed. There was certainly no going back to the storage facility now, but what they had managed to carry out was more than enough to take the team the rest of the way to Reflex Point. Once they finished here, of course.

Scott pulled Marlene aside while Lunk set about refueling the mecha energy systems. "We're going to have to go back up," he explained, his hands on her shoulders.

"Yes, I know."

He wanted to say more, but Lancer was now standing alongside them, urging Scott to hurry it up. "I don't mean to break you kids up, but we've got lots of work to do."

Embarrassed, Scott withdrew his hands. "See you," he said, blushing, and ran for the Beta.

Lunk and Annie remained with Marlene as the two Alphas and the now separate components of the Beta lifted off. *Hurry back*, Marlene was saying to herself when Lunk stepped up behind her.

"You miss him alread—"

An explosion erased the rest of his words and threw both Lunk and Marlene ten feet or more in opposite directions.

Marlene was first to come around. Unsure how long she had been out, she stood up and coughed smoke from her lungs. One section of the roof was holed and in flames, and she could hear screams of panic in the darkness. Lunk was on his back nearby, apparently unconscious; Annie was nowhere in sight. Someone yelled,

"Ariel," and for some reason she found herself turning around.

It was the green-haired woman they hadn't seen since the mountain attack. She was stepping from the flames that were licking at the armored legs of her towering command ship.

"Ariel," the woman repeated, and again Marlene felt something stir within her. "I am Sera, princess of the Invid, and I have come for you."

Trembling, Marlene stared at her. "But my name is ...Marlene. I don't understand why you've come for *me*...."

"Because you have turned against your people and I must know why, before we begin transmutation of our race. *Why* have you disobeyed the Regis?"

Marlene gasped. *What is this woman talking about?* "I don't believe what I'm hearing," she said, as if Sera were some hallucination she could banish through an effort of will. "I'm not an Invid."

Sera was taking steps toward her now, her crimson eyes flashing a kind of anger that burned deep into Marlene's soul. "You were placed among the people of Earth to learn their ways, so that we might profit from your discoveries. The Regis has been awaiting your reports, and yet you choose to ignore our commands. Do you expect me to believe that you have forgotten who you are and why you are here?"

Marlene shook her head back and forth; she tried to deny the words her heart seemed eager to affirm. "No ...it can't be."

The woman regarded her quizzically. "What can't be, Ariel? Search your thoughts, search them for the truth."

"You're lying! You must be!" Marlene screamed as an explosion tore up another section of the roof.

Sera leaned away to shield herself. "I must stop Corg, before the battle comes any closer," she said. Then her eyes found Marlene. "I will deal with you later."

Marlene watched Sera race off to her ship. Behind her,

Lunk was coming around, wondering aloud what had happened. But she hardly heard him.

It can't be true, she thought. *It can't be true!*

Down below, the battle was raging in the streets. Reconfigured to Battloid mode, Scott's section of the Beta was backed against a building, the rifle/cannon in both hands laying down a thunderous sweep of fire into the face of an advancing Trooper. Elsewhere, two Pincer Ships pursued Lunk through the city's right-angle canyons. Two more had ganged up on Rook's red Battloid, forced it into a corner, and were now attempting to open it with their claws.

She called for help over the net. "These cursed things are trying to rape my ship!"

Rand came to her aid a moment later, his Battloid hovering overhead and taking out each ship with a single shot. But the next moment he was facedown in the street, felled by a blast to the back by none other than Corg himself.

The Invid put down behind the crippled Battloid and moved in to finish it off, but Lancer blew it back into the air with a massive Bludgeon release from the reconfigured burly hindquarters of the Beta. At rooftop level, Corg countered with a wave of annihilation discs that pinned Lancer to the wall, but the Invid prince recognized that he was outnumbered and darted off to muster support.

Scott moved in to check on Rand's status, the rifle/cannon upraised and ready for action. Rook joined him shortly.

"Looks like they're pulling back," said Lancer, while his ship launched and reconfigured. "What do you say we call it a day, Scott?"

"We're not done yet; there's still the hive."

Rand whistled over the net. "The hive! Don't you think you're asking a lot out of four little fighters?"

"Yeah, Scott," Rook chimed in. "Have you got a secret army or something?"

"No, but I've got a plan," he told them. "Obviously the Regis never figured on a direct attack, or she wouldn't have had her workers build the hive in such an accessible spot. My bet is we can bring the whole thing down with a few well-placed cobalt grenades."

There wasn't much time to discuss the pros and cons because Corg had returned with three Pincer Ships to back him up. So the three Battloids launched to join their leader and boostered off toward the hive, the four Invid ships in close pursuit.

In the hive, the Regis's voice reached into the very thoughts of her unsuspecting children.

"Attention, perimeter guard: Four Earth fighters are preparing to launch an attack against the hive."

But Sera was nowhere to be found, and without her the Invid drones and Enforcers could do little more than scurry about in a kind of blind panic. And by the time Corg understood the Humans' intent, it was already too late to stop them.

The VTs had climbed to an altitude of several thousand feet and were now falling on the hive like metallic birds of prey. They directed their warheads into the conical summit of the tall structure that housed the hive, and the energy of the ensuing explosions funneled down through the building like a bomb dropped through the top of a chimney. The hive took the full force of the contained blast and blew apart, raining great clumps of organic mass to the streets.

Corg felt the collective deaths pierce him like a lance. In the face of the hive's collapse he broke off his pursuit and cursed the Humans for their barbaric act.

I will have my revenge for this day, he promised the stars.

Lancer insisted on saying good-bye to Simon.

"There's no way we can ever thank you for what you and your friends have done," Simon told him. "Why don't you stay here and leave the rest of it to them, Lancer? Surely you've done your part by now."

The city's survivors were leaving the subway shelters, taking stock of what had been leveled against them. Simon, Jorge, and the freedom fighters were near Carnegie Hall, having just finished loading the VTs with as much Protoculture as they could safely carry.

Lancer knew that Rand had heard Simon's remark and was waiting for his response. Lancer flashed him a brief look and said: "I've been with these people for a long time, Simon, and I plan to be with them right to the end."

Simon offered an understanding nod.

"This was just a skirmish in a much bigger war," said Rand.

"Well, I hope all of you will return someday. And when you do, we'll have the celebration you deserve." Simon embraced Lancer and wished him luck.

On their way out of the city (Lancer, Annie, and Marlene squeezed into the Beta's cramped storage space), the team flew over the remains of a metal statue that had once stood proudly in the harbor. It had once symbolized liberty, Lancer explained.

Scott regarded it and said: "I only hope we can return that to the world someday."

CHAPTER
THIRTEEN

> *Reflex Point consists of a central hemispherical hive (located close to what was once the city of Columbus, Ohio) and several attendant structures linked to it by numerous Protoculture conduits and instrumentality lines. There appear to be seven secondary nodes—one at twelve o'clock, a second at two, a third at four, a fourth and fifth at seven, and a sixth and seventh at eleven—along with an unattached and somewhat larger dome, south at six o'clock. And that's about the best we can offer you right now, fellows. We hope you'll be able to tell us more once you get down there.*
>
> An excerpt from the Mars Division premission briefing, as quoted by Xandu Reem in his biography of Scott Bernard

SHE WAS MOST DEFINITELY HUMANOID BUT OF INdeterminate, often variable height. The form was as close an approximation of Zor's as was possible for the Invid Queen-Mother; with her children she could work wonders, but to become like them she would need to divest herself completely, a thought beyond contemplation. Her cranium was well shaped but hairless, her large, exotic eyes a deep royal-blue, elongated to near slits, with sparse lashes and pencil-thin brows. She was attired in gloves and a full-length red robe whose curious collar encased her ears like a kind of neck brace. Two oval-shaped sensors were set into the robe's collar; they matched a third that was affixed to her breast.

She was deep inside the hemispherical hive that was the living heart of Reflex Point, positioned beneath an enormous globe of Protoculture instrumentality, her link with the outside world in which her children lived and died. The trigger point for the Flower of Life grew near, but the recent events had made her more fearful than encouraged by its timely approach. The experiment in racial transmutation had become hurried and desperate now, in the face of an imminent Human onslaught from the far reaches of space, from that very world that had once doomed her own Optera to death—the Tirol that haunted her memories and dreams.

How like those war-hungry creatures I have become in my drive to possess this world! she told herself. But wasn't this a condition of the body she inhabited?

It was strange that this very Human form should be deemed the one best suited to her designs for racial transmutation, that these very beings she and her children had labored to enslave should prove the form most suitable to the planet itself. And yet didn't she know somewhere in her heart that this would *have* to be the true form, the form that she had grown to love, the form that Zor had inhabited when he first seduced the secrets of the Flower from her innocent and trusting nature?

The Regis was well aware of the recent destruction of her outpost in the Human city of tall towers and artificial environments, and that the Robotech rebels who had so far eluded her were quickly closing in on the central hive complex. But she couldn't hold Corg or Sera accountable for their failures, or even Ariel, now that she understood. It was this physical form itself that was to blame; once instilled with consciousness, a subtle sabotage began to occur, an undermining of all spiritual vigor. It was like the Protoculture itself, that artificiality the Robotech Masters had conjured from her precious flowers. These bodies took over the stuff of soul and subverted its true purpose, enslaved it to emotions and whims and unfathomable interior currents.

But if these things were not far from her mind, they were at least somewhat removed from her priorities—the continuation of the Great Work. And the Human form, however gross, would have to serve them in this purpose;

it would merely represent a stage on the way to the final realization, the *transcendence* itself.

The sky above the western horizon was drained of color and angry with flashes of intense light, brighter than the midday sun. It was all the world's lightning in concert, a blinding stroboscopic show that could be seen and felt for a radius of one hundred miles.

Scott looked into the face of it, hands shielding his eyes from random bursts of unearthly whiteness. *The assault has begun*, he told himself with a mixture of excitement and terror. *Hunter's forces have arrived and are attacking the hive complex itself*.

The team was at the eastern perimeter of Reflex Point, Veritechs and Cyclones grounded after Scott's advance sightings and subsequent commands to regroup. They were in an area that had seen relatively recent tectonic upheavals, jagged outcroppings that looked as though they had been thrust up from the bowels of hell and had no place in this otherwise stable terrain of soft grasslands and rolling hills.

Annie stared at the sky in wonder. "Is it some kind of storm? A tornado, maybe?"

Rand and Rook exchanged grim glances. "I wish it were," Rand told his young friend. Bass sounds were rumbling across the sky, seconds late of the explosions that birthed them.

"It has to be Admiral Hunter," Scott said behind them. Squinting, he could discern dark shapes streaking through that celestial chaos. *Hundreds* of shapes—fighters, mecha, and surely the Invid ships launched to engage them. "Let's move in," he said firmly. "We can't just stand here and watch."

They kept to the high ground and began a slow forward advance. Oddly enough, the light show seemed to wane as they approached, and when at last they reached the arena itself—a wooded valley, host to a wide, meandering river—they understood why.

"We're too late," Scott informed everyone over the net.

They could see for themselves what he meant from their vantage on a cliff overlooking the battleground. The landscape was littered with the smoldering remains of Veritechs and Invid Pincer Ships and Trooper craft. Patches of forest across the valley were burning, and layers of smoke and gas hovered above the valley floor like some nefarious fog; it was as though the land itself had belched up fire and gas from its seething nether regions. In the distance, the uppermost portion of a hemispherical hive was visible, squadrons of Invid closing on it like wasps returning to their nest. A huge gunship crashed and burned while the team watched helplessly.

"It's too horrible," Annie sobbed, putting her face in her hands, and remembering Point-K and similar horrors. Marlene put her arm around Annie's shoulder and pulled her close. Lunk turned around in the front seat of the APC to stroke Annie's back.

"I've never seen ships like these," Lancer said from the seat of the Cyclone. Rand and Rook were nearby on their mecha. Of the three VTs, only the Beta had been moved in, and Scott was overhead now, hovering at the edge of the cliff.

"They must be the latest upgrades," said Lunk. "But I guess there's still some flaws in the design, huh?"

Scott heard the comment. "Can that talk, Lunk," he barked over the net. "This was only an advance group. The admiral is probably trying to ascertain the defensive strength of the hive complex. But he'll be back—you can count on that now."

Lunk grunted an apology.

"I'm going in to check things out down there," Scott continued, bringing up the Beta's rear thrusters. "Stay put until you receive my all clear."

"Somebody wake me up," Annie pleaded, rubbing her eyes. "This has to be just some terrible nightmare."

* * *

Scott's signal came an hour later, and the seven team members gathered by the river to honor the dead. Scott had looked everywhere but hadn't found a single survivor. The smoky aftermath of the battle was beginning to disperse, but the stench of death lingered in the cool air.

"What now, Scott?" asked Lancer.

Annie grabbed hold of Rook's elbow. "Can't we just leave? I hate this place."

Rook had turned to answer her, but the ground beneath their feet was suddenly quaking and rending open. Everyone fell back as an Invid Pincer Ship pushed itself up out of the earth. No blasters were drawn, however, because it was obvious that the thing was finished; it had been lethally shot and was leaking nutrient.

"Back!" Rand cautioned the others. The ship pitched forward on its face, spewing the viscous green fluid from its wounds. "You don't want to get any of that stuff on you!"

They all remembered when he had been slimed and couldn't get the smell off him for a week. Nevertheless, they were intent on watching the puddle spread and turned away only when they heard the sound of a muffled command ring out behind them.

"Hold it right where you are! Don't move!"

Scott swung around anyway, hand at his weapon, but stopped short of raising it. The source of command was a soldier who was aiming some sort of shoulder-mounted device at them, but underneath that shiny black helmet and gleaming body armor the soldier was Human, Scott was certain of that much.

"Who are you?" the soldier demanded in a curious voice, panning the device across the faces of the team. There was no hostility in the voice but a certain intensity Scott couldn't immediately identify.

"Are you with the Expeditionary Force?" he asked.

The soldier shushed him and fiddled with the controls of the device. Scott realized that it was a video camera.

"Let's try it again—and no questions this time. Now: who are you?" The soldier swung the camera on Scott.

"I'm Lieutenant Scott Bernard, Twenty-first Squadron, Mars Division, but—"

"Teeming Tirol!" The soldier exclaimed, pausing the shot. "Mars Division? And the rest of you?"

"These are my personnel," Scott began. "We've been together—"

"Freedom fighters! I got it, I got it!" the soldier said, recommencing to shoot the team. "Lieutenant—Bernard, did you say? ... Lieutenant Bernard and his ragtag band of freedom fighters, weary after their long journey to Reflex Point and disheartened by the devastating defeat suffered by the first wave of Admiral Hunter's assault group, contemplate their next—"

"That's about enough of that, mister!" Scott interrupted, taking a threatening step forward. "Just who are you and what the hell do you think you're doing?!"

The soldier shut off the camera and doffed the helmet.

Scott's mouth fell open. Not because she was that beautiful—although her long black hair and piercing green eyes *had* been known to stop men in their tracks—but simply because he hadn't figured on confronting a woman.

"My name is Sue Graham," the photographer was saying. "I'm a photojournalist attached to the Thirty-sixth Squadron, Jupiter Division."

"Then you're with the Expeditionary Force," Scott said excitedly. "When is the rest of the fleet due?"

"Soon," Graham answered him absently, training her camera on the fallen Invid's leaking wounds. "Maybe I can get a shot of you and the admiral shaking hands. That's something that should be included in the archives: Hunter congratulates one of his officers on a job well done." Graham looked at Scott. "You *have* been doing a fine job, haven't you, Lieutenant? Where are the rest of the Twenty-first?"

"Dead," Scott said nastily.

Graham glanced at the nearby wrecks of Veritechs and

troop carriers. "Guess that gives us something in common."

Scott glowered at her. "I don't think so, Graham. I didn't just stand around shooting footage while my comrades died."

"Oh, really? Just what exactly were you doing while your comrades were dying, Bernard?"

Rand snarled, "Listen, you," and started to move in, but Scott gestured for him to stay put.

Graham regarded Scott and his team. "Look, don't you think we should get out of here before the Invid show up? Or would you rather stand around and argue?"

"You heartless bitch," Scott seethed, bringing up his fists.

Lancer stepped between Scott and Graham. "Take it easy, Scott. If she can watch her friends die without so much as flinching, there's nothing we can say to put a dent in her."

Graham snorted. "Bunch of soft sisters."

Lancer had to get Scott in a full nelson to restrain him. But he might have broken free anyway had it not been for another of Marlene's early-warning-system headaches.

"Scott," she said, pained. "They're coming!"

Rook armed her blaster and looked around for cover. "Let's go, boys, let's go . . ."

"Push over your Cyclones," Graham shouted, scooping up her helmet and gesturing to the mecha. "Deactivate the systems so the Invid will think the pilots have been killed."

Rand made a face at her. "Jeez, space cadet, you think we need to hear that from you? We've been fighting these—"

"Here they come!" Lunk warned. Everyone turned their eyes west: The sky was dotted with hundreds of alien ships, black spots on the face of the setting sun.

Scott tore himself away from the scene and glanced nervously right and left; ultimately he fixed his sights on the mecha. "We better do as she says. Then make for the trees, everybody!"

* * *

More than a dozen Invid ships put down where Scott and the team had stood no more than an hour before—Pincer craft mostly, seemingly under the command of a blue leader. Curiously enough, they didn't fan out to search the woods but wandered around the battle wreckage instead, as though searching for something. On several occasions they came close to crushing the overturned Cyclones, and a mindless pincer swipe almost sent the APC off the slope (where it was supposed to appear crashed) and down into the river below.

From the edge of the woods, Scott's team of irregulars watched the aliens' movements with growing alarm. The search party represented more collective firepower than any of them had yet witnessed, and Scott couldn't help but wonder about it. He was saying as much to Rand, when Sue Graham suddenly stood up and began filming the Invid.

"Graham, what are you doing?!" Scott whispered from behind the fallen tree that concealed them. "You're going to give away our position!" It was getting dark now, but that was no reason to take chances.

"Every piece of footage adds to our knowledge, Lieutenant," she answered him calmly. "Besides, I don't have any decent shots of these things on two feet. Most of it's aerial sequences, and I'm not about to lose the opportunity now."

Scott reached over and grabbed her ankle, twisting it and forcing her to sit down. "You do that on your own time, Graham," he grated. "Not when there are other lives at stake."

A short time later, the Invid patrol left the area and the team began to relax somewhat. Lunk, Rand, and Lancer stole their way to the APC and returned with the sleeping gear and provisions. They made camp in a small cabin fifty feet into the woods.

Meanwhile, Sue Graham filled Scott in on what she knew about the Earth forces' imminent invasion. She had spent the past year aboard the SDF-3 as Admiral

Hunter's personal photographer, and she couldn't say enough good things about the man. She didn't say what had made her join the ranks of Jupiter Division, but it was obvious to Scott that there was some intrigue connected to the move. They spoke of Tirol and Fantoma, of Rem and Cabell, and of other notable people they both knew. Scott felt himself growing strangely homesick for deep space if not for Tirol itself, and even his attitude toward the journalist was softening somewhat. The red bodysuit she was wearing in place of the armor helped.

"The third attack unit is in preliminary maneuvers at a base on the far side of the moon," Graham was saying now. She had set her camera up to project some of the holographic footage she had shot, and everyone was gathered around. "Here's a shot of the site," she narrated as views of deep space and the warships of the Expeditionary fleet lit up the darkness.

"The admiral's fleet is due to rendezvous with the advance units any day now. Squadrons of new-generation Veritechs will arrive with the fleet. They've been code-named Shadow Fighters."

Scott, Lunk, and Lancer leaned toward the holo-image for a better view. The craft looked something like the standard VTs but were colored a nonreflective gray-black and had a more pronounced delta-wing design.

"Why 'Shadow Fighter'?" Lunk wanted to know.

Graham changed discs; technical readouts now filled the holo-field, replacing the space footage. "The Protoculture generators of the new-generation VTs have been redesigned to include a fourth-dimensional configuration that renders the Shadow Fighter invisible. The Nichols drive, it's called."

Scott had a hundred more questions in mind, but once again it was Marlene who threw him off track. She uttered a low moan and began to sink into that posture of agony they had all witnessed so often. Sue Graham looked at the red-haired woman skeptically and asked: "What's with this one, anyway?"

Scott ignored her and crept to the edge of the woods to

search the skies. Sure enough, the Invid squadron was returning, their thrusters blazing in the night. Scott ordered everyone forward, and silently they made for the valley floor to investigate the enemy's reappearance. Marlene, even though breathless with pain, was the first to notice that the cockpit of the blue leader was opening.

And out of the innards of the ship stepped what looked like a Human being: a young man with long blond hair in a tight-fitting broadly striped uniform of black and green. He issued a command the team strained to hear, and two of the Pincer Ships appeared to acknowledge him with raised claw salutes.

"Human pilots!" Graham said in amazement.

"Another turncoat," said Rand. "Just like that woman we saw . . . The Invid must have a thing for blondes."

"Quiet!" Scott told him. "I'm certain they know we're here."

"Maybe not, Lieutenant," said Graham almost casually, the camera perched on her shoulder.

Rook turned around to look up at her. "Then what? Some piece of Robotech mecha?"

"Exactly. A syncro-cannon."

Scott was the only one who knew what she was talking about; the rest of them were scratching their heads while he cursed Graham for not telling him earlier that the assault group had been equipped with such a weapon.

"It's a particle-beam weapon," he explained. "The cannon was developed by Dr. Lang for use against the Invid."

"It must pack one helluva wallop if the Invid are bothering to look for it," Rand commented.

"It does," Sue told him, still filming the aliens' movements. "That's why I hid it from them."

Scott shot to his feet and yanked the camera out of Graham's grasp. "Where, Graham? And no games."

"In a cave." She gestured without looking. "About a click or so upriver."

Roughly, Scott shoved the camera back into her hands.

"We've got to get that weapon before they find it."

"Count me out, Lieutenant," said Graham.

"Ever hear of loyalty, or self-sacrifice?"

She smirked. "We've all got our jobs to do. For me, it's this." She patted the camera.

"Please, Scott," Marlene said, cutting them off, reaching up for his hand. "Don't try to go out there. You'll be killed."

Scott squeezed her hand and smiled thinly. "I'll see that weapon destroyed before I see it fall into their claws." He turned to glare at Sue Graham. "That's my job . . . but I can't expect you to understand."

Graham laughed shortly, patting the camera again. "Just give me some good footage, hero. I'll make you a star."

CHAPTER

FOURTEEN

God knows Rick and I have had our share of difficulties, Max, especially during the weeks following his decision to join the Sentinels, as you probably recall. But this is worse than that, and it's beginning to prey on me. Sue's with him day and night lately, and Rick doesn't seem to mind it one bit—the lecher. He claims Sue sees him as some kind of father figure, but just who does he think he's kidding? She's infatuated with him, and I'm worried that he is going to fall for it one night— the loneliness of command and all that rot. Max, can't we just see about getting her transferred? Who'd be the wiser?

Lisa Hayes-Hunter in a letter to Max Sterling

ODDLY ENOUGH, SOME OF THEM MANAGED TO GET a little sleep. Marlene had made Scott promise to wait at least until morning before making an attempt to go after the syncro-cannon. He had given his word, proverbial fingers crossed behind his back, if only to calm her down. She had appeared especially stressed out for the past week, and Scott was worried about her, so he wasn't surprised to hear her call out in the middle of the night. He slipped out of his sleeping bag and went to her side; she seemed to sense his presence and come around, smiling weakly up at him in the moonlight.

"I feel so strange, so alone, Scott. . . ."

He reached out to stroke her luxuriant hair. "It's because we're so close to Reflex Point, Marlene. I was afraid this would happen; that's why I wanted you to stay with Simon. . . . " He was suddenly aware that she wasn't listening to him but staring instead at the holo-locket that had slipped from his shirt.

"You'll never forget her, the woman in your pendant. . . . She was very special, wasn't she?"

Scott held the heart-shaped memento in the palm of his hand and regarded it for a moment. "She *was* special, but so are you, Marlene." He placed his hand against her cheek. "I wear this to remind me. . . . Sometimes it's the only thing that gives me the strength to go on."

"I'm sorry I brought it up," she said sleepily, and rolled over in her bag.

Scott heard the roar of thrusters and went to the door and looked up. Through the trees he could see three Invid patrol ships streak across the night sky. Lancer was beside him now; he had the watch and had returned to the cabin at the sound of Marlene's cries. "Everything all right?" he asked.

Scott led him away from the doorway. "Nobody has enough strength left to hold on to, Lancer. If we don't finish this thing soon . . ." Scott let it go and uttered a soft curse aimed at the stars. "What's keeping Hunter? Doesn't he realize—"

"Don't, Scott," Lancer said, cutting him off. "We just have to keep taking things one step at a time."

"I suppose you're right." Scott turned to look back at his sleeping friends and teammates. "We've just got to— Lancer, where's Rand?!"

Lancer swung around and saw the empty bedroll— then another. "Annie's missing, too."

Scott stepped deeper into the woods to whisper their names in the dark. "They're with Graham, I'm sure of it," Scott told Lancer angrily. "Wake everyone up. We've got trouble."

Ten minutes later, what remained of the team was ready for action; Lunk and Marlene were helping Scott, Lancer, and Rook into their battle armor. "My guess is that Graham is leading them to the syncro-cannon," Scott was saying now. They were gathered at the edge of the woods and could see that the Invid were still patroling the area. "We have no choice—we have to get the Veritechs up."

"I can't believe Rand would be foolish enough to listen to that woman," said Lancer. "And to take Annie with him . . ."

Rook snorted. "Doesn't surprise me any. I think he's hot for that photographer." She disregarded the fact that Rand had tried to take Graham's head off earlier in the day.

"I know why he did it," Marlene offered, looking away from them. "Because I made such a scene about Scott going."

Lancer flashed her an understanding look. "Still, why would he take Annie?"

"That was probably Graham's idea," Scott answered him. "Can't you understand what she's up to?" he continued, seeing their puzzled looks. "The whole idea is to try to get some terrific action footage for herself. Think about it: Annie and Rand, two freedom fighters far from home."

Scott was correct on every count, including his hunch that Sue Graham had set the whole thing in motion. She and Rand and Annie were picking their way across a steep, rock-strewn incline now, nearing the place where Graham claimed to have hidden the Robotech weapon. Neither Rand nor Annie minded in the least that Graham was getting it all down on disc; after all, this was a heroic undertaking, and who along the long road they had traveled had taken such an interest in their actions? And while it was true that Rand had been affected by Marlene's concern for Scott's safety, his motivations were more selfish than considerate.

What Graham had termed a cave was actually a kind of pocket in the hillside, well concealed and protected by a broad earthen overhang. Several Invid patrol ships had overflown the area, but the cannon had thus far escaped detection. Rand wasn't all that impressed by his first sight of the thing. But the weapon was massive, he had to admit, with a boxcar-sized barrel that had a kind of mitered muzzle. There was an adjacent drive unit, its front cockpit portion enclosed by a bubble shield. The whole arrangement was mounted on a three-legged circular base that housed the weapon's thrusters and hoverports. It reminded Rand of some of the artillery used by the Army of the Southern Cross in the Second Robotech War.

Rand and Graham scrambled down the slope while Annie waved good luck from the overhead ledge. The photographer trained her camera on the young girl, then swung around to catch Rand as he was seating himself at the cannon's controls.

"On second thought, this thing looks awesome," he said, grinning for the lens. "But I'm sure I'll be able to handle it. Why, when I think back to some of the spots we've—"

"Get started!" Graham yelled from the ground. "I want to get a shot of you coming out of the cave."

Rand's face reflected his disappointment, but a moment later he was pushing buttons and flipping switches, the cannon's thruster fires roaring to life beneath him. He had had limited experience with Hovercraft of any sort, but what he knew was enough to send the weapon free of its rocky enclosure and place it to strategic advantage on a high ledge overlooking the valley floor, the river a dark, sinuous ribbon below him. Infrared scanners told him where the Invid patrol ships were thickest, and without much thought as to the consequences, Rand slipped on a pair of targeting goggles and began to arm the gun.

Back at Annie's side now, Sue Graham aimed her camera and readied herself for the shot.

The syncro-cannon erupted, spewing a flash of blue fire into the night. The first blast tore right through four Invid Enforcer ships, a streaking projectile through paper targets. *No more looking for vulnerable spots now*, Rand said to himself. He grinned and triggered three follow-up bursts, two directed into the midst of the patrol ships and one to take out the survivors that were making for the skies.

Suddenly patrol craft and Troopers were lifting off all across the valley. It was as though someone had tossed a smoke bomb into a bee's nest. And Rand kept firing, scorching earth and air alike with the cannon's devastating salvos. Then, out of the corner of his eye, he saw Graham, in her armor now and astride a black Cyclone.

"Hey, what are you up to?" he asked her over the tactical net. He saw Graham gesture to her camera.

"I've got work to do."

"But we're going to need you now that we've stirred everything up!" Rand yelled, but she was already gone.

Scott and the others took to the Veritechs at the cannon's first discharge. Rook hadn't witnessed such an incredible display of power since the early battles between the last of the Southern Cross and the first Invid wave. But even so, this was Reflex Point, not some low-echelon outpost hive staffed with Scouts and a couple of Trooper ships. For every ten Invid the cannon destroyed, there were ten more in the air, and Rook began to curse Rand for taking it on himself to confront them.

The three Veritechs had a bad time of it; that they survived at all was in no small way a result of the pandemonium Rand's shots were causing. Numerous though they were, the Pincer Ships and Troopers seemed to be buzzing around in a blind rage, desperate to counterattack but at a loss as to direction; in some cases they were even annihilating one other. Consequently, Scott, Rook, and Lancer were able to inflict a good deal of secondary damage as the syncro-cannon continued to send swaths of blue death into the field.

But the Invid ultimately located the cannon, and their forces proved to be more than Rand could handle. Recalling what Scott had said earlier—that he would rather see the cannon destroyed than fall to the enemy—Rand saw to it that that was the case, arming the syncro's self-destruct mechanism even as Pincer Ships were moving in to overwhelm him. He had rejoined Annie and was shielding her with his own body when the thing finally blew, taking twenty or more Invid ships with it.

"I didn't want to blow the damn thing up," Rand explained to Annie as dirt and rocks rained down on them. "But it was better than letting them get their steely paws on it!"

Shortly, the Beta was hovering over them, a rescue rope dangling blessedly from its undercarriage. Rand was shocked to find Marlene in the rear compartment, but Scott told him that they couldn't risk leaving anyone behind. Lunk was off somewhere in the APC. Rand sent Annie back to sit with Marlene and climbed into the Beta's rear cockpit seat.

"Prepare for mecha separation," Scott told him over the net. He said nothing about Graham and nothing about Rand's action, hoping to make Rand feel all the worse about it.

"I'm ready, Commander," Rand said by way of apology.

He then turned to the women and told them to brace themselves.

Sue Graham was overjoyed at the shots she had been getting: entire squadrons of Invid Pincer Ships reduced to slag heaps by blasts from the syncro-cannon; Veritechs and alien Troopers going at it tooth and claw in Earth's night skies; the ground-shaking self-destruction of the cannon itself—Invid craft clasped onto it like so many frenzied land crabs; the frightened look on the face of the young female freedom fighter as she climbed toward the safety of the hovering Beta Fighter. It was splendid stuff, fantastic—the kind of footage that would earn her awards.

She knew that Lieutenant Bernard had caught sight of her once or twice during the chaos and was well aware of what he thought of her. But she found it easy to dismiss him from her concerns. It might be a bit uncomfortable later on, Sue told herself, but with the main fleet already

overdue, she wouldn't have to put up with the lieutenant's
flak for very long. She had to admit, though, that he had
certainly provided her with some of the day's best action
sequences—especially now that his Beta had undergone
mecha separation and his motley band had all reconfigured their fighters to Battloid mode. It had been a long
time since she had seen techno-knights dishing it out. She
kept her camera trained on the skies for a time, singling
out the red Alpha and its attractive pilot.

But suddenly her lens found an even more interesting
subject: the blond Human who had stepped from the
Invid command ship the day before. She had seen his
craft off and on during the battle, but now she had him
fully in her sights. And so, apparently, did the pilot of the
Beta's rear component—that daredevil Rand. The two
ships, Battloid and Invid commander, exchanged hyphens
of laser fire and flocks of heat-seeking missiles; they
darted across the valley like two insects in a kind of death
ritual. But in the end it was the Earthling who prevailed;
his missiles tore into the hovering, perhaps depleted ship
and holed it top to bottom, blowing away one of its cannon arms and sending it into a lethal dive.

Sue reconfigured her Cyclone to Battle Armor mode
and zoomed in to meet it, a gleaming figure in black hop-
ping across the battle-scarred terrain. Most of the drone
ships had also taken note of their commander's demise
and were fleeing the arena in the direction of the central
hive.

Sue raised her camera and took a few steps toward the
fallen ship, its pilot on the ground motionless beside it.
He had scampered out of the ruined cockpit and collapsed, but Sue was certain he wasn't dead. As she
stepped closer, the blond man got up, gasping. She centered him in the lens brackets and asked: "Who are you?
How long have you been fighting for them? What's the
Regis really like?"

The pilot dropped to his knees, hands tight against his
abdomen and stared at her uncomprehendingly. Then he
was on his feet again, taking shuffling steps.

Sue heard the angry rasp of thrusters behind her and turned to look up at the source of the sound. It was one of the few remaining Pincer Ships, evil on its mind. She broke into a wild run, but the first discs were already on their way. For a brief instant her eyes met those of the blond pilot, before white light erased the world. . . .

Scott got off a few rifle/cannon shots at the retreating Pincer Ship, but the thing got away. He ordered a sweep of the area, then put down where he had seen the command ship crash and Sue Graham shoot her last footage. Lunk, Lancer, and the rest joined him after a moment.

"Hey, is this guy really an Invid or what?" Lunk said, standing over the body of the blond man as though afraid to touch it.

Scott went over to the photographer and gently removed her helmet. Alive but mortally wounded, Sue let out a long, deep moan. Scott tried to cradle her head in his lap, but the bulky armor of the Cyclone prevented it. He pushed her hair away from her face.

"It seems I've got pictures of an Invid with the body of a Human," she managed to say, looking up at Scott through glazed eyes.

"Were they worth dying for, Graham?"

Behind him, Annie was making disgusted sounds. She and Lunk and Marlene watched as green blood pulsed from the pilot's wounds. "Anybody that bleeds green blood must be an Invid," she announced. "But how come they look like us all of a sudden? I mean, he looks almost Human, doesn't he, Marlene?"

"Like that other blond pilot," said Lancer. "That woman."

Annie turned around to find out why Marlene wasn't answering her; she saw that Marlene was staring wide-eyed at a wound she had received to her left shoulder. Alarmed, Annie reached out. Then she noticed the blood.

It was green.

Annie collapsed to her knees in disbelief. Was it possible that through all their months together she had never seen Marlene bleed? *It had to be some kind of mistake—a hallucination!*

Annie's actions had drawn everyone's attention, and all eyes were now fixed on Marlene. No one knew how to react: someone might as well have told them that Marlene was suffering from a fatal disease. The pale woman looked from face to face, then put her hands to her head in a gesture of complete shock. "No! No!" she screamed, tossing her head back and forth.

Scott left Sue's side to calm Marlene, uncertain himself and denying the evidence with each step. He put his hand out to touch the wound, to see for himself if this wasn't just some trick of the night. . . .

The two of them exchanged looks of dismay as they regarded the blood on his fingertips. "Marlene . . ." he stammered. "I . . ."

She stared at him, tears streaming down her face, turned, and ran off. Only Rand made a move to stop her, but Scott restrained him.

"But we can't just let her leave!"

Scott's lips were a thin line when he turned to his friend. "She'll be back," he promised. "I don't know what's going on here . . . this pilot, now Marlene . . . but I know she'll never be able to live among the Invid again. We're her family, Rand. *We're her family!*"

■ ■■ ■ ■■ ■ ■■ ■ ■■ ■ ■■ ■ ■■ ■ ■■ ■ ■■ ■ ■■ ■

CHAPTER

FIFTEEN

Captain, there's something wrong with the engines! They're just not responding!

Remark attributed to someone in the SDF-3 engineering section

ON THE FAR SIDE OF THE MOON, THE WARSHIPS OF the main fleet dematerialized from hyperspace—sleek, swanlike destroyers with long tapering necks and swept-back wings. They were enormous battlecruisers shaped like stone-age war clubs with crimson underbellies; dorsal-finned tri-thrusters and Veritech transports that resembled clusters of old-fashioned boilers; and of course the squadrons of new-generation assault mecha, the so-called Shadow Fighters.

On the bridge of the flagship, General Reinhardt waited for word of Admiral Hunter's arrival, while the rest of the fleet formed up on his lead. Filling the front viewports was the Earth they had come so far to reclaim. Reinhardt regarded the world as one would a precious stone set on black velvet. *Almost sixteen years*, he thought to himself. *Is this a dream?*

He shook his head, as if to clear thoughts of the past

from his mind, and turned his attention to the monitors above the command chair. Here were displayed views of local space, Earth's silver satellite, and the gleam of a thousand hulls touched by sunlight. But there was still no sign of the admiral. Reinhardt slammed his thin hand against the chair's communicator button. "Anything yet?"

"No sign," the astrogation officer responded.

"That damn ship's jinxed," Reinhardt muttered to himself. "I told Hunter something like this would happen. . . ."

The bridge controller flashed him a look across the bridge. "Recommend we initiate attack sequence, sir. We can't afford to wait much longer for the SDF-3. All approach vectors have been plotted and locked in, and conditions now read optimum status."

Reinhardt drew his hand across his face. "All right," he said after a moment. "Issue the codes."

The controller swung around to his console and tapped in series of commands, speaking into the mikes while his fingers flew across the keyboard.

"All units are to proceed to rendezvous coordinates Thomas-Victor-Delta. Attack group three will remain and await instructions from SDF-3 command. Attack group two will continue to objective Reflex Point, activating cloaking device at T minus five minutes and counting. . . . Good luck, everyone, and may God be with us for a change. . . ."

Ground force units and their companion VT strike groups had already landed. Scott and the team had been on hand to greet them, and in the ensuing excitement everyone forgot about Marlene for a few moments. She hadn't been seen since dawn, when the painful realization of her identity had led to her flight.

Sue Graham was dead.

The Invid hadn't shown themselves either, which in itself was a positive sign. Scott still didn't know what to make of the Human or humanoid pilots they were apparently using. He wanted desperately to believe that Marlene was in fact the amnesiac captive he had come to love—that that green blood was something the Invid had done to her—and that they would reunite when all this was finished once and for all. But there were just too many reasons to think otherwise, and for the first time in over a year he found himself recalling Dr. Lang's theories concerning the Invid Regis and her ability to transmute the genetic stuff of her children into any form she chose. These were fleeting thoughts, however, glossed over while preparations got under way for a full-scale invasion of the central hive.

The irregulars had been attached to the ground forces under the command of Captain Harrington, a dark-haired, clean-shaven young man who thanked Scott for the recon information he had gathered and promptly dismissed it. They were all in a group now, atop a thickly wooded rise that overlooked Reflex Point's centermost and largest hive, a massive hemisphere of what looked like glowing lava surrounded by five towering sensor poles and a veritable forest of Optera trees—those curious thirty-foot-high stalk and globes that were the final stage of the Flower of Life. There was no Invid activity, ible activity, except for random flashes of angry lightning, which in their brief displays suggested a domelike barrier shield that encompassed the hive itself.

"At last . . . we finally made it," Scott was saying. He was in Cyclone battle armor, as were Lancer, Rook, Rand, Lunk, and most of Harrington's troops. Veritechs had taken up positions in the woods all around the hive, and the grassy slopes to the rear were covered with squads of Cyclone riders.

"I don't want to burst your bubble," said Harrington, "but we've still got a Protoplex energy barrier and a couple of thousand Invid Shock Troopers to get through."

Scott had a defensive reply in store for the captain but let it go. How could the man be made to understand what Reflex Point meant to Scott's team? True, the Expeditionary Force had come a long way for this showdown, but Scott reckoned that the distance of the overland journey to this moment as incalculable.

"I want to make certain that the main Alpha force stays out of this until we punch a hole in the barrier," Harrington was advising his subordinates. "We don't want to repeat yesterday's mistake and get them too stirred up. We'll let them think we're of no consequence." Harrington turned to Scott. "Lieutenant, I'm counting on you to be ready with your fly-boys as soon as you receive my word, understood?"

"Sir!" said Scott. Lancer and Lunk joined him in a salute.

"I'm so excited I could just scream!" Annie enthused from the sidelines.

"It's going to be awesome," Rand said beside her.

Scott threw Rand, Rook, and Annie a stern look. "Forget it, you're not coming. This is strictly a military operation."

"You're lucky to be out of it," Lancer added at once and almost cheerfully, hoping to mitigate Scott's pronouncement somewhat.

Rook went from sadness to anger in an instant. "Well, we sure don't want to interfere now that the big boys have arrived, do we? I mean, all that action we've seen together—that was just *play fighting*, right?"

Rand, too, was seething but was determined not to show it. "Personally, I'm in no hurry to get myself killed, *Lieutenant*, so it's fine with me."

Annie looked up at her two friends, then over at Scott, Lancer, and Lunk. "But it's not fair to break us up like this just 'cause you guys were soldiers. We're still a team —a *family*! You can't just tell us to split up!"

Rook tried to soothe Annie while she cried. "I suppose this is good-bye, then." She had packed away all her snide comments. "Good luck, Scott."

Harrington gave orders for the attack to begin before Scott could answer her. Veritechs configured in Guardian mode lifted out of the woods to direct preliminary fire against the hive, filling the air with thunder and felling

scores of Optera trees. And as fiery explosions foun-
tained around the hive, awakened Invid Shock Troopers
emerged from the ground to engage the Earth forces one
on one. Scott rushed to his fighter, but Lancer stopped to
say a farewell to his friends, even as Veritechs roared by
overhead.

"I can't say it's always been fun, but it's certainly been
terrific," Lancer yelled over the tumult. "You three take
care of yourselves, okay?"

"*You* take care," said Rand. "Remember, I expect to
see Yellow Dancer perform again."

Lancer smiled coyly. "Don't worry, you will."

"You promise?" Rook asked.

Lancer leaned over to kiss her lightly on the cheek.
"Till we meet again."

It was a little too sweet and fatherly for her liking, but
Rook said nothing. Lancer behaved the same toward
Annie.

"Now, don't go and get married behind my back."

"I won't," Annie said tearfully.

Lunk pulled up in the APC to wave good-bye as
Lancer headed for his Alpha. "I'm a soldier again," he
shouted, gesturing to his spotless battle armor. "I'll be
seeing you guys!"

Rand watched his friend drive off. "A soldier again?
What the heck does everyone think we've been doing this
past year?" He frowned at Rook. "They're all riding off
into *battle*, right? So how come I feel like we're the only
ones without invitations to a party?"

A short distance away, Scott waved good luck to Lunk
and threw a salute back to his former teammates.

"That tears it!" Rand cursed. "I should've figured he'd
say good-bye like that. A robby, through and through."

"Would you want it any other way?" Rook asked him,
returning Scott's salute and smiling.

Rand thought it over for a moment, then brought the
edge of his hand to his forehead smartly.

Scott turned to his console and displays, lowering the
canopy and activating the VT's rear thrusters.

Good-bye, my friends, he said to himself. *Whatever happens now, at least I'll know the three of you will get out of this alive.*

Veritechs and Invid Shock Troopers were clashing throughout the field now. Hundreds of Pincer Ships had joined the fray and were buzzing around the hive in clusters four and five strong. Only a few Cyclone riders had reconfigured their mecha to Battle Armor mode; most of them were riding against the hemisphere in a kind of cavalry charge, pouring all their fire against the hive's flashing barrier shield.

Bursts of blinding light strobed across a sky littered with ships and crosshatched by tracer rounds and hyphens of laser fire. Rand watched from the edge of the woods as Veritechs swooped in on release runs and booster-climbed into the sunlight. The sounds of battle rumbled through the surrounding hills and shook the ground beneath his feet. He could see that the battalion was meeting with heavy resistance, despite what Captain Harrington had said about underplaying their hand. The Invid knew exactly what was at stake, and they weren't about to be tricked.

I can't do it, he thought. *I can't just stand here and watch them go!*

Without a word to Rook or Annie, he donned his helmet and made for his Cyclone. They called out after him.

"I'm not going to sit it out after coming this far," he told them. "I figure the time has come for a little well-meaning insubordination."

Rook tried again to stop him, to talk some sense into him, but her words lacked conviction—even *she* didn't believe what she was saying. "That idiot's going to get himself killed without somebody to look after him!"

Annie saw what was coming but didn't bother to try to stop her other than to shout a halfhearted, "Wait!"—and that was only because she didn't want to be left behind. She began to chase after them, leaving the woods and risking a mad unprotected dash across the battlefield, but it was Lunk she ultimately caught up with.

He had been riding escort to various Cyclone squads, adding his own missiles to the riders' laser-array fire, when an Invid command ship he had finished off with heat-seekers almost toppled on him, sending the APC out of control. Suddenly he was flung into the shotgun seat, and the vehicle was skidding to a halt in the thick of the fighting. And the next thing he knew Annie was in the driver's seat, practically standing up to reach the pedals and shouting: "I'll show you how to handle this thing!"

"What the heck are you doing here?" he demanded, grateful and concerned at the same time.

Annie accelerated, pinning him to the seat.

"What's it look like I'm doing?!"

"Come on, Mint, gimme the wheel—"

"Forget it!" she yelled into his face as he made a reach for it. "I'm not gonna be left behind anymore, Lunk!"

Lunk backed off and regarded her. She was a trooper, he had to admit, a regular workout.

Deep within the hive, the instrumentality sphere glowed with images of the battle—a Cyclone charge, an aerial encounter, death and devastation. A living flame of white energy now, the Regis beheld the spectacle and understood.

"The Earth people have risen in great numbers against us," she addressed her troops, in position elsewhere in the hive. "And now they dare to attack our very center, to threaten all that we have labored to achieve. But this time we will put an end to it. Corg, I call upon you to defend the hive. Destroy them, as they would us, for the greater glory of our race!"

"It will be my pleasure and my privilege," Corg answered her from the cockpit of his command ship. Behind him, his elite squad of warriors readied themselves as the hive began to open, the subatomic stuff of the barrier shield pouring in to fill the drone chambers with white radiance.

But Corg was suddenly aware of a Human-sized figure silhouetted against that blinding light. "No, wait! You mustn't!" it shouted.

Ariel, in her Human guise and garb, was below him, searching for sight of him in the cockpit. "So, you've returned. . . . What do you want?"

"I want to speak to the Regis. Let me through—this madness must be stopped!"

"Madness?!" he shouted, stepping his ship forward menacingly. "What are you saying?"

Ariel gestured to the outside world. "They're only fighting to regain the land that is rightfully theirs . . . the land we've taken!"

"You've lived among them too long, Ariel," Corg told her. "Or should I call you *Marlene*? . . . Now stand aside!"

Corg leapt his ship over her head, nearly decapitating her, but she had ducked at the last instant and was on all fours now, weeping, Sera's pink and purple ship towering over her.

"Sera, you must listen to me," Marlene pleaded, getting to her feet. "Have we forgotten our past? You yourself opened my mind to these things. Have we forgotten that our own planet was stolen from us? What gives us the right to inflict the same evil on these people?"

Sardonic laughter issued through the ship's externals. "So suddenly our Ariel remembers," sneered Sera. "And you would have us surrender. . . . Well, we have traveled too far to concern ourselves with this barbaric life-form's needs. Soon this will be our world, and our world alone."

"We've traveled far, and yet we have learned nothing."

Sera engaged her ship's power systems and leapt into the light, the roar of the thrusters drowning out Marlene's anguished pleas.

Outside, the barrier had been breached by antimatter torpedoes delivered against it by two Veritechs and subsequent blasts from the battalion's destabilizer cannons. Cyclone riders and Battloids were now punching through the rend and battling Pincer Ships on the ground nearest the hive wall.

The outpouring of Protoculture energy released from the shield was working a kind of seasonal magic across the landscape, reconfiguring not only local weather patterns but the life processes of the flora itself. Rand and Rook, riding at the head of a contingent of Cycloners, moved from winter to spring in a matter of seconds. Spores and pollen clusters the size of giant snowflakes were wafting through the newly warmed air; young grass was spreading like some green tide across the valley, and trees and flowers were blossoming in vibrant colors.

"*This* sure wasn't in the forecast!" Rand commented over the net.

"Look at all these wildflowers! Poppies, marigolds—"

"Yeah, but I don't like the look of that big cornflower up ahead."

Rook saw a blue Enforcer ship surfacing in front of them, its cannon tips already aglow with priming charges. "Fan out," Rand ordered the rest of the Cyclone group as energy bolts were thrown at them. The two freedom fighters launched their Cycs and changed over to Battle Armor mode.

"Draw its fire!" said Rook, boostering up and off to the left.

Rand remained at ground level, taunting the blue devil with trick shots, while Rook came in from behind to drop the thing. But a second Invid suddenly appeared out of nowhere and swatted her from the air with a cannon twist that smashed one side of the armor's backpack rig, shearing away one of the mecha's tires. She went into an uncontrolled fall with her back to the larger ship, but Rand swooped in to position himself between the two of them.

"It's okay, I've got you covered."

"Leave it to me!" she told him, voice full of anger, as Rand triggered off a series of futile shots.

"If I'd left it to you, you'd be a pile of smoking rubble by now, and I'm just too fond of you to let that happen!"

"You're what?!"

Rand risked a look over his shoulder at her. "You heard me—I'm fond of you, dammit!"

It was a hell of a time to be confessing his feelings, she thought, but it was turning out to be one of those days. "I—I don't know what to say. . . ."

Rand swung back to his opponent and saw that the Invid ship's cannons were about to fire. "Don't say anything," he yelled in a rush, "just *moooove!*"

The cannons traversed and followed the Cycloners up, but the pilot's aim was off, and Rand managed to sweep in and bull's-eye the ship from behind.

"Nice shooting there, cowboy," Rook said, coming alongside him later. "I bet you try to impress all the girls that way."

There was a sweetness in her voice he had never heard before and a smile behind the faceshield of her helmet that lit up his heart. "No, only the ones who can outshoot me," he laughed.

They were both some fifty feet off the ground, almost leisurely in flight, as though the battle had ended. Then, without warning, there was something up there with them: a kind of towering diamond-shaped flame of white energy inside of which, naked and transcendent, was a Human female with long, flowing red hair. . . .

The vision, if that indeed was what it was, also appeared to Lunk and Annie, who were down below in another part of the arena.

"What the devil is that thing?!" Lunk said, back behind the wheel of the APC now.

At that the flame seemed to tinkerbell across the sky, as though calling to them. Annie swore to herself that she was seeing Marlene up there but dismissed the thought as wishful thinking. The flame, however, *did* seem to be beckoning to them.

"Do you get the feeling it wants us to follow it?"

"That seems to be the idea," said Lunk, putting the vehicle into gear. "And I've learned that you never say no to a hallucination."

* * *

At the same time, almost directly over the hive, where the fighting had been fast and furious, Scott and Lancer were reconfiguring their fighters to Battloid mode in the hope that some of the Expeditionary Force fly-boys would follow their lead. The air combat units had been sustaining heavy losses, and Scott reasoned that the boys had been flying far too long in zero-gee theaters. He recalled the fear he had felt when Lunk first surprised him with the Alpha—and back then he was only going up against two or three Troopers ships, nothing like the swarms of Invid craft that were in the skies today.

Reconfigured, the two teammates demonstrated what a year of guerrilla fighting had taught them; they dropped down close to the hive, rifle/cannons blazing, and took out one after another Invid ship—even the most recent entries to the aliens' supply: the Battloid-like Retaliator ships, upscale versions of the Invid Urban Enforcer street machines. Lancer went so far as to bat a couple of them with the rifle/cannon, showing just how to make gravity work to one's advantage.

Then suddenly there was a kind of flame whisking along beside them, tipped on its side and incandescent.

Lancer said: "It's some sort of vapor cloud, I think. But I can't get a decent fix on it. See if you can get close to it."

Scott banked his fighter toward the apparition and trained his scanners on it. But it was his eyes that gave him the answer: Inside the flame cloud a naked figure swam, larger than life and recognizable.

No, it can't be! Scott thought.

All at once Lancer's voice pierced the cacophony of sounds coming over the tac net.

"I'm hit, Scott! The gyro-stabilizers are shot! I can't get myself turned around! Can't get the canopy up, either. I'm down and out, buddy! . . . A memory!"

CHAPTER
SIXTEEN

One of the intriguing (and unanswered) questions of [the Third Robotech War] is how Ariel/Marlene accomplished her minor miracle in the skies above Reflex Point. Nesterfig (in her controversial study of the social organization of the Invid) advances the theory that Ariel somehow "borrowed" Protoculture energy leaking from the hive barrier shield—the same that so affected the surrounding countryside. But this does not really answer the question. Neither Corg nor Sera was endowed with similar abilities, and most experts agree that they were the most highly evolved of the Regis's creations. The Lady Ariel herself was never able to shed light on this curious incident.

Zeus Bellow, *The Road to Reflex Point*

IN THE COCKPIT OF HER COMMAND SHIP, SERA FLASHED a self-satisfied smile at her display screen. The Human pilots had hoped to get the better of her troops by reconfiguring their craft, but, vastly outnumbered, they were sustaining the same losses in Battloid mode as they had in Guardian. But suddenly her scanners revealed that Lancer's fighter had been one of those to feel the Invid wrath, and although his ship had not been destroyed, it was plummeting toward Earth, hopelessly out of control. As she watched him fall, memories of his face played across the screen, and when she could bear no more of it, she engaged the thrusters of her ship and fell in to rescue him.

Ariel's words came back to her now: *We have learned nothing Sera, nothing!* And she answered back: "You're wrong, Ariel. I have learned to love at least one of our enemies, enough to betray my own people."

Lancer caught sight of the rapidly approaching Invid command ship and guessed that it was coming in to finish him off. He had been struggling with the canopy release switches but had since abandoned any idea of freeing up the jammed mechanisms. His teeth were gritted now, and he was resigned to death. But all at once the Invid was actually scooping up his wounded ship in its armored arms, and far from annihilating him, the enemy was pulling him out of his fall. He glanced up and saw through his canopy and the enemy ship's bubble cover that it was the blond woman pilot. Whether she was XT or Human had yet to be learned; but whoever, she was saving his life.

"Why?" he shouted. "Why?!"

And somehow her voice found its way through the VT's command net to answer him: "Don't ask me to explain," she told him. "But in saving your life I have forfeited my own!"

At the same time her ship let go of his, but the Alpha's systems were revived now, and the foot thrusters were able to maintain it at treetop level. Lancer had the Battloid's rifle/cannon raised, and it would have been a simple matter to destroy the command ship, but instead he let it escape unharmed, confused by this latest turn of events.

Closer to the hive, Scott was still staring at the flame cloud Marlene inhabited. Several other Battloids were similarly suspended, awed by the sight.

"Marlene . . . is it you?" Scott asked the thing hesitantly. "Is it really you?"

In response, the flame leapt toward the hive. Cocooned within its radiance, Marlene, like some living filament, stretched out her arms, and sinuous waves of lightning leaked into the sky.

Scott engaged the VT's boosters and shot after her. Lancer was right behind him.

Corg's ship was not far off; while he watched the two Earth mecha streak off in pursuit of Ariel's projected image, the voice of the Regis entered his ship, informing him of Sera's betrayal.

"She did what?" Corg said in disbelief.

"It is true, Corg," the Regis repeated. "She has saved the life of one of the Robotech rebels."

"Then she is as tainted as Ariel." How was it that this Human species could make his sisters abandon their duty? he asked himself.

He vented his rage against two Battloids and three Alphas, destroying all of them with blasts from the fore-arm cannons of his ship; then he soared after Ariel and her rebel friends.

But if the flame had begun to alter itself, so had the weather. The land had suddenly passed from spring to summer, and now autumn leaves were falling. Rand and Rook were still following Marlene's form, a flickering sun trailing tendrils of light.

"Marlene," Rand shouted over the net, hoping she could hear him. "What does all of this mean?! What's going on?"

If they had any doubts that what they were seeing was truly Marlene, the voice they heard put an end to all of them.

"Can't you understand?" the flame seemed to ask, oscillating as it moved, its naked filament regarding them over her shoulder, long red hair streaming out behind as though it were a part of the light itself. "We are only trying to find a place where we can live in peace and security."

"Yeah, but you forgot something," Rand reminded her angrily. "This planet is our home, not some Invid retire-ment community."

"You must believe me, it was never our plan to destroy Humanity."

Marlene's flame shot ahead of them, a free-floating electrical disturbance against the crimson and yellow sur-face of the hive.

"Then what was your plan?"

"I am neither Human nor completely Invid. I am a new form of life that is a blending of the two. I see that now, although my Regis does not. I can see that it was never our destiny to remain in this Human form. But I must somehow make her understand."

Even though they were scattered, the rest of the team —Scott and Lancer, Lunk and Annie—were monitoring the conversation.

"And this new form of life is planning to replace the old one, I suppose," said Lancer, still thinking about the humanoid pilot who had saved his life.

"My friends, follow me into the central core, the heart of the Invid civilization. There all your questions will be answered."

With that the flame dove into the hive, opening a radiant portal in the side of the dome.

"She went in," Annie said in an amazed voice from the shotgun seat of the APC. "You're not going to follow her, are you?" she added, tugging on Lunk's arm.

"You better believe I am," he told her firmly. "Listen, Mint, if you're scared, you can hop out. I'll be back for you."

"I'm not *scared*," she harumphed, turning her back to him. "I don't think. . . . "

They were approaching a blinding white hole in the side of the hive now, driving entirely out of their own world, destined perhaps never to return.

It was a little like being underwater or within a living bloodstream, replete with cells and corpuscles. In the distance they could discern a blinding white sphere, bisected by a horizontal ray that spanned the field from one side to the other.

And Marlene's form was still leading them in.

"I can't believe it," Rand said to Rook over the net. "We're *inside* Reflex Point. I thought we were supposed to be destroying this place, not taking the grand tour."

"I think I prefer the view from the outside. Where do you suppose she's taking us?"

"Over the rainbow," said Rand.

Almost everyone emerged at the same moment: Rook and Rand, still in Battle Armor mode, Lunk and Annie in the APC, and Lancer and Scott in their fighter mode Alphas. The place was a huge cavernous chamber, filled with light and supported by what seemed to be webwork strands of living neural tissue. Suspended overhead was an enormous globe of pure Protoculture instrumentality, a kind of veined bronze sphere with dark shadows moving and shaping within it, responding to a will that was fearful to contemplate.

They were all shocked to see each other, but where Annie was excited, Scott was angry; he threw off his "thinking cap," raised the canopy of the alpha, and hopped out, storming over to the two Cycloners.

"I thought I told you two to stay put," he began. "You're not soldiers!"

Rand marveled that the man could even be entertaining such thoughts given the circumstances.

"Well, since we're not soldiers, we don't have to follow your orders, do we?" Rook threw back at him, raising the faceshield of her helmet.

"Marlene led us to this place," Annie explained, climbing down from the APC.

Scott looked around uncomfortably. "She led all of us here, I guess."

Suddenly Rand was pointing up to the sphere; its interior was growing brighter by the second. The glow culminated in a flash of threatening light.

"Foolish Humans," an omnipresent deep but female voice began, "you have come here seeking to look upon the face of the Invid Regis. . . . So be it. You shall see her."

Over the rainbow, indeed! Rand said to himself.

The next thing anyone knew, someone had pulled the

plug, plunging the Regis's inner sanctum into darkness, except for the inner glow of that sphere, directed down on them now like stage light. Then a towering flame formed beneath the base of the sphere. It was similar to the one that had encompassed Marlene earlier, only this one was larger and more menacing. And within it they could discern a hairless humanoid figure, thirty feet high and dressed in a long red robe and strange gloves that dangled a kind of tail.

"Behold, I am the Invid. I am the soul and the spirit. I have guided my people across the measureless cosmos, from a world that was lost to a world that was found. I have led my people in flight from the dark tide of the shadow that engulfed our world, one that threatens to engulf us even now. I am the power and the light. I am the embodiment of the life force, the creator-protector. In the primitive terminology of your species, I am . . . the *Mother*!"

While she spoke they had views of nebulae and star systems, the journey the Invid had taken from Optera to Tirol and on to all the worlds that had led them eventually to Earth.

Light returned to the chamber, and they had a full view of the blue-eyed creature, the Invid mother.

"You are surprised. . . . So were we, when we discovered that the planet to which we were led by the Flower of Life was inhabited by the very species who had destroyed our homeworld."

"I'd say 'inhabited,'" Rand started to say.

"That is of little consequence. . . . Your species is nothing when weighed against the survival of my people. . . . The Invid life force will not be denied. . . ."

"No, that's not right!" a small voice rang out to argue with her. Everyone turned and saw Marlene enter the domed chamber from somewhere, just as they remembered her in her yellow jacket and blue denims.

Scott called to her.

"So, Ariel, it is true: you *are* a traitor. Was it you who led these children of the shadow into the hive?"

"They are not children of the shadow," Marlene contradicted her. "They have a life force almost as strong as our own."

"They are the enemies of our race."

"If they oppose us, it's because we are trying to do the same thing to them that was done to us so many years ago!" She turned to her friends now. "Scott, listen to me: Perhaps if we could begin again, we might be able to find a way for our two races to share this planet together, in peace."

Scott closed his eyes to her and shook his head. "I'm sorry," he told her. "But you must realize that's impossible."

"So you'd rather have the death and destruction continue?"

"That's right, Marlene," Lunk cut in. "To the bitter end if we have to!"

Marlene made a stunned sound; she had not expected this.

"Lemme tell you something," Lunk continued. "Maybe you've forgotten that your species invaded our world—*remember*?!"

"I do remember," she said softly.

At the edge of Earthspace the third attack group was moving into position above Reflex Point, the Shadow Fighters that rode its wake dematerializing as the command was received for activation of the Protoculture cloaking device.

"There are still no signs of the SDF-3," the controller updated. "All other ships are present and accounted for."

"*Jinxed*!" Reinhardt muttered.

"Ground forces report successful penetration of the hive barrier shield, with heaviest losses sustained by the Veritech squadrons. Invid command is either unaware of our presence or unconcerned. My guess is that the cloaking device has been successful."

"All right," the commander said, turning to the forward viewports. "Signal the fleet to form up for final attack formation and prepare to engage." Reinhardt exhaled slowly, exhausted by the weight of his responsibility. His confidence had been bolstered by the controller's report, but he couldn't help but dwell on the possible consequences of failure. Hunter had called for the use of neutron bombs, which while sure to annihilate the Invid would also spell doom for much of the Earth's population.

Over the battlefield Corg was taking out ship after ship in an effort to offset Sera's betrayal. And now his sensors were indicating the presence of Robotech mecha inside the hive itself. He dealt out death to two more Veritechs and headed through the remnants of the shield into the heart of the hive.

In the inner sanctum, the alien the Humans knew as Marlene was still trying to get over Lunk's remarks. "But you've traveled with me," she was telling him, the hurt evident in her voice. "I even thought that you liked me, or at least accepted me. I'm no different now than I was then, Lunk. So why have your feelings changed?"

"What d' ya mean, you haven't changed?" Lunk's face was red with rage beneath the lifted faceshield of his helmet. "You're an *alien*! You think we woulda taken you along if we knew that? You're a spy!"

"But the fact that I *could* travel among you as a friend should tell you something, Lunk. Isn't it possible that we're not so different, after all . . . your people and mine?"

The Regis had been following these exchanges with interest, and she learned more about the Humans in the past few minutes than she had in the past three years. But Ariel still had a lot to learn. "Look at these friends of yours," she said to Ariel and directly into the minds of the Humans. "Notice how they stare at you in fear and confusion—emotional states that in their species inevitably lead to hatred . . . and *violence*!"

"Yes, they're confused because they feel I betrayed them," she argued, "but they're not full of hatred."

"Your contact with them has blinded you to their true nature, my child. It is their genetic disposition to destroy whatever they cannot understand."

"Now just wait one damn minute, Dragon Lady!" Rand interrupted her, willing to risk a step forward. "I've had about enough of this! How do you know what we're thinking? I'm willing to take Marlene as she is—and I think Lunk feels the same underneath all that armor of his. I don't *hate* her. Especially now, knowing what she stands to lose by coming to our defense like this. But *you* are another matter. As far—"

No one saw the crimson paralyzing rays until it was too late; they seemed to bubble up out of her blue eyes like dye, and they knocked Rand off his feet—the proverbial look that could kill—but his battle armor saved him.

"It is natural to them," she explained to Marlene/ Ariel, barely missing a beat. "As natural as breathing itself. Their entire history is a catalog of murder, conquest, and enslavement, all directed against others of their own species."

"That's not true!" Sera now threw back, suddenly materializing in the chamber. "Ariel's right, Regis. Forgive me, please, but I too have begun to doubt whether we are any better than they are." She looked briefly at Lancer before continuing. "You say this species is guilty of murder and enslavement, but how is that any different from what we're doing to this planet?"

"So, Sera, you *and* your sister have been turned against us."

Sera, Lancer thought to himself, watching her.

Ariel was now gesturing toward the Humans. "Look at them, Regis. They're not . . . animals or barbarians. They are a brave and noble people trying to protect what is rightfully theirs, just as we tried to do." She offered Scott an imploring look, hoping he would understand and forgive her. Something in his eye told her he would.

Corg had by now joined them also, not in the flesh like

Sera but via the instrumentality sphere, where his image appeared five times life size.

"Have all of you gone mad?" he shouted. "How did these Humans gain entrance to the hive?! Sera, remove them at once!"

Sera thrust out her chin. "I was not aware that I had to obey your orders, Corg."

He scowled at her. "Your contact with the rebels has made you weak and spineless."

"And it has made a monster out of you," she returned. "Consumed by vengeance and evil passions. *You* are a child of shadow, Corg, not the Humans."

"What are you saying?" he bellowed. "This pathetic species you've become so fond of cannot be allowed to stand in the way of our future. Have you forgotten what we have been called to do?"

"If you keep fighting, there won't be a future for any of us," Lancer said from the floor of the chamber.

Corg dismissed the threat without a word. "Enough. I am called to battle—where my duty lies!"

"I've got to stop that lunatic!" Scott yelled, ignoring Marlene's pleas for him to wait and racing for the cockpit of his fighter.

The Alpha gave chase to the alien ship through that same netherworld of moving cells Rand and Rook had navigated earlier. *I've got you now!* Scott thought, training his weapons on Corg even before the two of them had left the hive. But the XT swung his craft around and loosed a stream of discs before Scott could get off his shot, and an instant later they were outside, dogfighting in the skies over those recently altered autumnal forests. Red-tipped heat-seekers and anni discs cut through the air as the two aces put their ships through their paces, dodging and juking, climbing and dropping against each other.

Views of the battle were displayed inside the chamber, where the rest of the freedom fighters were still gathered, along with Ariel and Sera.

"I don't like just standing around and watching this," Rand told Rook. "What do you say, do we stay here or go out there and help him?"

"I don't know anymore, Rand. I'm all confused. . . ."

All at once the sphere's images de-rezzed, only to be replaced by space views of the approaching Expeditionary fleet.

The Regis's lapis eyes narrowed. "No! They have come! The dark tides of the shadow have come to engulf us again!"

"It's the rest of Hunter's fleet!"

"Wow! I didn't expect so many ships!"

"Well, that does it," Lancer said softly, filled up with a sudden despair. "Any hope of a peaceful settlement has just gone down the drain."

CHAPTER
SEVENTEEN

Throw water on her! Throw water on her!

Remark attributed to Rand (unconfirmed) on seeing
the Invid Regis for the first time

MOST OF EARTH'S POPULATION WAS UNAWARE OF
the Expeditionary fleet's arrival, let alone of the Olym-
pian battle that was taking place in the skies above Reflex
Point. But even as far off as the remote areas of the
Southlands, people knew something was up. The Invid
were suddenly taking their leave—from cities, towns,
communications outposts, and Protoculture farms, a
steady stream of Troopers and Pincer units, all headed
north for some unknown purpose.

Meanwhile, in one small section of those embattled
northern skies, a green and orange Invid command ship
was going one on one with a Veritech, each oblivious to
the ferocious fighting going on around them, as though
these two had been chosen representative combatants.
And in some ways they had. . . .

For Corg, the alien prince, there was no thought of
defeat, only the glory of victory. Showing a malicious

grin, he raised the right cannon arm of his ship and loosed
a bolt of red death at the approaching fighter.

But Scott was well prepared for it and already thinking
the Beta through an avoidance roll; he returned two
bursts to Corg's one, reconfiguring to Battloid mode as
the VT came full circle.

Corg darted left and right, almost playfully, then threw
his ship into a frontal assault, even as the Battloid's rifle/
cannon continued to pour energy his way. The two crafts
collided and grappled in midair, thrusters keeping them
aloft while they flailed at each other with armored fists.
Scott tried to bring the cannon down on the ship's crown,
but Corg parried the blow and punished the VT with
body blows. Scott twisted and hurled his opponent way;
once again he brought the cannon into play, and once
again Corg seemed to laugh off the attempts.

The alien's voice seethed over the tac net: "Your pitiful
attempts make your defeat at my hands all the more
pleasurable!"

Scott snorted. "I'll be satisfied with boring you to
death, then!"

The Battloid had the cannon in both hands now; the
first volley missed, and the second impacted harmlessly
against the command ship's crown. In response Corg
loosed a flock of missiles from his ship's shoulder-
mounted racks, and Scott met the stakes with an equal
number of his own. The projectiles destroyed themselves
in midair between the two ships, but Corg had followed
his missiles in, emerging from the smoke and bringing the
metalshod foot of his ship against the VT's control mod-
ules before Scott had an opportunity to take evasive action. Electrical discharges snapped around the inside of
the Beta's cockpit like summer lightning as circuits fried
and systems shorted out. Scott sat defenseless in the seat
as shock poured through his armor and the displays cried
out last warnings. Corg's ship was behind him now, cannon raised. Scott thought he would feel the final blow
against the Battloid's back, but Corg played his hand for

insult instead. He targeted and zapped the Beta's thrusters, incapacitating the ship.

The Battloid commenced a slow facedown descent, trailing thick smoke from its leg and neck. . . .

Corg watched it for a moment, laughing out loud in his cockpit, then turned to deal with the half dozen fighters that had suddenly appeared to avenge their commander.

"How quaint," he sniggered to himself.

He positioned himself central to their assault and let them take their best shots, which he avoided with ease. Then, as they came in at him, he showed his teeth and counterattacked, taking out the first as it swooped past him, then a second, third, and fourth as they strived to ensnare him.

At the same time, Corg's Troopers were taking the battle to the edge of space. The so-called Mollusk Carriers and squadrons of Pincer units a thousand strong had moved in to engage the main fleet. Laser fire crisscrossed and lined local space, spherical explosions blossoming like so many small novas.

Hundreds of Invid ships were annihilated by mecha they could not even see, let alone fight. Squadrons of Enforcers and Pincer ships were wiped out; Mollusk Carriers exploded before they could even release their brood. And yet they continued to come, more and more of them.

On the bridge of the fleet flagship, Reinhardt received the latest updates. "Estimate of Invid troop capability is coming in now, sir," Sparks reported.

"I want a full status report on the assault force entry into Reflex Point," he demanded.

"They're continuing to meet heavy resistance, sir."

Reinhardt studied the monitors and displays. "If push comes to shove we're going to be forced to use the neutron S missiles."

"But our troops . . ." said Sparks, alarmed.

"I'm aware of the consequences," Reinhardt answered him grimly. "But is there a choice? Either we eliminate them and reclaim the planet or give it all away. We can deal with the ethics later on."

"I understand," Sparks said softly.

"Shadow Fighter launch is complete," a female tech said over the comlink.

"This is it, then," said Reinhardt. "Wish them Godspeed for me, Lieutenant."

In the hive chamber, Lancer, Lunk, Annie, and Sera had their eyes fixed on the Protoculture globe as glimpses of the battle in space were relayed to the Regis's *sanctum sanctorum*. It was obvious to the Humans that the Regis was growing concerned now; she was no longer the omniscient being they had first met.

"All units regroup," she was telling her troops. "Repel the invaders at all costs!" As she swung around to face her small audience, her eyes found Sera. "Your defection has cost us much, my child."

No one really understood what she meant by it, least of all Sera. It was true that she had stayed her hand when it had come to killing Lancer, but it was beyond her how her presence in the current battle could have affected things or altered the outcome any. "It can't be," she answered her Queen-Mother, knowing guilt for the first time.

Lancer was about to add something, when he saw one of the cells of the communication sphere black out. It was the third time he had seen it happen now, and it suddenly occurred to him that the sphere was tied in not only to the Regis in some direct way but to her offspring as well. He turned his attention to the battle images again: A squadron of Enforcers was being decimated by laser-array fire erupting from what seemed to be empty space; and as the last of the ships were destroyed, another cell faded and was gone. Annie noticed it, too.

"Hey, look at that!" she said, pointing to the dark patch on the underside of the globe.

"It loses power with each Invid loss," Lancer explained. "Isn't that right, Regis?"

The alien looked down at him imperiously. "You are perceptive, Human.... And as you have observed, our entire race feels the loss when even one of our children ceases to exist."

The pain she must have known, Lancer found himself thinking. Even over the course of the past year, to mention nothing of what had happened before, with the Tirolian Masters, then Hunter and the so-called Sentinels....

"Those Shadow Fighters are chewing them up!" Lunk enthused as more and more Invid ships disappeared in fiery explosions and seemingly sourceless cross fires.

Lancer took a step toward the pillar of flame that was the Invid Queen-Mother. "Your forces can't detect those fighters," he told her. "Your children are defenseless, don't you understand? Now you're the only one who can end this destruction."

Unmoved, the queen regarded him. "Twice in our recorded history we were forced to relinquish our home and journey across the galaxy.... But this time we shall not leave!"

"Don't you know when to take no for an answer?!" Lunk shouted at her. "Your children are dying!"

Sera glanced at Lunk, then looked up to the Regis. "Mother, perhaps we should listen to him...."

"You have the power to transform any world you choose," Lancer argued. "Some planet you won't have to fight for!"

"You cannot understand," the Regis said, almost sadly. "The Flowers of Life exist on this world and this world only. They are our strength; they are our life. Without them, we would perish."

Scott opened his eyes to Marlene's face and a world of pain. He was in his battle armor and propped up against a tree not far from the smoldering remains of a crashed fighter. He had no recollection of the events that had landed him there.

"Scott," Marlene was saying, dabbing at his head with a moistened rag. "Is your head any better?"

Scott saw blood on the rag and raised his fingers to the wound. Even this slight movement brought a wave of pain along his left side; at the very least his ribs were cracked under the armor's chest plate. "Agh...what happened?" he groaned.

Marlene gestured to the VT, "You were shot down. I saw you fall and—"

"Where's the Beta's component?" He tried to raise himself and collapsed; Marlene laid her hand and cheek against his chest.

"You shouldn't be moving, Scott. Stay here with me!"

"I've got to get back...." He saw that she was staring at him in a peculiar way and couldn't understand it. The revelations of the previous day and the sequence inside the chamber of the hive were lost to him. "Marlene, what's wrong?" he asked her, almost warily.

"I...I don't know how to explain it," she stammered. "I feel so strange, so concerned about you....Do you think you could love me, Scott? Even if only for a little while?"

Some of it was coming back to him now, scenes of battle, memories of *Corg*! He looked at her like she was crazy to be saying these things. "Marlene, I'm capable of only one thing, and that's fighting the Invid!" Refusing her offered lips, he managed to struggle through the pain and get to his feet.

Marlene chased after him as he ran off. "But, Scott," she screamed, "I love you!"

Elsewhere, two Battloids were moving through the chaos like lovers taking a Sunday stroll in the park. Rand's had just suffered a near miss, and Rook was teasing him about it over the tac net.

"I think you need some lessons in how to maneuver, kiddo. My grandmother could do better than that."

"All right," he told her in the same teasing voice. "But the next time you're in trouble, don't come to me for help."

"*Who'll* come to *who* for help?"

Rand smiled for the screen. "Love you, too."

"Same goes for me," Rook started to say, but Corg's approach put a quick end to the flirtation.

He split them up with fire from his hand cannon. They had arrived on the scene too late to see what the alien had done to Scott, so it took Rand by surprise when Corg moved against him hand to hand—something seldom done in midair—effortlessly knocking the rifle/cannon from the Alpha's grip. Rook stared out of her cockpit amazed, watching the two ships begin to duke it out, moving in to exchange rapid flurries of blows, then separating only to thruster in against each other all over again, trying to punch each other's lights out. But Rand was nothing if not resourceful, and somehow he managed to get the Invid ship in a kind of full nelson, which left Corg vulnerable to all frontal shots.

"Okay, I've got him!" Rook heard Rand yell over the net. "Blast him!"

Rook tried to depress the HOTAS trigger button, but her fingers simply refused to obey the command. If she didn't catch the alien just right, Rand would be destroyed along with him. Her face was beading up with sweat and the HOTAS was shaking in her grip as though palsied, but she couldn't bring herself to fire with Rand's safety at stake. He was screaming at her, telling her not to concern herself. . . .

Corg was just as confused as Rand: the red Battloid had a clear shot at him, but instead of firing the pilot was throwing herself against him, trying to batter him with the mecha's cannon. It was a tactical blunder and one that gave him all the time he needed to reverse the Battloid's hold. Corg grinned to himself and fired off a charge into his opponent's right arm, taking it off at the elbow; then he threw open the command ship's arms to propel the Human mecha backward. Engaging his thrusters now, he fell against the red ship, striking it with enough force to stun the mecha's female pilot.

Rook came around as Corg's ship was surfacing in her

forward viewport, the hand cannon primed and aimed at her. But just then Rand rammed the thing from behind, and although he had managed to interrupt Corg's shot, he received the blast that had been meant for her.

Rook could hear his scream pierce the net as his crippled Battloid began a slow backward fall, bleeding smoke and fire and sustaining shot after shot from Corg's weapons. Rook came up from behind to try to slow his descent, but Rand protested loudly:

"Rook, it's useless. . . . He's coming in for another run. You've gotta save yourself!"

"You're out of your gourd, mister," she told him, "I'm not letting you go now!"

Corg had the two Battloids centered in his sights and was preparing to fire the one that would annihilate them both, when an energy bolt out of the blue impacted against the back of his ship.

Scott's voice came over the tac net as Rook saw the component section of the Beta come into view.

"Get Rand out of here. I'll take care of things up top."

"Roger," she exclaimed, wrapping the arms of her mecha more tightly around that of her crippled friend.

The Beta and the alien mecha went at it again, only this time both of them knew it would be for keeps. Enough of Scott's memory had returned to make him aware of what Corg had done to him.

The two ships spun through a series of fakes and twists, drops and booster climbs, slamming each other with missiles and volleys from their cannons. Again, flocks of projectiles tore into the skies and met in thunderous explosions, throwing angry light across the field. But then Scott saw a way to prey on the alien pilot's technique: He made a move as though to engage Corg hand to hand, then surreptitiously loosed a full rackful of heat-seekers as Corg hovered open-armed and defenseless.

Even Corg wasn't aware of how much damage the Bludgeons had done to his ship and sat for a moment, complimenting the Human pilot on what had been a clever if underhanded maneuver. But all at once his ship's autosystems were flashing the truth, even as the first explosions were enveloping him, searing flesh and bone from the humanoid form that had been created for his young soul. . . .

Scott shielded his eyes: Fire and green nutrient seemed to gush from the ship at the same instant as the explosion quartered it, arms and legs blown in different directions. But as important as it had been for him personally, Scott knew it for what it was: a minor battle in a war that was still raging all around them.

Scott put down a few minutes later to see about his friends. His mecha's missile supply was virtually depleted, and it was time to let the fleet VT squadrons take charge of things for a while. He asked Rand if he was all right, but instead of the thanks he thought he was due, Rand said: "What the heck did you say to Marlene?"

"Yeah," added Rook, "we can't get a word out of her."

"I'd rather not talk about her," Scott started to say. But without warning Rand was all over him, head bandage or no, his hands ripping at the armor at Scott's neck.

"You're gonna *tell* me whether you like it or not! You think you can just walk out on this thing? She's got some crazy idea that she loves you—as if she had some idea of what that means. But you're gonna see to it that she understands, pal! I think you would have loved her, too, if you hadn't found out she was an Invid."

Rook separated the two of them. Then she had a few things of her own to say to Scott. "Stop torturing yourself over your dead girlfriend and come back to life, will you?"

"How can I ever forget that she was killed by the Invid—by Marlene's race?"

"So you're going to hold that against Marlene?" Rand seethed. "It wasn't like she pulled the trigger, you know. Besides, what about all the Invid you and the rest of Hunter's troops killed? This war has made victims out of all of us. When are you going to realize that the Invid are just our latest excuse for warfare?"

"Rand, you've lost it—you've gone battle-happy. *They* started it; they attacked our planet—"

"Listen, there were wars before we even heard of the Invid or the Robotech Masters or the Zentraedi. You might've lost your Marlene fighting other Humans."

Scott shook his head in disbelief, but even so he sensed some *rightness* in Rand's words. Not the way he was phrasing it; more in the sentiments he was trying to express, the sensibilities. . . .

After a moment, he said: "If only we could have avoided this. . . ."

Scott Bernard might as well have asked to negate his own birth.

*The so-called trigger point was that point at which Flower
production would have provided the Regis with adequate supplies of liquid nutrient for the conversion of her hibernating
hive drones to quasi-Human form. Once this had been accomplished, her soldiers (with their Protoculture-fueled ships—the
Troopers, Pincers, and Enforcers, would have been turned
loose to eradicate the remaining Human population, including
those who had comprised the labor force in the Protoculture
farms, which (with more than enough Protoculture on hand to
maintain a standing army) would have been shut down.
Presumably... But would this then-reformed race have taken
up where they had left off on Optera? Would they continue to
employ the Flower that had been central to their society there?
Would they have become somewhat Humanized by the
Reshaping?... We are open to suggestions.*

Zeus Bellow, *The Road to Reflex Point*

WITH THE ARRIVAL OF THE INVID LEGIONS FROM
the Southlands the tide began to turn on the Expeditionary Force. It was a matter of sheer numbers.

Even though the Shadow Fighters had been initially
successful in decimating the enemy ranks, the odds had
now changed. The alien hordes were now punching
through Reinhardt's forward lines and launching strikes
against the fleet warships themselves. Consequently, con-
tingents of Shadow Fighters had fallen back to protect
their mother craft, leaving vast regions of space unprotected and vulnerable to infiltration. And though the hive
barrier shield had been breached, the Terran ground
troops had yet to gain entry to Reflex Point itself. Reinhardt, of course, had no way of knowing that six Humans

not only had been inside the hive but had met the Invid Regis face to face.

"Three cruisers wiped out!" Sparks reported from his duty station as the flagship was rocked by another volley of enemy fire. "They're all over us, Commander. Even the Shadow Fighters can't stop them!"

Reinhardt swiveled in the command chair to study one of the threat board displays. "Blast it! What in heaven's name is preventing Harrington's men from getting into that hive?!"

"Sir, the Second, Third, and Fifth Divisions are reporting extremely heavy casualties. I can't raise the Fourteenth at all."

Reinhardt cursed. If the fourteenth was wiped out, it meant that responsibility for the entire assault had fallen to the Cyclone squadrons. And they would have to accomplish that without air support.

"At this rate we won't be able to hold out for more than a few hours," Reinhardt muttered. "Order one of the Shadow squadrons to prepare for a direct assault against the hive. I don't care how they accomplish it— even if we have to pull everyone back for a diversionary move. Tell the air wing commander that I'm instructing cruisers in the fleet to concentrate their firepower in sector six. We'll guarantee a hole, but the rest is up to them."

Sparks swung to his tasks.

Reinhardt sucked in his breath and waited.

In the hive chamber the Regis regarded the Protoculture globe with growing alarm. Though her children were meeting with success, the battle was far from won. And could it ever be? she began to ask herself.

"This planet retains the malignant spirit of the Robotech Masters," she said out loud to Sera and the three Humans. "Whether one race or the other emerges victorious is of little consequence now, because such lingering hatred will only breed greater hatred into the race that

survives. This world is contaminated, and I am only just
beginning to understand. . . .

"The conflict will rage from generation to generation
unless every last Human is wiped out, and that still won't
be enough. Because *we* have inherited that evil bent. Our
gene pool is polluted by it."

Cocooned within her column of cold white fire, the
Regis turned slowly to gaze down upon Sera. "My child,
this is not what we seek. This is not what we have traveled so long to achieve. But I begin to see a way clear of
the treachery that has ensnared us . . . the truth I refused
to grasp on Haydon IV. It is almost as if *he* were speaking
to me across the very reaches of space and time . . . as
though he had some inkling of the injustices he unleashed
even then, when his Masters first directed their greed
against us. . . . "

She could see Zor's image in her mind's eye, and it
came to her now that the Flower that had been the cause
of it all was about to bring their long journey full circle.
That the Protoculture he had conjured from its seeds was
to provide her with the energy she needed to complete
the Great Work and ascend with her children to a higher
plane, the noncorporeal one at last, that timeless dimension. *No earthly chains to bind them* . . . no emotions, no
lust, only the continuous joys and raptures to be found in
that realm of pure thought.

But could he really have seen this all along, been so
omniscient? she asked herself. Such a precise vision, such
an incredible realtering and reshaping of events . . .
Sending his ship away to this world, then drawing the
Masters and their gargantuan armies here, only so that
the Flower could take root and flourish, so that the Invid
might follow.

And now these returning ships with their untapped res-
ervoirs of Protoculture—destined from the start to be her
mate in the new order.

She had been so misguided in assuming his form; in so
doing she had been captured by the rage and fears and
emotions that blinded her to Protoculture's true purpose.

It was not simply to supply mecha with the ability to transform and interact with its sentient pilots; it was meant to merge with the race that had passed eons cultivating its source. They had used the Flowers for nourishment and sustenance and spiritual succor, and for all these millennia the Flower had been trying to offer them something more.

And Zor had played the catalyst.

"My child," the Regis continued, "I see now the new world that calls to us. And we shall consume and bond with that blessed life that provides our passage."

"Do you understand what she's saying?" Lancer asked Sera as the Regis seemed to reincorporate with the chamber globe.

Sera nodded, her attention still fixed on the battle scenes displayed there. Lunk and Annie gasped as the latest view was flashed into the inner chamber: Shadow Fighters, visible now, piercing through the hive's protective envelope.

And Reflex Point was beginning to react to their entry. Colored lights began to strobe into the chamber from unseen sources, dissolving the weblike neural arrangements supporting it and eliciting a threatening tide of organic waste and refuse from those collapsing cells.

"Well, the takeoff may be decided, but she just ran outta time," said Lunk.

Sera started off in the direction of her command ship, but Lancer put his arm out to stop her. "Let me go," she pleaded with him. "I must protect the Regis and the hive until she has assured our departure."

"I want to help you," Lancer told her.

She stopped struggling and turned to him. "You will be fighting against your own people."

Tight-lipped, he nodded. "If they knew what I know now . . . they'd understand."

"*We* understand," Annie encouraged him. She grabbed hold of Lunk's arm and led him toward the APC. "Now let's get out of here before this whole place comes apart."

* * *

Word of the Shadow Fighters' successful penetration of the hive was relayed to the flagship, but Reinhardt was still not encouraged. Six cruisers had been taken out in the past hour, and it had required over fifty fighters to get a mere four through the hive's defenses. And if those few survivors didn't make it into the central chamber, Reinhardt asked himself, what then?

"Sir?" Sparks said from his station.

Reinhardt looked at him wearily. "I have no choice. . . . I want all neutron missiles armed and ready for an immediate launch against Reflex Point."

Sparks swung around to his console. Reinhardt listened while his orders were radioed to the rest of the fleet. He wondered what the other commanders must be thinking of him. But there was no alternative; they had to realize that. . . .

"T minus fifty and counting," he heard Sparks say.

At the edge of Earthspace, the thrusters of two dozen mushroom-shaped droneships flared briefly, propelling their armed warheads toward the target area.

The hive corridor was oval-shaped and surgeon's-gown green. Lancer had no idea as to its purpose or its direction. But Sera appeared to know where she was going, and that was all that mattered. She was at the controls of her pink and purple command ship; he was alongside her in a Cyclone he had taken from the VT, reconfigured in Battle Armor mode.

"I consider it an honor to be fighting side by side with you," Sera told him over the comlink.

Yes, we're both fighting on the same side now, he thought. And in a sense they were a nonallied counterforce, separated from the Human as well as the Invid cause.

"You know, I've been thinking about how we met. . . . " he said leadingly.

"Lancer, would it be possible for you to love one of my race?"

He thought back to Marlene. And Scott. "I think I could. And what about you?"

She sighed over the net. "I only hope we have time to find out."

Two Shadow Battloids were fast approaching them from the corridor terminus.

"T minus ten seconds and counting," the tech reported.

Reinhardt was standing at the control center now, Earth's beautiful oceans and clouds filling the bridge veiwports. Short-lived explosions flashed across the field, and off to port a holed cruiser floated derelict in space. He had already inserted the override key into the console lock; he gave it a quarter turn and commenced arming the main switches as the countdown continued.

"Seven, six, five, four..."

Reinhardt hit the secondaries and slammed home the final crossover; now the S missiles were beyond anyone's control, no matter what followed.

"Three, two, one, *zero*!"

Reinhardt could discern bursts of white light below him against the seemingly tranquil face of the planet.

"God forgive me," he said under his breath.

The Regis's voice boomed out, omnipresent. It was as if she had become the entire hive now, and each part of it her.

"The final attack has begun. And a terrible error has been made. But in seeking to reach our own goal we shall see to it that these creatures have a chance to reach theirs as well. The shadow of the Robotech Masters has been allowed to rule this world for too long.... Now it will be dispersed!"

Sera's ship took a hit to the shoulder from one of the Battloids in the corridor, but she rallied and returned fire, taking out not only the one who had shot her but two more. Lancer hovered clear off to one side, unable to assist. But he had already done his part by destroying the first two, and it pained him even now to think about those Human lives he had taken.

Suddenly two more Shadow Fighters streaked into view.

"We'll never be able to stop all of them!" he shouted to Sera.

She was about to reply when unexpected fire from behind them devastated the intruders. Lancer twisted around to find Scott's VT behind them in the corridor.

"Figured you could use some help," the lieutenant said flatly.

"You're a welcome sight, Human" Sera told him.

"Yeah, well I'd love to stay and chat about that," Scott said after a moment, "but I suggest we get ourselves out of here on the double."

Lunk and Annie made it out of the hive before the three pilots. Rook and Rand and Marlene were also in the clear, a few miles off when the hive began to undergo the first changes.

In the shotgun seat of the APC, Annie gulped and found her voice. "Lunk," she said, pointing, "tell me what's happening!"

As if he could explain it.

The hive had gone from a crimson, almost bloodred color to steely blue. It was also more transparent now, and some sort of huge spherical nodes had been made visible in the deep recesses of the dome—perhaps those same round commo devices Lunk and Annie had stood beneath only minutes before. With the barrier envelope disappeared, the Shadow Fighters had direct access to the Regis's lair, but they couldn't get near it because of the intense electrical discharges that were surging up throughout the area.

And somehow the voice of the Invid queen was reaching all of them where they fought, died, or waited.

"Hear me, my children," she intoned. "When we sensed the first faint indications of the Flower of Life resources on this world, we thought we had at last found the home for which we searched."

The hive was barely visible now. It was engulfed in a kind of swirling storm of blinding yellow light from which rays of raw energy poured into the sky, while a crazed network of lightning and electrical groundings danced overhead. It was more like a contained explosion than anything else, as though the hive had become an epicenter for all the world's random energy, as though the very processes of universal creation were gathering together and being run through at an extraordinary pace. The hive had become the vessel for the Great Work, the merging of opposites—the pleroma. Here was the meeting place of the red and white alchemical dragons: the point of transcendence. The air was crackling, local storms unleashed and billowing clouds tearing through darkened skies as though in a time-frame sequence. And the land was changing and reconfiguring. The trees surrendered their leaves as an intense chill swept in from all sides, minitornadoes swirling around the sunlike fires that glowed within the hive. Invid ships—Scouts, Troopers, and Pincers—were streaming into it like insects drawn to the flame that annihilates them.

"We had called together all of our children scattered throughout the galaxy to begin life anew on this planet. We began rebuilding a world that had nearly been destroyed by evil. And we constructed the Genesis Pits in order to pursue the path of enlightened evolution. But it was not enough."

Suddenly light and shadow seemed to reverse themselves, and the world drained of color. Where the hive had stood there was now only an impossible tower of radiant amber light, launching itself through hurricane clouds with blinding determination, a pillar of raw but directed energy.

It was a mile-wide circular shaft of horrific power that erupted from the hive, mushrooming up with a rounded, almost penile head into that feminine void above, a million blast furnaces in concert.

* * *

Overhead, at the edge of the envelope that was Earth's protective shield, the neutron missiles were falling toward their target, but now that target was now coming up to meet them, with a face as different as any could be, a face only the once-dead would recognize. . . .

Reinhardt and his bridge staff saw it coming and would not have been able to move away from it had they had the power to do so; they were transfixed, in awe, in some sort of splendiferous, almost holy, reverie. Before their eyes the light was changing shape even as it pierced through Earth's atmosphere and entered the vacuum out of which it had been born. It was anthropomorphic here, contorted into a dragon's face there, with its fanged mouth opened wide, its tongue a lick of solar fire, ready to engulf all that dared stand in its way. It struck like a serpent, twisting and flailing about as though charmed by its own existence, charmed by its own imminent swan song.

Reinhardt saw the creature—for that's what he termed it to be, a living light: energy and life combined on some new and unimaginable scale—encounter the warheads he had launched against it, and he saw those alloyed death machines slag and melt away in the creature's wake. And he realized that this was to be his own fate as well. . . .

There was nothing but brilliant yellow light in the viewports now; throughout the fleet men and women stood naked before it, unable to comprehend what was happening but aware that it was something that had never occurred before. They were unable to understand that they had come all this way to meet death face to face, like the Zentraedi and Robotech Masters before them. It was as though they had been chosen to reap the whirlwind that had blown in from the other side of the galaxy. And they were unable to understand that they had been chosen to unite with the Invid in some inexplicable way, in the same manner that the Invid were uniting with the wraiths of the Protoculture. They were the homunculi, the Micronians who had been used by the conjurer Zor in the carrying out of the Great Work.

Some people, in ships at the perimeter of the fleet, saw that tower shoot up from Earth's surface like a lance of pure light, only to be joined as it pierced the night by coils of unequaled brilliance delivered up from the planet itself, encircling it for a brief moment like the shells encompassing an atomic nucleus. For this really was a kind of cosmic orgasmic fusion.

"Come with me!" the Regis's voice rang out, like the music of the spheres. "Discard this world and follow the spirit of light as it beckons us onward. And let our leave-taking heal this crippled world and reshape its destiny."

Then that light contacted the warships of the main fleet and digested and assimilated their strengths and weaknesses as it had the bombs sent against it, incorporating into itself all the contradictions and ironies and, most of all, Humankind's ability to wage war.

The dragon seemed to yawn and bellow its triumph as the light streaked on into the void.

"Our evolutionary development is complete," the racial voice continued.

"To all of my children scattered throughout the cosmos . . . Follow me to a new world, a new plane. Abandon this tortured life and follow the spirit of light as it spreads its wings and carries us to a new dimension. . . . "

And those few who survived told of the ray's complete and total transmutation. To a feline face with bright blue eyes, through one that was surely Human in form. And then it had collected itself into one mass . . . like a phoenix on the wing, a radiant bird with outstretched wings wider than the world it was leaving behind, soaring away quicker than thought to another plane of existence.

EPILOGUE

Which came first: the Flower or the Protoculture?

Louie Nichols, *BeeZee: The Galaxy Before Zor*

Life is only what we choose to make it;
Let's just take it,
Let us be free.

Lynn-Minmei, "We Can Win"

THERE WERE FEW SALVAGEABLE VERITECHS LEFT
after the Transformation, but Scott Bernard had managed
to secure one of them. Most of the crew and ships of the
main fleet had perished with the Invid's departure—*gone
with them*, as some were saying.

A month had passed, and Earth was indeed beginning
to heal itself, as the Regis's voice had promised it would.
Grass and nascent forest covered what had been waste-
land before, and regions that had been hot since Dolza's
rain of death were showing markedly lower levels of ra-
dioactivity. Even the devastated area around the central
hive had been sanitized by the light's leave-taking.

But two of the Regis's children remained. . . .

Scott was saying good-bye to one of them now on a
rise overlooking the scene of what was to be Yellow
Dancer's last concert, an outdoor amphitheater not far
from the city that had once been called New York. People
had been drawn to the concert from all over the Northlands and Southlands, seeking some explanation for what

had occurred, almost as though the Invid's departure had been something of a Second Coming. There was a sense that the Earth had come to play a pivotal role in events that were beyond anyone's ability to comprehend, that the world had been used somehow to further one species' progress toward an end that awaited all of them. And in the process Humankind had been saved from self-annihilation, so that Earth, too, might someday follow along the same path.

A feeling of peace prevailed, of lasting calm few had ever known. War had been placed out of reach. And if one were to be fought, it would have to rage without Protoculture, for almost all that precious substance, along with all the Invid Flowers, had vanished from the face of the Earth. It would have to be a war fought with sticks and stones by a species that had been returned to a kind of primitive innocence; to childhood, perhaps.

But these issues were far from Scott's teammates' thoughts that day; rather, they were dwelling on endings and beginnings of a different sort. For now that they had done their part in allaying everyone's initial fears and confusion, the time had come for them to think about their own individual paths and the inevitable farewells those steps toward the future would entail. And amid all that returning splendor, there was an awkwardness they had never experienced with one another.

As for Scott Bernard, his mind was made up. The SDF-3 had never appeared out of spacefold, and Scott was going out to look for it aboard the only fleet cruiser that had survived the Transformation.

"But why?" Marlene wanted to know, raising her voice above the music booming out from the concert shell below them, where Yellow Dancer held center stage.

"Really, Scott, what's the point?" Rand said, backing Marlene up even though he knew it was futile. "You can start a new life here."

"I've got to go back," Scott insisted, turning the "thinking cap" over and over in his hands.

"But how will you figure out where to begin looking?"

Annie asked him. "I mean, couldn't you be happy staying down here on Earth with your friends and everything? Gee," she added, tears welling up in her eyes, "I miss you already."

How could he explain it to them? That although their friendship had meant so much to him this past year, he had other friends as well. Dr. Lang, Cabell, and so many others. He *had* to find out what had become of the SDF-3. And more to the point, space was his home, more than the Earth ever was and perhaps more than the planet would ever be.

He looked down at Annie and forced a smile. "Admiral Hunter's lost out there, and someone's got to find him and his crew. We've got to try while there's still one ship left with enough reflex power to make the fold." He glanced over at Rand and Rook, Marlene and Lunk. "Fate brought us together for a journey none of us will ever forget. But we've reached the end of that road, and there're only individual ones left for us now." Scott shook his head. "I don't know, maybe to spread some of what we learned while we were together. Does that make any sense to you?"

Rand caught Scott's eye and smiled broadly. *So it's not meant to be a winding down, after all*, he told himself, *but a gearing up for new quests. . . .*

"Well, good luck," Lunk said dubiously, walking over to shake Scott's hand. "I think I'm through with the road for a while." He gazed appreciatively at the green hills above the festival grounds. "I'm going to do a bit of farming, try and pay back the debt I owe to good ole Earth for shooting it up the past coupla years. Especially now that I've got some real fine volunteer help," he added, looking over at Marlene and Annie and grinning.

"What about you, Rand? Any ideas?" Rook asked leadingly. The two of them were sitting side by side in the grass, their backs against a tree.

Rand leered at her fondly. "Well, yeah, I do have a

notion or two. I'm thinking of going back to the Southlands to write my memoirs."

Rook grimaced. "You've got to be kidding. Who the
heck cares, anyway? Besides, you're just at the beginning
of your life, not the end of it."

Rand thrust out his chin. "Hey, I think people would
be interested to read about some of the adventures we've
been through."

"*We*?" she said excitedly. "Well, that's different! But I
think those books are going to need a feminine point of
view, just to keep things balanced, of course."

"And you're applying for the position."

"I am uniquely qualified to edit you, rogue."

Rand was about to agree, when a tremendous cheer
rose from the crowds down below.

But the cause of the commotion wasn't Yellow Dancer,
who had just finished her rendition of "We Will Win"—
the anthem of the First Robotech War—but Lancer himself. He had thrown off his wig and female attire and was
now attempting to explain himself to the audience.

"Thank you, everyone, thank you. You've made Yellow Dancer's final concert the greatest ever. Thank you
all, you're wonderful!"

Those in the front rows saw that he was directing a lot
of his delivery to one person in particular: an unusual-
looking woman with short spiky green-blond hair and
eyes that glowed like embers . . . For who else but an out-
of-this-world woman was so well suited for Lancer?

Only he wasn't getting the response he had expected;
the audience seemed almost *indifferent* to his visual con-
fession. In fact, they were prepared to follow him in any
guise he chose; after all, it was just *the stage*, wasn't it?

Up above, Scott had kissed Marlene good-bye and was
headed for the cockpit of the Alpha. What would become
of her and Sera? he wondered, and found himself thinking about Max and Miriya Sterling's daughter, Dana.

He waved to his friends as the VT lifted off, tuning his
receiver to the broadcast frequency of Lancer's concert.

He really did it, Scott chuckled to himself. *It was certainly a month for revelations.*

"I want to dedicate my last number to a very special group of friends," Lancer was saying from the stage. "And to one friend in particular. . . . He's leaving Earth behind, and with it the most precious of possessions: his friends—the people who love him most. But I want him to know that when he returns, we'll be here to welcome him home with open arms."

As Scott listened to Lancer's latest composition, he found himself recalling the names and faces of the people who had emerged as heroes during Earth's quarter of a century of devastating warfare. Rick and Lisa Hunter; Max, Miriya, and Dana Sterling; Lynn-Minmei and Bowie Grant and Louie Nichols . . . And all those who hadn't lived to see this day: Admiral Gloval, Roy Fokker, Claudia Grant, Rolf Emerson, and countless others. Scott felt a bittersweet wave pass through him as Lancer's words crept into his mind, Earth dwindling now in the Alpha's cockpit display screen.

> She finds him strong and brave
> And how she wants him so, so much
> So much she knows she needs that touch
> To lead the way to love.
>
> He spies a gentle soul
> Waiting for her to find someone so
> So very sweet and kind
> To lead the way, the way to love.

"The Way to Love," Scott repeated, meditating on the words. And it suddenly occurred to him that it was love after all that had tipped the scales in each of those terrible wars. Love had won out over the greed, the hatred, and the betrayals, redressing the evil the Robotech Masters had first unleashed, and perhaps even atoning for some unknown sin that was Zor's alone.

> And now they have their space
> They've run the final race
> Love's given them a place
> Where love can live
>
> Heaven is where they are
> With love, they have no need to roam
> Just look at them to see how she,
> She led them to love
>
> They are in love
> They are in love . . .

Marlene! he thought, leaning out as though to catch a glimpse of her. But there were only Earth's oceans and clouds now, and stars winking into view above him. And he made a promise on one of them: a promise to return after he had found that jinxed ship and its long-lost crew.

Scott listened a moment more, choking back his sadness, and hit the Alpha's thrusters, boostering up and away from the world he had helped to liberate, one he hoped he would see again. . . .

Far below, Lunk, Marlene, and Annie had climbed into the battered APC and were headed down to the festival grounds to pick up Lancer and Sera. There were wisps of sunset clouds in a warm-looking sky, clear all the way to tomorrow. The Moon was rising, brilliant and seemingly closer than it had ever been. Lunk glanced up at it and said:

"You know, sometimes I think that's the most beautiful sight in the whole world. And I don't know why anyone would want to leave it behind."

Annie saw the VT's contrails caught in the western sky's final moment of color and sighed.

"And it might be a long time before anyone leaves it again." She smiled.

Marlene put her arm around Annie and hugged her close.

"Good-bye, Scott," she said softly. "May you find what you're after. May all of us."

ABOUT THE AUTHOR

Jack McKinney has been a psychiatric aide, fusion-rock guitarist and session man, worldwide wilderness guide, and "consultant" to the U.S. Military in Southeast Asia (although they had to draft him for that).

His numerous other works of mainstream and science fiction—novels, radio and television scripts —have been written under various pseudonyms.

He currently resides in Dos Lagunas, El Petén, Guatemala.

ROBOTECH
THE SENTINELS

In 2020, members of Earth's Robotech
Defense Force decided to send a secret
mission to the Robotech homeworld to try
to make peace with the Robotech Masters. This mission, led by Rick Hunter and
Lisa Hayes, set forth aboard the SDF-3 and
spent years in space. Meanwhile, back
on Earth, the Robotech Wars continued
unabated—and everyone wondered
what fate befell the people on the SDF-3,
now known as The Sentinels.

It has remained a mystery...until now! For
the first time, the full story of the SDF-3 Expeditionary Force is about to be told. At last...
the story you have been waiting for is

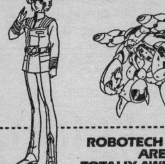